DANGEROUS
GAMES

Edited By
JONATHAN OLIVER

Featuring
CHUCK WENDIG
LAVIE TIDHAR
PAUL KEARNEY
LIBBY MCGUGAN
SILVIA MORENO-GARCIA
BENJANUN SRIDUANGKAEW
HILLARY MONAHAN
GARY NORTHFIELD
TADE THOMPSON
REBECCA LEVENE
YOON HA LEE
MELANIE TEM
IVO STOURTON
GARY MCMAHON
ROBERT SHEARMAN
HELEN MARSHALL
NIK VINCENT
PAT CADIGAN

SOLARIS

First published 2014 by Solaris
an imprint of Rebellion Publishing Ltd,
Riverside House, Osney Mead, Oxford, OX2 0ES, UK

www.solarisbooks.com

ISBN (UK) 978-1-78108-265-2
ISBN (US) 978-1-78108-268-3

Cover by Nicolas Delort

Designed & typeset by Rebellion Publishing

Printed in the US

CONTENTS

For Joel Lane (1963-2013)

Friend and Inspiration

INTRODUCTION
JONATHAN OLIVER

GAMES ARE UBIQUITOUS – even if you don't consider yourself a 'gamer' it's likely that at least some of your leisure time is spent gaming; whether that's casually on your iPhone or tablet, or attempting to complete a crossword to while away the time on a journey. Games are a part of our lives from the earliest age and *Dangerous Games* explores some of our reasons for playing.

Often the player of a game is setting out to prove something to themselves – athletes regularly push themselves to their limits and beyond – and this anthology kicks off with Chuck Wendig's 'Big Man' in which the recently-divorced protagonist finds himself involved in a curious game of one-upmanship on the freeway. Endurance and risk-taking also feature in Tade Thompson's 'Hounourable Mention' in which a traditional board game is given a surprising twist. The reasons for Tito, Tade's penniless protagonist, to play are clear, but it's the price he pays that gives this story its bite. Ivo Stourton gives Russian Roulette a science-fictional twist in 'Two Sit Down, One Stands Up' and in doing so produces a story which not only questions the motivations of players, but also looks at the very fundamentals of what it is to be human.

This being an anthology concerning itself with games, it's not surprising that some of the stories are playful. After all, writing itself is something of a game; creating something from nothing and allowing the imagination to roam in a fictional space. Silvia Moreno-Garcia's 'The Yellow Door' has a somewhat tongue-in-cheek feel in its use of a Lovecraftian trope, though in telling it straight, Silvia also explores the risks taken by gamblers. Gary Northfield's three page comic strip 'Captain Zzapp!!! – Space Hero from 3000 AD' is laugh-out-loud funny but may also make one ponder the nature of videogame violence. Robert Shearman has always been a playful writer, mixing humour with pathos, linguistic trickery with emotional complexity and 'The Monogamy of Wild Beasts' certainly shows Shearman at his best. The three humans onboard the second Ark play games with the animals on board in order to produce the strongest couplings, but the players soon turn on themselves in this poignant and darkly funny tale.

Games of cruelty and games with deadly consequences have been part of genre for almost as long as genre itself. In Lavie Tidhar's stark 'Die' it's a game of human against human, to the death. This short-sharp-shock of a story demonstrates why Tidhar is considered one of genre's rising stars. The macabre subject matter of Melanie Tem's 'Death Pool' cleverly masks a story that's about the importance of hope. 'The Bone Man's Bride' by Hilary Monahan blends a Depression-era tale of desperation with a gruesome pagan ritual.

Unsurprisingly, card games are a part of this anthology, though I *was* surprised that I didn't receive more stories using cards as a narrative. Pat Cadigan's 'Lefty Plays Bridge' is all about what's happening between the cards being laid on the table. It reads like a pleasant conversation between the players, but trust me when I tell you that this story is as dark as Hell. Nik Vincent's 'The Stranger Cards' shows how much can be achieved within the confines of the short story. This is a great little thriller. A seemingly innocuous game of Clock Patience played by a convicted serial killer on death row becomes something so much more. Killers, of course, have their own games, the rules and motivations for their method of play inexplicable to all but the killer themselves. Gary McMahon has written extensively about such folk and 'Ready or Not' shows us a childhood game gone horribly wrong. Rebecca Levene's 'Loser' reveals the effects of a damaged childhood on a young man and how playing games helps him to cope with the cruelty visited upon him.

Of course one of the reasons we play games is to win, and this is no better demonstrated than in Libby McGugan's 'The Game Changer' in which the father of a terminally ill child discovers a game that may just help his son. 'South Mountain' by Paul Kearney features a cadre of American Civil War re-enactors facing the realities of warfare and receiving a stark reminder of why some battles are worth fighting.

To those not involved in the mechanics of a game, the rules can seem strange and overly complex. The confused looks I get from those non-gamers to whom I try and explain roleplaying games is a case in point. Yoon Ha Lee's 'Distinguishing Characteristics' features a very unusual roleplaying game, one which appears to be being played for a political purpose. Yoon's world is strange and her characters oblique – which of course makes for a satisfyingly strange story. In 'Chrysalises' Benjanun Sriduangkaew has produced a story full of startling imagery – poetic while sometimes horrific, one is reminded of the body horror of Cronenberg's early films. Benjanun's game may be being played in one reality or many, it's up to the reader to immerse themselves in this fantastical tale. There is a lot of cruelty in Helen Marshall's 'All Things Fall Apart and Are Built Again' as games are played with the emotions and upon the body of the protagonist. There's a lyrical sadness to much of Marshall's fiction, and it's present here as the old men roll the bones at the end of the world.

So here then are the players and the played. It's time to take your place at the table, time to shuffle the cards and roll the dice. There are eighteen games for you here, and a whole host of possible outcomes. Win or lose, *Dangerous Games* are always worth playing.

Jonathan Oliver
August 2014, Oxford

BIG MAN
CHUCK WENDIG

Those of us who drive will already be more than familiar with the dangerous games some choose to play on our roads. You'd think people would be more considerate when the stakes are so high. In a story reminiscent of Richard Matheson at his best, Chuck puts an extreme twist on road rage in a story about a man just trying to prove himself...

RICHIE REVS THE engine.

The line from that movie, the Bill Murray movie, goes through Richie's head as he presses down on the Subaru's accelerator: *Don't drive angry.* He's thinking to himself – yelling to himself, even, inside the hollows of his own head, *I'm not driving angry, shut up, fuck you, it's fine,* even as his foot gains weight and density like a star collapsing, even as it presses down harder and harder on the Go-Fucking-Faster Pedal.

Beneath the car: the rain-slick highway. Greasy mist on windshield – the wipers are shitty, honking with every swipe, *shree-wonk, shree-wonk, shree-wonk.* Tires hissing on wet road. He comes up behind a tractor trailer, gets caught in the gray spray. Tries to pass. Fails. Fuck. He bites at a hangnail on his thumb. He just makes it worse, like now he's afraid to pull any further because he'll unzip his skin all the way down to the elbow, and yet he keeps nibbling. A bead of blood wells up like the head of a red pin.

An image clear in his head – sudden and sharp, like a mirror shard whipped in front of his face. He sees her. Marie. Sees that face of hers staring at him in the courtroom just, what? Twenty minutes ago?

God, that look of disappointment. Like a soggy piece of bread. A crumpled paper airplane. She wasn't pissed. Not anymore. Just sad. Sad because he *made* her sad.

Richie remembers being a kid and how his parents would always be disappointed in him. The real hell of it was feeling angry about it... not because it wasn't earned but because they were *right* about him, because their disappointment was *righteous*. He'd always done something to deserve it. Terrible grades. That time he broke their front bay window with his backpack. The permanent marker on the wall. Stealing Mom's Pontiac to go into Philly to see that show by that band he loved so much then, a band whose name he now can't remember no matter how hard he juices his brain.

He tries to pass the tractor trailer, but another big truck – this one, a dumper with a rust-chewed back end – comes up alongside him.

"Goddamnit," he says, and slams a fist down.

The rod controlling the wipers snaps.

And flicks into the passenger seat.

The wipers go faster. *Shree-wonk shree-wonk shree-wonk.*

He can't turn them off.

He screams. Silent from the outside, loud from the inside.

Divorce, man.

Divorce.

She's going to take Sadie away.

She wants full custody.

Because he can't be trusted. That's what they said. *Actions unbefitting of a parent.*

They pulled out those photos, flashed them up on the pull-down screen like it was a slide-show of somebody's vacation instead of hasty snaps from some private detective: and there the judge and the lawyers and Marie all looked on grainy images of a man that was clearly Richie tangled up in various, uhh, *dalliances* with many women. The secretary at Air Products. The redhead from the Applebee's. The escort from the Hilton.

Many, many women.

And again he screams because that makes him a shit-bag. He knows that. He *gets* that. But it also doesn't make him unfit as a father, right?

Divorce. Custody.

The dump truck presses on and eases past on the left, and Richie again hits his blinker (at least he hasn't broken *that* lever, yet) and just as he starts to slide into the passing lane –

Wonk! A horn blasts.

Richie quick jerks the wheel, wobbles the Subaru back into the lane just as a brand new, lemon-yellow Dodge Charger whips past. Bumpers shiny as a knife blade. Doors so glossy Richie can see his own car reflected.

He leans on his own horn. The Subaru has a horn like a child's tricycle. Less a raging bleat and more a polite clearing-of-the-throat.

He wants a *honk*. He gets a *beep*.

The Charger zips past, but then eases back so it's running parallel to Richie's car. Richie can't see much with the foggy spray coming off that tractor trailer ahead of him, but just the same he sneers in that direction and offers up a middle finger so tall and proud it's like a straining erection.

The rain-spray dies back for a moment.

The passenger side window of the Charger is down.

The driver is leering. Young guy. Younger than Richie, anyway. Mussed up black hair, black like an artful scribble of ink. Sunglasses in pink-frame plastic. Big boomerang grin with white, too-white, teeth.

The driver laughs.

Richie rolls down his own window, yells *fuck you*, but it's lost to the highway sounds.

The Charger's driver lifts a cup, a big-ass cup like a 64-ounce Thirst Aborter from Your Local Convenience Store, and gives one last pull off the straw, then grins and lifts it up like he's toasting to Richie.

Then: a casual flip of the cup.

It spirals out the Charger's side window.

Spinning. Already spilling, too – still half-full, this cup.

Jesus, it's gonna –

The cup hits the Subaru windshield. A spray of brown liquid – iced tea, maybe, or fizzy Coke, coats the glass. The now-empty cup spins away as Richie jerks the wheel, the car taking a drunken swerve, tires grinding on the rough stone of the highway shoulder, the wipers swiping away the spill –

As Richie rights the car, he sees the Charger is already gone. Just a brush of yellow and a smear of red taillights.

But even over the highway noise, he hears it:

The Driver's laugh.

Braying. A bro-boy frat-fuck laugh. Smug donkey.

That guy coulda killed me.

Richie's pissed. Another day, he might've let this go. Not worth it. But today: oh, it's so fucking worth it. It's the only thing that matters. A bright, shining crystal – an inverted pyramid digging its peak into the meat between Richie's shoulders, bunching up his muscles, tightening his neck, drawing his jaw tight and his teeth together.

The Subaru's an Outback – some kind of mash-up between an SUV and a station wagon. Ugly car, like a rust-red shoe with wheels: a roller-skate on an ill-shaped foot. Richie doesn't know what it is, but the car has something called a 'continuously-variable transmission.' All he knows is, when he needs it, the car has a little punch, a bit of give – it's not like his wife's old Honda hatchback, which had all the get-up-and-go of a hungover ladybug. The gas pedal's tiny, made for women or small Japanese men, but he slams his foot down just the same and cuts the wheel sharply to the left –

He careens into the passing lane.

Ahead, he sees a flash of yellow. Pair of taillights. Red and bright like cigarette cherries, like demon eyes.

Motherfucker.

Richie knows – abstractly, distantly, like he's someone else watching himself on television or through a window – that this is road rage. This is raw, red, throbbing *highway fury*. But it feels just. It feels earned.

Both right and righteous.

He accelerates past the tractor trailer. Through the spray.

Behind: dark clouds. Ahead: a band of sunlight, garish and white. Rain's over but he can't turn his wipers off and so they just keep squeaking and honking across the now-dry glass.

Accelerate. Drive, drive, drive.

The Dodge Charger is disappearing.

The Subaru doesn't have the juice.

The windshield wipers, they keep going –

Shree-wonk.

Shree-wonk.

Shree-wonk.

You're weak.

So weak.

He slams the pedal to the floor. Hard enough where he thinks he might go full-on Fred Flintstone: feet breaking through the bottom of the car all the way to the asphalt, scrabbling and running and pushing the car along with the urging energy of his own molar-cracking *pissed-offedness*.

The Subaru spurs forward. Like a horse, pushed too far, run to a froth. The steering wheel shudders in his hand like it wants to come off.

Big man.

Those two words. Clear as a wind-chime tinkle.

That's what she said to him. They were leaving the courtroom – barely a courtroom, really, nothing like what you see on *Law & Order*, couldn't seat more than fifteen people – and he went up to Marie and he was mad but sad, too, and he said how sorry he was again and how he desperately wanted to find some middle ground here. For Sadie. He offered to take Sadie for half the week, to share custody – he said he knew the divorce was a foregone conclusion because he screwed up. He told her, *I accept that, but let's not sacrifice Sadie on this altar.*

Richie said, *I wanna do my part.*

And Marie, dead-eyed like her eyes were buttons or nickels, just said:

Big man.

Then she joined her lawyer and it was over. Richie didn't bother talking to his own lawyer afterward, even though they were supposed to have a 'confab' – all he could do was get in his car and drive away. And now here he is, windshield sticky with some asshole's soda, trying hard to race to catch up to a car he can never catch.

But then –

Ahead, two more tractor trailers. One passing the other like a pair of whales racing in icy waters. Logjam.

The Charger doesn't make it past. Gets caught in the block.

Richie hears himself laugh. A mad, musical sound.

The Outback accelerates. He imagines himself slamming the Subaru right into the back-end of the Dodge, jamming his car so far up the ass of the other that he ends up in the backseat, where he can punch that cocky Driver asshole right in the throat with a hard fist. The stark, staggering violence of that image rattles him –

Is that who I am?

Big man.

Shree-wonk shree-wonk shree-wonk.

Wee man.

So weak.

He stills his heart and tries to will blood back into his knuckles.

He wants to see the asshole who threw the cup. He looks

around his car, thinks, *maybe I can throw something back at him*. Not much around – couple quarters, that'll do. He needs them for tolls when he hits the turnpike again but he tells himself he can stop along the way, get change at a McDonald's or something, so instead of giving the Charger a big ol' hot-steel Subaru enema, he grabs a fistful of change and eases up alongside the Charger on the right, both of them again caught in the aerosolized rain-cloud of not one but *two* tractor trailers, the first a tanker, the other a flatbed –

Someone else is in the Charger.

A girl. In the back seat.

She presses herself against the window. Her eyes are ringed with bruises. Her nostrils, crusted with blood. A crooked swatch of duct tape sits across her lips. The girl – young, not teens, maybe 20s – shoves her forearms against the glass, a look of panic like lightning in her eyes, the gleam of handcuffs jangling –

And then she's gone. Back down.

The Driver shows his shiny Tom Cruise teeth in a big grin.

Ahead, the tanker trunk lurches forth, and the Charger sees a space – however small – and guns it into the gap.

Richie drops the change in his own lap, feels his palms go wet with sweat. Pulse-beat fluttering in his neck like a moth pinched between two fingers. Everything is changed.

The road rage – the road *race* – is something else now.

Call it in. You can't handle this.

He fumbles for his phone.

Tries to keep an eye on the road as he looks down. The Subaru drifts, but he rights it again when a pickup behind him honks.

Phone on. Two numbers pressed –

9.

1.

Then:

BATTERY WARNING.

And the phone goes dark.

"Fuck!" he tries to turn the phone back on, as if the battery's a gas tank with hidden fuel in it or a doorknob you just need to jiggle to work, but of course it stays dead because that's how batteries work. "No, no, no."

Deep breath.

"Okay. *Okay*. Okay!"

He pitches the phone into the backseat. Worthless technological turd.

It's on him. He's gotta do this. Gotta handle this. Gotta catch up.

Gotta *man* up.

For the girl. That poor girl.

Big man.

Shree-wonk you're weak shree-wonk so weak.

He pulls the Subaru into the gap left by the Charger. Richie eases the car ahead. Easy to imagine all his fear and anger over everything funneling into the car – hot, red lines of energy. Magma. Burning lava. Acceleration.

The Charger zips through traffic like a needle closing a wound. Richie takes off after, praying to whatever gods that govern the universe that the bullshit parable about that rabbit and that turtle – "Slow and steady win the race!" he shouts – turns out to be an actual thing.

But every opportunity to catch up, the Driver ahead shuts it down. Every opening, the Charger closes. Ahead of a white SUV. Around it. Blocking it. Between two tractor trailers and then ahead of them – gone, suddenly not there at all, like the yellow sports car just vanished into the fog now rising off the wet, sun-touched highway. And Richie thinks, *Oh, shit, it was never there to begin with. This was all in my head.*

Big man.

Can't save the girl.

Can't save yourself.

But then: a flash of yellow in his rearview.

The Charger's behind him.

He sees the leering, smug-fuck face of the Driver there. Tongue out, waggling in the space between two fingers forming a crass 'V'. The Charger flashes lights, honks its horn. Wobbles left, then right, then back left again.

Suddenly the car is on the shoulder to Richie's left. Bounding and bouncing up alongside him, tires grinding on rough-hewn ground.

Richie yells: "Pull over!" He bellows a lie: "I called the police!"

Again that Driver's laugh – ha ha, haw haw, hee, woo. And then the Driver is holding up a hand and in the hand he has something, something that might be playing cards, Richie doesn't know, and just like with the cup the pompous prick flips his wrist and all the playing cards go flying –

Up, ahead of the two cars, then on the wind, breaking apart –

Richie sees colors, so many colors –

Faces? Bodies?

They're not playing cards. They're *photos*.

They hit his vehicle. Whipping against the Subaru's hood, spinning away into the mist, disappearing under tires. Except one.

One sticks under the driver-side windshield wiper.

Shree-wonk.

Shree-wonk.

You're weak.

She knows.

It's a picture of Richie. And another woman. Blurry. From outside a motel room window. He knows this picture. He remembers when it happened and he remembers just seeing it in the courtroom *today*. It's him with the Applebee's waitress. The one with the band of freckles across her nose and cheeks like a galaxy of stars, the one with the big lush hips but the narrow middle, the one who – there, right there in the goddamn picture – mounted him like he was the mechanical bull and she was the rodeo rider.

The wiper flips the photo away. Spinning off into oblivion.

Richie can barely breathe.

This clown, this prick, he's messing with Richie. He *knows* Richie, somehow. Was he in the courtroom? Did his wife hire him? Is his wife *fucking* him? Jesus. God. What is happening?

The Charger is already gunning it. Doing what its name suggests, and hard-charging up through the line of cars.

Richie screams again.

And punches the vertical pedal on the right.

The Subaru lurches like a dog whipped with a belt. *Catch up, catch up, catch up.* But the Charger, again, has the edge.

Ahead: orange construction pylons. Jagged diagonals. Marking an exit that's closed off. Exit 35B – the 309 exit. Closed because highway 309 is closed here on this stretch. Making a new bypass, if he remembers right.

The Charger veers toward that exit.

Is he really gonna –?

The Dodge blasts through the pylons. And takes the dead exit.

Richie spins the wheel and carries his car across the left lane, cutting in front of a minivan. The van swerves and honks and he sees some big-haired woman shaking her fist and screaming at him like he's the devil, and he gesticulates a floppy, flappy-bird hand in the air as if to say, *yeah, yeah, sorry, lady, but this is important business, sorry again, fuck you, bye.*

He drifts toward the fallen pylons –

But then swerves suddenly back onto the road.

No. That's the wrong move.

This is like a – a what? A chess game. Think several moves down the line. Don't chase the opponent. Get ahead of your foe.

He's been reacting this whole time. Passive. Letting this asshole set the meter and tempo.

Time to act, not react. Time to be active.

Richie knows ahead by a half-mile is another closed exit. Take you to the same closed-off highway from the other side – going north instead of south. That'll get him ahead of the Charger.

He laughs again. It's not a happy sound.

Marie will see what he's capable of. He'll confront this sonofabitch, and Marie will see that her efforts to… thwart him, to destabilize him, were for nothing. Zero, zip, zilch. Sorry, baby. Then she'll know. She'll know why he cheated on her in the first place – always so controlling. She'll see that he's tough, a real man, a *big man*. This dumb fuck Driver should've never locked antlers with him. He'll come out ahead. Marie will see that.

And then it'll all be over.

She won't divorce him. Because she'll know who he is.

Big man.

Shree-wonk.

Shree-wonk.

Not weak.

There's the closed off exit.

The Subaru hits the orange pylons like a fist punching through a stack of plastic party cups. A few more orange cones get sucked under the tires.

Richie rounds the curl of the exit ramp, cuts the wheel as the back-end skids on a carpet of limestone gravel, then suddenly he's up on old highway 309. Construction equipment on the side of the road, abandoned due to the storms that just passed through here – the road, empty, abandoned, almost apocalyptic like it's just him and the Driver.

Tired grumble. The car judders. The highway here isn't broken up – but it's fallen to disrepair, crumbling and cracking. Chipped and cratered like broken windshield glass. All of it down to one narrow lane.

Then, as if on cue:

A shimmer of something in the distance.

The gleam of sun on a knife-shine bumper.

The Charger.

Richie whoops.

Then he does a thing he's read about – he slams on the brakes, yanks on the emergency brake, and cuts the wheel. The Subaru's back end slides forward as the front end shifts backward, and then the car rocks and starts to tip and he thinks, *oh, shit, oh, no,* he's about to flip the damn thing, he's literally gonna roll end over end because of some amateur-hour stuntman trick he thought he could pull –

But then the car skids to a halt and rocks back down on its tires.

The Subaru is now perpendicular to the road.

Blocking it.

Construction equipment on one side. A high barrier closing off the shoulder on the other. The Charger has nowhere to go.

Richie cuts the engine. Under the hood he hears: *tink tink tink*. The wipers freeze in the middle of the windshield like eyes half-lidded.

He gets out.

The Charger keeps on coming.

The engine growls. Louder, not quieter.

It's coming faster. The Driver isn't slowing.

Richie feels that twinge in his gut. Panic shoots through his heart like a saline flush. His bowels go to ice water. He wants to leap back in the Subaru, start the car, speed off –

Or maybe just run away. Leap over the barrier. Disappear into the distant trees. Never come back.

But he stays.

His feet, rooted to the macadam.

The Charger keeps on coming. Roaring. Headlights flip on – just pinprick smears of light in the bright day, but on just the same.

Richie shuts his eyes.

The car blasts his horn.

The engine roars.

The Driver laughs.

Then –

Brakes squeal. The ground beneath him trembles.

And when he opens his eyes –

The sports car is stopped twenty feet away. Cocked at an angle. The engine, cut. A faint hissing.

Mist rises off the wet road.

The door pops open. And out steps the Driver.

Hair mussed. Collar popped. Tongue licking those bright whites.

"You," Richie says, his voice a squawking croak. "You sonofa –"

The Driver pulls a gun out of his back waistband. Big, nickel-plated pistol. A hand-cannon with ivory grips and a pair of red-beaded sights like little Devil horns. The gun barrel swings up, points at Richie.

"Calm down, Richie." The Driver reaches in his pocket. Pulls something out: a set of car keys. He jingles them in the air like he's trying to distract a cat. Then he pitches them forward in a hard underhanded arc.

Richie steps back, catches them right in the center of his chest.

A flash of pink – a pink rabbit's foot attached to them.

"You won the race," the Driver says.

"What? Race? What is this? Who are you? Did Marie send you?"

"Big man, Richie. Big man."

"Fuck you. Tell me who you are. *Tell me what this is about!*"

The Driver tilts his pink-frame sunglasses down and stares over the plastic. He smirks and sneers. "Enjoy the ride."

Then he shoves the gun under his own chin and –

The shot is muffled. It's not some dramatic thing like you see in the movies. The head shakes like someone just punched him, and a little fountain pen *squit* of blood squirts from the top of the Driver's hair.

The gun falls away.

Velvet smoke drifts from his mouth and nostrils.

Then the driver doesn't topple so much as he crumples – a Jenga tower tumbling down upon itself.

The Charger hisses.

The Subaru *tink-tink-tink*s.

Richie stands there for God-knows-how-long. Shaking. Wondering if he's pissed himself. He's almost afraid to check.

Eventually, he pats down there. Nothing wet.

The girl.

He swallows hard, hurries over to the Charger – around the body, giving it a wide berth because, well, he doesn't know why. Maybe the Driver will reach for him. Maybe he doesn't want to be caught for the murder. Maybe he just doesn't want to see it anymore.

Richie goes to the Charger.

Sees movement in the backseat. A glimpse of dark eyes. Doe eyes.

He gets in the driver seat. Not sure why he does that, either.

Black leather seats. Warm, not too warm. He sinks in. Like it's cradling him, somehow. A hand cupping him, keeping him safe.

The keys are cold in his palm.

He draws a deep breath, wills himself to look in the backseat.

The girl is there. The tape is off her mouth, hanging there off her red, chafed cheek. Lipstick smeared. Her eyes glimmer.

"You ready to drive?" she asks him.

She sits in the back next to a black duffel. The duffel is open. He sees the stock of a shotgun or rifle sticking out. A rope tied into a noose next to it. Sex toys lumped around it like coiled, black snakes – dildos and dicks and nylon harnesses. Next to the bag, a tackle box – that's open, too. Pill bottles inside. Most full. And next to that, a photo album. Also open because, Richie thinks, now everything is open. All things are open to him, nothing is forbidden, all is permitted. In the book he sees photos. Of him. With women. Women he hasn't been with, women he doesn't know. One of them is him with Marie. Him fucking her from behind on a beach somewhere. They've never been to the beach. She never liked that position, either.

"Wh... what is this?" he asks.

"You're the Driver now," the girl says. "Big man." Then she takes her hand and presses the tape back over her mouth. She's smiling behind it.

Richie turns back around.

Get out of the car.

Get out, get out, get out.

He puts the keys in the ignition and starts it up.

Above him, a holder built into the console. For sunglasses. He pushes it, it clicks, then it drops open.

A pair of plastic pink-frame sunglasses sit in there.

He grabs them, puts them on.

Ahead, bright sun. Behind, black bands and a low grumble of thunder.

Big man.

So strong.

Richie revs the engine.

THE YELLOW DOOR
SILVIA MORENO-GARCIA

Silvia's story plays on the theme of gaming as an addiction, and for some this is certainly a reality. However, as you will see this is a weird tale, an otherworldly piece. It's not so much the game that should give you pause for thought here, as the soup.

IN CHINATOWN, WHEN Chinatown was vibrant, lit bright with electric signs and buzzing with neon. A garish, delightful urban haven for the night moths. The Bamboo Palace and Ming's and the Terrace are gone. And of course, The Yellow Door is gone, too.

It wasn't much of anything, The Yellow Door. At least, from the outside. You couldn't even get to it without very specific directions. Which was, of course, part of the allure. Part of the reason why we ventured there in the first place.

It was located in the middle of a long, narrow alleyway, tucked around the corner from a busy street, far from the vendors who hawked dried fish and shrimp in the daytime; away from the late-night restaurants with their fake golden pagodas or the shops with geese hanging at the window. That first time we walked there we couldn't find it.

"Maybe you got it wrong," Carrie told Jean Baptiste and Jean Baptiste shook his head.

"No. I don't have it wrong," he said.

"Who told you about this place again?" Carrie asked.

"James Winters. The law students like to come here."

"Winters is a candyass," Carrie said, frowning.

"Maybe he is," Kendall said, "But I want to play."

"We should go home," Carrie replied. "I'm tired."

He was very handsome, Roger Kendall. Tall and thin, with a practiced air of mockery always upon his face. His hands were those of a pianist, though he played poorly; the fingers long and elegant. On his right hand he always wore a simple little silver ring with an onyx stone that had belonged to his grandfather and was reckoned lucky. I admired Kendall's taste and I'd spent two months trying to find a similar stone for a modest price, but everything was out of my range. Unlike Kendall I did not come from a wealthy family. My clothes were not fashionable, my shoes a tad worn.

"Go then," Kendall said.

"It's a bad area," Carrie muttered, as if that might deter Kendall. He was fearless, stubborn, magnificent, wild. He knew every joint and every eatery and every club in town, and he was a bit offended that someone had not bothered to tell him about this game parlour. The Yellow Door. He came here because he was a completist and he could not abide that someone knew of a den he hadn't tried; because he had to taste everything there was.

"What do I care?" he said. "Run back and hail a cab if you want."

As he spoke he took out a cigarette and his lighter. It was then that some piece of glass or metal reflected the blooming flame, catching our attention so that we turned our heads and found the yellow door.

It was not quite yellow, though. Dirt and grime had streaked it, the paint had peeled off in parts, making it hard to distinguish its original colour, though here and there was a patch of jaundiced wood. We could make out no name above the door, just as we'd been warned. No wonder that in the dark people might pass it by.

"Well, it doesn't look like much," Carrie said. "We ought to have gone to Pussycat tonight, this whole evening has been a bust."

"Knock," Kendall told Jean Baptiste.

Jean Baptiste knocked and the door opened a crack. Jean Baptiste took out a tiny piece of yellow paper – the invitation Winters had given us – and then the door swung open and we were let in. We walked down some steps, pushed aside a yellow curtain, and emerged into a large room with intricate woodwork and detailed red and gold wallpaper. Showy, with great chandeliers. Not your usual cheap dim sum joint with bare walls and a sad, lonely calendar in the corner.

It was crowded, everyone smoking, drinking, playing mahjong around little tables. Some players had grim faces while others sipped tea and smiled.

We paused by a great tank that was so clouded with algae and muck it was impossible to glimpse any fish, though there was the vague suggestion of movement in its dark waters. We moved aside to let a few people pass and then the fellow leading us, the one who had opened the door and had not spoken until then, raised his voice.

"A private room?"

"Why not?" Kendall said.

He took us to the back of the parlour and pulled open a door that looked more like a filigree screen and we went into a little room decked in the same gold and red wallpaper that covered the rest of the venue, a table and four chairs at its centre. There was a mahjong box on the table. It was heavily carved; the handle, sides, front and back, all decorated with a sinuous pattern. The tiles were all neatly stacked inside little drawers.

We sat down and Jean Baptiste, who had played the game before, began explaining the rules and showed us the tiles. A server in a yellow dress walked in and nodded at us.

"What will you be having?" she asked.

"Beers all around," I said.

"Oh, please no, what a bore," Carrie said petulantly. "A Martini for me."

"And to eat?"

"Shoggoth soup," Kendall said.

"Didn't James say he got sick with that?" I asked.

"James would get sick from eating anything other than potatoes and rice," Kendall said.

"We don't always serve the soup," the server said, making a face.

"Come now," Kendall said taking out a few bills and flicking them on the table. "I can pay."

So that was that. Jean Baptiste explained how we would draw tiles and make different melds. I looked at my tiles, the bamboos and flowers and circles, and then at Kendall, who was smirking and tapping his foot to the rhythm of some music that was piping in through a concealed speaker. He already knew how to play and he wasn't paying attention to Jean Baptiste, instead staring at the wallpaper with that distant, careless look he sometimes got. And I wasn't paying too much attention to Jean Baptiste either, already too drunk to bother much with the rules and the kongs.

The result was I lost miserably the first round and had scarcely any points. Kendall won and we all clapped, and then Carrie – who was perhaps drunker than me at this point – declared she was going to bet her shirt in the next round.

That's when they brought the shoggoth soup. It arrived in a covered silver dish and when the server placed it on a little table next to the bigger play table he removed the lid. Smoke curled up, a pungent smell invading our nostrils. It was... it smelled... like the seaweed you find strewn along the beach when the tide has pulled back. Brine. And something else. Something meaty. But I thought of truffles, too. I did not like it.

Kendall picked into the silver bowl, stirring it with a ladle and took a sip.

"It's not awful," he declared, and then he ordered another round of beers.

A couple of hours later we staggered out into the street. Kendall vomited just a few steps from the game parlour, staining his shoes with yellow bile. He wiped his mouth with the back of his hand and then he laughed loudly. We found a cab willing to drive us to our respective homes and called it a night.

A WEEK LATER Kendall knocked on my door and announced we were going out, which was the usual way things went with Kendall. He did not give you fair warning. You had to simply comply with his demands and go wherever and whenever he wanted; it had been this way since we'd met. But everyone loved Kendall, everyone followed Kendall, and none of us resented him for it because Kendall was fun and Kendall was generous. Last summer he'd bought me a new coat, the one I wore almost every day now, because he knew I couldn't afford it. He treated me, us, to meals, drinks, outings. Plus, I liked him. He offered me a view of a different world than the one I'd lived in all my life, the little kid on a scholarship with the bad teeth and the awkward face. With Kendall, you felt like royalty and were treated as such.

"It's Reading Week and I've got a whole book to go through," I said.

"Bullshit," Kendall replied. "No one reads during Reading Week. I certainly am not reading a single line."

"That is because you've dropped out of all your classes and you don't need an education when you have that much money."

"Well, that's the beauty of money, isn't it? It allows you the chance to throw your life away on idle pursuits. Come on, I do need a fourth."

"For what?"

"We are heading to play mahjong. Jean Baptiste and a friend of his, David Wong, another law school kid."

"It's not my thing."

But he'd already grabbed my keys, which had been dangling by the door, and was walking down the stairs. I fetched my coat and followed him to his car, a Corvette Stingray – his latest purchase, only two months old – and nodded at Jean Baptiste and David Wong.

"Hey," I said as I sat up front.

"Hey," said David.

David Wong was a thin, well-dressed young man who smiled a lot during the ride to The Yellow Door. His good humour evaporated when we sat down in the private room and a server came by.

"Shoggoth soup," Kendall ordered.

"You better be careful. That stuff will kill you, you know?" David said, sounding earnest and serious.

"So will alcohol and I'm further ahead on that score," Kendall said and grinned.

"What's so bad about the soup?" I asked.

"I just wouldn't recommend it," David said.

I played without interest, pausing a few times to stare at the gold and red wallpaper, the pretty spiral patterns catching my fancy. David talked about mahjong superstitions. Wear red for luck, if you have a losing streak wash your hands to get rid of bad luck, do not eat pau when you play.

I was distracted, tired, and at the first opportunity excused myself and hurried back home.

ONE NEVER LEFT without Kendall's express permission. Parties did not end until he said so, neither did excursions nor drinks. I'd sinned against him and knew to expect a short period of silence followed by a random invitation to participate in the night's revelries.

A month later Carrie called and I thought she was going to invite me to one of Kendall's parties. I'd have to show contrition, but I'd done that before. Instead, she told me Kendall had broken it off with her and she needed a favour. She'd left some important books at his place and needed them back.

I was to be an intermediary.

I asked her if she couldn't just pick them up herself, but Carrie didn't want to run into Kendall.

"He's behaving like a perfect ass," she told me. "I never want to speak to him again."

How melodramatic, I thought, but I owed Carrie a favour and she wanted it repaid.

I told her I hadn't spoken to Kendall for several weeks and that I'd see about it. After she hung up I decided I'd better go to Kendall's place that same day. There was no need to put it off.

Kendall's apartment was huge, very elegant and refined. Kendall had installed three great mirrors in the living room which spanned from the floor to the ceiling and when he threw parties and invited me over I saw myself reflected in them and felt my drab appearance was not so drab after all. Reflected in the beauty of that room, duplicated, I was almost fascinating. Though never as interesting as Kendall, who burned in the middle of the room, a glass of wine in his hands, his head thrown back in laughter. Sometimes, when you walked by, Kendall would tap you on the shoulder for a second and smile, a benign god holding court. At his right was Jean Baptiste, his roommate, but I was at his left.

Kendall didn't need a roommate, but he didn't like being alone, so he'd convinced Jean Baptiste to go live with him. Jean Baptiste had the temperament for it. He could also cook omelettes or pancakes or some other little breakfast for Kendall on the weekends, and kept the liquor cabinet stocked.

It was noon by the time I walked into Kendall's building,

which was the perfect time to visit Kendall because he'd be getting up right now, ready and eager for brunch, happy for a chat, perhaps even willing to forget that I'd ditched him four weeks before.

"Hey," Jean Baptiste said when he opened the door, rubbing his eyes, and I could tell he'd been on a bender the night before just by the way he was standing up. "You are here. Are we supposed to go somewhere? Did Kendall ask you to organize something?"

"No. I've come for Carrie's books. She said Kendall was going to put them in a box," I said.

"He didn't tell me anything about that."

"He probably forgot. Is he awake yet?"

"No. We were at the Yellow Door two nights ago. He's still there."

"Still there?" I said panicking. "Jean Baptiste, he probably tried to stumble home hours ago, fell asleep in an alley. We should go find him and bring him home."

"No. He's done it before. You have no idea. We've been going to The Yellow Door almost every other night. Well, every night this week. I wasn't drinking last night. I'm just exhausted from this week and trying to recover, but Kendall wouldn't come back and it was three a.m. so I split."

"Two nights ago?"

"Yes. Friday at 3 a.m., I told you so."

I turned around, ready to head back down the stairs.

"I don't know if you should go. He's really weird lately."

"He's in one of his moody phases. Give him a week. He'll pick up painting or collecting porcelain tea cups or something else to keep himself distracted," I said. Kendall was not exactly constant.

"No. He's weird," Jean Baptiste said and paused. He looked suddenly afraid. "He's not well at all."

*   *   *

KENDALL DID NOT look at me when I walked into the private room. He was alone, moving tiles around with an index finger. There was a faint, unpleasant smell in the room and the soft piping of music through the concealed speaker.

He looked thinner. Hunched over the table, I could make out the outline of his spine against his shirt. The tips of his fingers seemed jaundiced and I thought, dear God, his liver has failed him. But no. That couldn't be it.

"Do these tiles look yellow to you?" he asked all of a sudden, raising his head.

They were ivory tiles painted red or blue or green. No yellow on them. I shook my head.

"No. We should get you back home."

He had dark circles under his eyes and he was very pale, like laundry that's been bleached out in the sun.

"You should have come earlier. I finished the soup."

He gestured towards the silver bowl sitting in a corner.

"Time to go, Kendall," I said.

I thought he'd refuse to come with me.

He agreed and I was thankful.

Kendall managed to make it to the doorway of his apartment, but he almost collapsed once we crossed the threshold. Jean Baptiste had to help him to his bed.

"Phone the doctor," I told him.

Jean Baptiste babbled a little because Kendall hated doctors and when he came back to his senses he'd be pissed, but I prevailed. The doctor came and declared Kendall malnourished.

"What has he been taking?" he asked. "This is not a little bender and a puff of weed."

I said I did not know.

Truly, I did not. I intended to find out.

JEAN BAPTISTE GAVE me David Wong's address and I paid him a visit, but David Wong didn't have much information about the shoggoth soup, except that they'd always warned him about it in his family. But there were dire warnings about almost everything in his family and David had not thought to ask. He did know someone who could tell me about it: his aunt Bai, who smiled a toothless smile when David introduced me to her.

"I need to know about shoggoth soup," I told her. "Is it a narcotic? Does it have a toxin?"

"You've been to The Yellow Door," the woman replied and her eyes fixed on me, searching for something.

"Yes. With my friend. And now he's hooked on that – shoggoth – I think it is. I want to find out…"

"You drink alcohol, don't you?"

"I do," I said.

"You drink it and most of the time you are fine. A light buzz in your head and a feeling of effervescence. But simple people drink alcohol and they don't feel so well. They get sick."

"It's a drug, then."

"It can do things… it can change you," the woman said.

Kendall certainly looked changed, but what I wanted to know was exactly what kind of drug we were dealing with. Was this some opium derivative? Something else?

"I have to –"

"Poor child. You have to keep your friend away from The Yellow Door," the woman said, patting my cheek.

She would not say anything else. I was floundering and exhausted. I phoned Jean Baptiste and told him under no circumstances was he to let Kendall out of the apartment, though judging by his condition it was doubtful Kendall would be able to walk to his car, much less drive himself to The Yellow Door.

TWO WEEKS PASSED. I went to see Kendall, even helped him into some of his clothes. He had ugly welts and marks over his torso. Circular bruises that were turning from purple to yellow as they healed. Ugly abrasions on the neck. He'd lost a whole nail and chewed the rest. Aside from gambling and indulging in drugs, had he also been in fights? It was likely, judging by the state of his poor body.

But each day seemed to bring back his strength, his smile fluttering for a moment. He didn't have the stomach for solids yet and was stuck eating mush, chuckling.

"Like a baby," he said and despite his thinness there was much of the old Kendall there, that smug, lofty grin.

He talked about the summer trip we were going to take. To the Charlottes, where we'd have to camp in a tent and be wary of bears, but it would be fun.

Carrie even came to visit Kendall, bringing some daisies to cheer him up. Later, when she stepped out of his room she spent a good amount of time telling me how all this was her fault. The breakup had driven poor Kendall into a deep depression. Kendall was too self-centered to behave in such a way, but Carrie had already built herself her own version of events and I wasn't very interested in correcting her. I was relieved when she did not return for a second visit.

Overall, it was going well. In a year, I thought, we'd look back and laugh at this incident. Remember that time… and we'd descend into hilarity. Kendall's wild antics. Kendall's follies.

And then Jean Baptiste phoned late at night, waking me up.

"Kendall's gone," he said in one breathless sentence.

"What do you mean Kendall is gone?" I asked, already putting on my shoes, which I'd left by the bed.

"Gone! I walked by his room and he's not there and the car is not downstairs."

"Christ. You stay there. I'll go grab him."

"I'm afraid."

"God damn it!" I yelled into the receiver.

I took my coat and rushed out. It was starting to rain and

by the time I'd made it to The Yellow Door it was definitely pouring. The taxi driver wouldn't drop me off in the alley. I had to walk it and was soaked in two seconds flat.

I went all the way to the back, to Kendall's usual room. He was there, of course. Where else would he be? He had spread the mahjong tiles all over the table. There was a steaming dish of shoggoth soup waiting for him, on a little side table. He stirred the tiles with his index fingers, rearranging them.

"I had a dream about an ocean with no stars," he said.

He held a tile up, towards the light.

"Did you dream?" he asked me.

"I didn't have any dreams last night."

"No, just now. There was an ocean made of sequins. Made of tiles, each one nestled against the next. And the sequins that are tiles, they are gold. Sequins, tiles, embroidered, glistening, below the velvet night. Do you hear me now?"

I thought Kendall's health had been improving but he seemed worse off now that I looked at him. There was a nasty pustule on his hand and the way he sat, you'd have thought he was an 80 year-old man, his spine bent by the weight of time.

"Sit down," he said. "If we get two more players we can have a game."

"We are not going to play."

"I'll ask some others."

"I doubt anyone else will want to play with you in your state."

"But they are already here."

I flinched at that though truly it was just the two of us in the tiny private room with the rich wallpaper and the speaker.

"Kendall, it's time to leave," I muttered.

He glanced at me, his eyes very dark, though… there seemed to be a film across them. He rubbed them, absentmindedly and the film – a trick of the light, perhaps – was gone. But he still looked like hell. Stooped over the table, his hands shaking just a tiny bit.

"If you look at the tiles carefully you can see things," he told me.

"What things?"

"The lines. The colours move." He turned his head, looking at the wallpaper. "The patterns move. Strange moons. An oracle. I am an oracle. I will be. Can you hear it? See. This tile is yellow."

He muttered something intelligible, all sharp consonants, and I lost my composure. I could not take any more of this.

"Listen to yourself, Kendall. You are so fucked out of your skull that you can barely speak full words. Come on."

He'd taken off his jacket and rolled up his sleeves, so when I grabbed his arm and tried to pull him up I touched his skin, which seemed feverish to the touch. And also seemed... rubbery. Not skin at all, but something slick and moist and sick. He shivered, and that was the worst part. The shiver seemed to rack his whole body, from the top of his head to the soles of his feet, rippling through his flesh.

"Let go of me," he said. "I hate you. Let go of me."

I released him and could not help my disgust. He must have noticed my revulsion. He stood up, his hands resting on the table, and threw me a look of such venomous contempt I took a step back.

"You are pathetic. Always following me around, like a dog nipping at my heels. Always paying attention to every word I say and everything I do, and wanting to be me. Oh, I know how you envy me. It's not my fault, though, not my fault I am who I am and you are... that."

He smirked, brushing his shaggy hair from his face. It was sweaty; the filthy pelt of a beast. His clothes were dirty and there were specks of mud, something dark – perhaps oil – on his trousers. The awful smell had returned. As though Kendall had rolled in one of the dumpsters in the alley and walked right into the gambling den. Perhaps he had. I could picture him scrabbling in the alleys, muttering gibberish to himself.

He surprised me when he spoke. His voice was so loud and strong; quite at odds with his present condition.

"Do you know what they say of you?" he asked me and pointed a finger at me. "They say you are a pathetic social climber and that I should just get rid of you. Carrie said it, you know. And Jean Baptiste. And James, too.

"You think you are smart and capable, but you are never going to amount to anything at all. That is why you hate me. And the only reason why I keep you around is because you amuse me. Because you are such a clown!"

"Don't, Kendall," I said. "I'll take you home."

"I don't want to go home and I certainly don't want you to take me there. You're not fit to wipe my shoes, much less drive my car. Who do you think you are?"

"Kendall."

"You were good for a laugh! In your mended trousers and your used jackets. But I'm tired of you. You bore me."

It would have been better if we'd come to blows. It would have stung less. Because it was true. All of it was true. Suddenly I could picture them, the lot of them – Carrie, Jean Baptiste, James, even David Wong – chuckling in a corner. Why'd you invite this one again? It was good once for a lark, but now... I could hear Carrie's bird-like laughter and Jean Baptiste's deep guffaw.

He turned his back towards me. I took off my coat, the one he'd bought me with a smile, and tossed it on the floor. I didn't want his crumbs. Then I walked outside. It was still raining, but it didn't matter. As I walked down the streets the neon lights of Chinatown were reflected in black puddles.

THE COPS CAME knocking soon after that. I was expecting them. The only surprise was when they said the name "Jean Baptiste." They had to repeat the whole story twice and still I didn't quite believe it.

Jean Baptiste had been found dead in the apartment he shared with Kendall. It had been an ugly, miserable death. He'd been stabbed nearly twenty times. The apartment was torn apart, the great mirrors smashed to pieces and shards of glass strewn all over the floor. Books had been pulled from the shelves, their pages torn and smeared with a dark, foul liquid. Kendall's expensive clothes had been shredded wildly. Kendall himself was missing and they were looking for him. I told them Kendall and I had fought and were not on speaking terms.

I didn't tell them about The Yellow Door. I guess a part of me thought Kendall might be there and I didn't want them to find him, despite everything. I returned to The Yellow Door a few days later, but he was nowhere to be seen. I kept coming back every few weeks. But he was never there.

They cleaned Kendall's apartment. Jean Baptiste's body was sent back to Montreal for burial. The crime did not take much space in the newspapers. It was a robbery gone wrong. Kendall's family hushed the whole affair as much as they could: money was good for more than idle pursuits. I thought perhaps they'd aided Kendall's escape and pictured the rich boy, off in some tropical island, walking by the seashore. If they had, they wouldn't have told me, so I didn't bother them and I didn't talk to the police about my suspicions.

Still, I paused by The Yellow Door once in a while.

The last time I went into the gambling parlour it was October. It had been a long summer, but now the rains returned. I did not play the previous times when I visited the parlour, and this time it was no different. I just stood by the fish tank, adrift, awash in melancholy.

I listened to the incessant click-clack of tiles against wood and watched the smoke of cigarettes curl up in the air.

There was a light tap and I glanced at the murky glass of the fish tank. It still had not been cleaned. It was dark and filthy with algae and slime. I did not think any fish could survive in there but clearly some did because there was movement in the darkness and I squinted, peering closer.

It darted out of the shadows for a few seconds. A brief glimpse was all I got. But it was unmistakable. Kendall's silver ring with the onyx. The beautiful antique ring. His lucky charm which he never took off, even when he went swimming. There, floating in the tank.

I opened my mouth.

Something dark, which could not have been a hand; which was the vague, fuzzy memory of a hand retracted, slipped back, and the ring was gone.

I closed my mouth and I walked out.

I didn't scream until a long time later.

DIE
LAVIE TIDHAR

In a story reminiscent of the notorious Milgram Experiment, Lavie asks us how far we would be prepared to go in a game where our life is at stake. What follows may feel at times entirely without hope, but there are glimpses of humanity, a refusal to succumb to the loss of identity that torture can bring. Lavie demonstrates yet again why he is one of the most extraordinary writers working in genre today; an author with an uncompromising vision and deft hand.

54.

THERE IS A room. It is a white room, with white walls. It smells very faintly of paint and something like Listerine.

There are two people in the room. They are watched by hidden viewers. The two people sit facing each other across a table. Before each one is a single die.

On the table between them is a pistol.

"Throw," a voice says. It is a cool, calm voice. The two people each pick up a die. They throw.

No. 54 gets a five. No. 12 gets a four.

No. 54 reaches for the pistol. No. 12 falls back. No. 54 fires the pistol. The bullet catches No. 12 between the eyes. She falls back, dead instantly. No. 54 stands there with the pistol in his hand.

A buzzer sounds. The door opens.

"The winner is No. 54," the voice says, monotonously. "No. 54 is the winner."

No. 54 places the pistol on the table and leaves the room.

55.

No. 54 sits in the room. No. 55 sits opposite 54 in the room. No. 55 is tall and thin and pale. No. 55 is a boy.

Before each of them is a single white die.

On the table between them is a large, sharp knife.

"Throw," the voice says.

They throw.

No. 54 gets a two.

But No. 55 gets a one.

No. 55 backs away as No. 54 grabs the knife. 54 is left-handed. His palm is sweating. He stabs down with the knife. The boy No. 55 says, "No, no, no." The knife slashes him across the arm and blood gushes out.

"No, please, please, don't," 55 says.

He backs away against the wall. No. 54 stabs wildly, his eyes blurred. Blood splashes everywhere. The boy, 55, is silent. A jagged line trails down from his ear to his chest. Blood bubbles out of the wound in his throat, but no words come, will ever come again.

A buzzer sounds. The door opens.

"The winner is No. 54," the voice says, monotonously. "No. 54 is the winner."

No. 54 tosses the knife on the floor and leaves the room.

61.

"My name is Simon," No. 61 says. He is a small, nervous looking boy.

A buzzer sounds. No. 61 shakes in pain as an unseen electric current runs through the bracelets on his arms and around his ankles. He clamps his teeth tight and doesn't cry.

"Fuck you," No. 61 says, when the current subsides.

This time when the buzzer sounds he does scream.

"Throw," the voice says.

They throw.

"Shit," No. 61 says, softly.

He'd thrown a five. But lucky No. 54 has thrown a six.

There is a vat of acid on the table between them.

"I'm sorry," No. 54 says. The current hits him then and the acid splashes all over No. 61, and Simon screams, and screams, and screams, and then he's silent.

The buzzer sounds. The door opens.

"The winner is No. 54," the voice says, monotonously. "No. 54 is the winner."

No. 54 hobbles out of the room.

67.

"MY NAME'S RAY," he tells No. 67. "My name's Ray Walker."

No. 67 looks at him in contempt. "Fuck you, fifty-four," she says. The buzzer sounds a moment later and they're both electrocuted, but 67 is grinning all the while.

"Throw," the voice says.

They throw.

There is a hammer on the table.

Ray has thrown a three.

67 has thrown a three.

"Draw," the voice says, but 67 is already moving, pushing back the chair in her rush to get the hammer, and her hand closes on the handle a moment before 54 makes his move. 67 swings the hammer at 54 and catches him on the shoulder. The pain explodes in his arm but he ducks down and tries to lift the table up, to throw it against her, only it's bolted to the floor.

67 grins.

"Fuck you, fifty-four," she says again. The hammer swings but 54 is fast, and he ducks under the swing and comes down behind her and he grabs her arm. She kicks back at him and he grunts with the pain but he won't let go.

They don't speak any more, all their energies are focused on the hammer, it hovers in the air as their muscles strain, a strange deadlock has taken them.

At last 67 screams and tries to turn, to shift the balance, but she stumbles, and 54 twists her arm, forcing the fingers loose, taking hold of the hammer. She cowers away from him. "What's your name?" Ray Walker says, and again, desperately, "What's your name?"

She looks this way and that, trying to find an angle of attack, when he brings down the hammer, again and again, cracking her skull like a shell.

The buzzer sounds. The door opens.

"The winner is No. 54," the voice says, monotonously. "No. 54 is the winner."

Ray Walker looks at the dead girl on the floor and the hammer drops from his fingers.

"The player must leave the room," the voice says softly, coldly. Still Ray Walker stands there looking at the girl.

The buzzer sounds. Electric shocks sear Ray Walker's flesh. He turns and leaves the room, still shaking.

89.

"I'M MATTHEW," No. 89 says.

The buzzer sounds. Matthew screams.

"How long have you been here?" Matthew says.

The buzzer sounds. Matthew screams.

"Will it hurt?" Matthew says. "Will it hurt to die?"

The buzzer sounds. Matthew screams.

"Throw," the voice says.

"No," Matthew says.

The buzzer sounds. Matthew screams.

"Throw," the voice says.

"I am not scared of you," Matthew says.

The buzzer sounds. Matthew screams.

"Throw," the voice says.

Matthew cries tears of pain. He cups the die in his hand. His eyes look into Ray's. His lips form into an O but never speak. Ray holds the die. They throw.

"No," Matthew says.

He's thrown a six.

Ray's thrown a one.

There is a small sword on the table.

Ray looks at Matthew. Ray sits motionless. "I'm Ray," he says, and there is something liberating about it, about saying his name, about losing. "I'm Ray."

"It's nice to meet you, Ray," Matthew says, trying to smile.

They stare at each other across the table.

Matthew's hand closes on the handle of the sword. He lifts it in the air.

Ray stands. He is taller than Matthew. "Do it quickly," he says.

"I will, Ray," Matthew says.

Ray keeps his eyes open. He watches Matthew. Matthew holds the sword in both hands. He raises the sword. Then he cries out and brings it down, not on Ray but on himself.

The sword enters Matthew's soft belly. It cuts through skin and tendons, though muscle and lining. Intestines spill out of the wound, the rank smell of semi-digested food, acids, blood. Matthew's eyes flutter. His lips move without sound. Ray watches him, numbly.

Ray watches him die.

"Forfeit," the voice says.

The buzzer sounds. The door opens.

"The winner is No. 54," the voice says, monotonously. "No. 54 is the winner by default."

Ray walks out of the room.

* * *

120.

"HE WAS THE bravest little guy I ever saw," No. 54 says.

No. 120 is a big muscled guy. He looks at 54 with no change of expression as the buzzer sounds and the electric shock hits 54.

"Throw," the voice says.

They throw.

The big muscled guy looks down at the dice without expression. He'd thrown a two. No. 54 has thrown a three.

There's a garrotte on the table.

No. 54 is a little bit scared, but the big guy doesn't move, just looks at him. No. 54 picks up the garrotte. He walks behind the big guy, No. 120.

"Just make it quick, motherfucker," No. 120 says. "How the fuck did you survive this long?"

No. 54 loops the garrotte around the big guy's neck and pulls, hard.

"I guess I'm just lucky," he says.

The buzzer sounds. The door opens.

"The winner is No. 54," the voice says, monotonously. "No. 54 is the winner."

No. 54 walks out of the room.

200.

"I JUST DON'T think I've ever loved anyone the way I've loved you," No. 200 says. She looks at him seriously. The buzzer sounds but she ignores it. He sees it in her eyes. Like him she's learned to ride the currents. She looks at him, in pain, earnest. "How many?" she says.

He says, "I don't know. You?"

"I don't know," she says. "Too many."

"We're the lucky ones," he says.

"Yes," she says, nodding seriously. "We're the lucky ones."

"I love you too," he says. "Do you want to know my name?"

"No," she says. "No names. There are no names."

"No," No. 54 agrees. "There are no names."

"Throw," the voice says.

They throw.

"Three," she says.

"Five," he says.

"I knew it would be you," she whispers. "It's why I've loved you, I've always loved you."

"I won't do it," he says.

"You will do it," she says.

"We could throw again," he says. Bile rises in his mouth from the repeated electric shocks.

"But it wouldn't count," she says.

"I thought you would be the lucky one," he says.

"I *am* the lucky one," she says.

She smiles. On the table between them is a double-barrelled shotgun.

"I think my name was Annie," she says, just before he shoots her.

Her body blasts back against the wall. She crumples to the floor. Her lips are still smiling, still holding the last vestige of her name.

The buzzer sounds. The door opens.

"The winner is No. 54," the voice says, monotonously. "No. 54 is the winner."

No. 54 walks out of the room.

612.

IT'S JUST ANOTHER day, another game. No. 54 sits in the room. No. 612 sits in the room. There are dice on the table between them. There is a canister of petrol on the table between them. There is a box of matches on the table between them.

"Throw," the voice says.

They throw.

"Two," No. 54 says.

"One," No. 612 says, dully.

No. 54 reaches for the petrol. No. 612's lips move, almost without sound. It takes a conscious effort to make out the words.

"Our Father who art in heaven, hallowed be thy name," No. 612 says.

No. 54 douses No. 612 with the petrol.

"Forgive us our trespasses," No. 612 says, almost inaudibly. His eyes are closed, his face shining.

Ray Walker strikes the match.

"And lead us not into temptation," No. 612 says, "but deliver us from evil."

Ray Walker tosses the match. It flies through the air, the flame flickering. It hits No. 612 in the chest.

No. 612 alights in a blaze of fire.

He begins to scream. He smells like crackling.

The buzzer sounds, much later. The door opens, allowing in some air.

"The winner is No. 54," the voice says, monotonously. "No. 54 is the winner."

No. 54 walks out of the room.

813.

IT'S JUST ANOTHER day, another game.

No. 54 sits in the room. No. 813 sits in the room. There are dice on the table between them.

They throw.

Later, much later, when No. 813 is dead, the voice speaks.

"You win," it says.

The room is silent. Ray Walker stares at No. 813's ruined face, his unblinking eyes. He breathes heavily, steadies himself. "What did I win?" he says.

The door remains closed. The room remains silent. There is no answer. Ray Walker grips the edges of the table. "What did I win?" he shouts.

The sound bounces off the white walls. Faintly, in the room, is the smell of fresh paint and something like Listerine. There is no answer.

"What did I win?" No. 54 shouts. "What did I win? What did I win? What did I win?"

The buzzer sounds. The door opens.

Defeated, Ray Walker exits the room.

xxxx.

IT'S JUST ANOTHER day, another game.

No. 54 sits in the room. No. xxxx sits in the room. There are dice on the table between them.

They throw.

CHRYSALISES
BENJANUN SRIDUANGKAEW

Most of us will be familiar with the analogy of war as a game, but Benjanun takes this trope and puts her own fascinating twist on it. I'd say there's body horror here, but that's perhaps too simple an assessment, because there is actually a great deal of beauty to be found too; the ambiguity and fantastical imagery in Benjanun's stories ensure I come back to them time and again, finding fresh treasures on each occasion.

As THE CITY of cities burns down, its queen is offered a choice.

She sits in a throne of quantum questions and nascent narratives, contemplating a skyline of flame and nuclear smears. For centuries she has ruled and built; a thousand nations pay her tribute. Her domain fell in a matter of weeks.

Before her an entity of uncertain appearance kneels, shreds of noon and scraps of dusk sutured together by tendons of smog. The creature holds forth a game board, a set of pawns.

"Tell me the rules," she says. Her palace is mortared in syncretic logic and armored in singularity paradoxes. For the moment she is safe, though that will not last.

"A battle game," the entity says. "To a point it reflects the players and your circumstances will heavily weigh the game against you. Your units will be weaker – growth rate, recovery, numbers. Victory conditions are impossible and winning is not the objective."

"Then what is?" If she listens the queen may hear the sound of houses and temples shattering, of conundrum shields sundering beneath ballistic blasts. She will not flee; escape is beside the point and beneath contempt.

"The game has a lateral relationship with reality. I have activated its causal bridge. The troops you generate as you play may translate and cross over, if you choose, to act at your behest."

"Nothing comes of nothing. What will give them embodiment and power?"

The entity's mouth curves, a parted parabola. Its teeth gleam jagged in the dark. "At this juncture, does it matter?

"No." She engages the board and begins.

MONSOON SEASON AND everything is budding fast: mangoes and rose apples heavy on the branch, cocoons ripe and brilliant on forearms and wrists. Janthira, surgeon by trade and entomologist by hobby, heads the collection that harvest.

The extraction process is individual and arbitrary, and no one has a knack for it quite as Janthira does. At an orphanage she coaxes a chrysalis from a boy by wrapping it in glittering foil, persuades another to detach by clicking red-hot scissors at a teenage girl's jaw. It is not a threat she means to carry out, but the cocoons have been known to show unexpected sympathy for their hosts. Those newly unburdened would shiver in relief, rid at last of a weight that has been gravid upon them for a year. A few sigh, wistful, already impatient for the next turn.

In the hothouse, they sort the harvest like fresh fruits. Janthira enjoys the variety, though the entomologist in her is slightly offended: no two chrysalises split alike. The first to hatch has the abdomen of a blue-banded bee, the complicated wings of a swallowtail butterfly, a pair of antennae dusted with gold. The second is mostly an orchid mantis, graceful petal-limbs and toothed forelegs, a proboscis like viscous brass.

Collection is done within the first week of monsoons, cultivation within the second. They have to work fast, but Janthira takes time to admire the insect-forms when she can.

They grow on a specific, exclusive nutrient. Most feeders are from the nursing home, a wealth of decades to spend and spare. Janthira is the second youngest at thirty-eight, Prae the youngest at twenty: neither offers much to nourish the pupae. Still Prae gives up her memory as though she possesses an octogenarian's worth, pouring minutes and weeks and years; monarch butterflies grow marvelous on Prae, scarabs sleek and bees brilliant. Of all the insectoids hers are matchless in speed and strength.

Janthira hears that, in a distant country, Prae fought in a war. At ten, twelve. Their town used to be so quiet and remote that the idea one of their own might've been a child soldier seems risible. Yet Janthira is inclined to believe: Prae's gaze is quick, sharp, feral. She admits to no parent or sibling, barely a surname. Janthira has seen Prae with a knife, has glimpsed the scars.

At the end of the day Janthira's hands are raw, her vision a kaleidoscope. Alien senses seep into hers, a view of the world through compound lenses. They slice away a moment of five-year-old Janthira in a kindergarten playground, sip from a bright day sticky with candied tamarinds.

It's not so high a price, she thinks as the colors and sweetness of that noon leach away. One hosts or feeds. Everyone has a duty to keep the town alive.

THE BOARD IS cut from the hide of unsleeping giants and the husk of ruined engines. The pawns are whittled from black light, dead trilobites, and packed ashes collected from the sites of genocide. The queen handles them with care.

She assesses the strength of her real-world troops, counts the evacuating ships. Too few remain; fewer will escape. "How do you perceive the board?" When she speaks diaphanous wings unfurl, wet, and shudder into brittle glass.

"An odd question to ask." The entity's outline distorts. Its limbs may be chainsaws sheathed in black exhaust, its fingers long rivets dripping rust. "I may see it in raw data and unorthodox geometries. Most likely I see it as you do, a simple physical object."

Since the game began the queen has been seeing the board as a canvas of butterfly blots and dragonfly smudges, but this she does not say. "In the crevices of abandoned moons began a race of itinerant gamblers who cross the stars as I would a doorstep. They derive endless life from the probability backlash of reversed fortune. To imperiled species they give indelible ink-roads with which to escape dying planets. In conflicts of perpetuity they arm the beleaguered with negation storms and obliteration shrikes. The turning of tides, the transformation of defeat to victory or otherwise – this is their passion and purpose."

"Such beings may exist. I concede the possibility." Its fingers graze over the board's edge. The metal ripples with percussive echoes. "But more immediately, Majesty, it's in your best interest to give the board your undivided attention."

SOME NIGHTS JANTHIRA dreams of lamplight eyes and smoke hands. Each time this happened – like a warning – she would steal away from the shelters, find a spot where she could observe the fighting.

A lighthouse, for the town bordered a sea once. What happened to the shore and the waves and the fish no one knows: relocated elsewhere, gobbled up by the swarm, never there in the first place. Janthira climbs the steps quick and quiet, tracing marks and stains that might have hosted her girl-self playing hide and seek, playing at being an explorer in the dark. No telling – she gave up those years long ago. She's never believed childhood more precious than any other part of life, if anything thinks it less: the hazy repetitive days where she had no say over herself and did not know what she wanted.

She parts gray cobwebs and sepia dust, reveals a window under harsh flashlight. On her knees she waits; she doesn't whisper monk-taught mantras, having fed those to the chrysalises too.

When the swarm comes the world stops, listens, strains taut.

They are factory parts and assembly noises, pipes and razors coated in oil, turbine-guts and pistons coiled in rust. Janthira imagines gasoline heat for eyes, rotating saw-fangs for ears, but the swarm perceives and hunts by other senses.

The insect-forms make their own answer. Flesh-hatched and memory-fed, they move too quickly to see, proboscides and stingers and formic acid vivisecting the swarm.

It is over fast, always it is – the swarm slows, ripples. Its constituents fall in geometric patterns, fluorescent circuits and schematics for impossible machines.

Janthira leans forward, clutches the windowsill. Her breath momentarily bruises the glass.

The insectoids circle the lighthouse, thinking hive thoughts, sampling human memories, or perhaps nothing at all. By dawn they will spin into the horizon, to find their next life-phase or better climate like migrating birds – everyone theorizes; no one knows. The insectoids protect the town for one year and not a day more. The next batch replaces them and the cycle lurches on; without the chrysalises there is no defense against the swarm.

A flashlight beam strobes between haloes of slag, rectangles of shrapnel. Pauses. Moves again, settles on shredded wings that glint like bottle shards.

Distance and night make it difficult to be sure but Janthira tracks the figure with her eyes, becomes certain. On knees gone numb and trembling, she watches Prae collect the broken bodies of moth-ants and gather antennae as long as arms, holding them close.

*   *   *

ON THE BOARD, the queen makes an illegal move, testing the boundaries of play and daring the algorithms of rules.

The entity cocks its head; its chuckle is a hard, motorized stutter. "I approve. I always like it when someone tries to break the game itself rather than contend within its criteria. What you did won't work, I regret to say, but may have gone a little way to sway the odds in your favor."

"These brokers of fortune," she says and judges how long it will be until the protections of her hall give. "At the end they exact payment, the forms and measures of which – so it is said – can be quite particular."

"Possibly," it concedes. "But it's fair to pay for goods received, don't you think?"

"Others still speculate that, though these brokers may slip from one end of the universe to another as I stride the length of my palace, they do not always find catastrophes of a scale suitable for their needs – eternity can be expensive; a little earthquake here or supernova there simply won't do. And so they engineer unwinnable sieges, incurable plagues, extinction events. It's a neat strategy; they create demand for services which they alone can supply, and thereby reap immortality in the bargain."

"Now that, I am sure, is pure fantasy."

IN THE MORNING the lighthouse grounds are empty, soot on the pavement and oil slick in the rain puddles. Prae stands over them like a general surveying a battlefield. "We've got fewer every year, you know," she says without turning. "Their numbers are probably constant. The way they disappear, maybe they reincarnate right away. Recycle. Whatever. We're never going to win and there's only one way for this to end."

Prae has a high, young voice. Twenty: she should be in university, fresh-faced and uniformed, navigating her first romances and sophomore classes. Janthira wonders if it is condescending to pity her. Probably it is. "What makes you think that?"

"I keep count. Old folks die and babies can't host. You can do a lot with lesser numbers but when you're fighting attrition... what do you think moves the bugs? They're good, intelligent even, but it can't be the memories of cooks and shopkeepers and schoolteachers that give them tactical sense. And what makes them fly away after the year is up?"

"Instinct?" Janthira says. This is the most she's ever heard Prae say at a time.

"It bothers me. Weapons you can't understand; that should appall anyone. But it's all we have."

"Last night," Janthira begins.

Prae turns around, abruptly. The moment of tension passes and her arms fall slack at her sides, her stance loose. "I eat them. They don't taste the best but if you season and cook them right, it's tolerable. Wings and torsos mostly, you don't want to risk the stingers. They are always some casualties on our side, I might as well put them to use."

"What?"

"Recycling. You only have so much to feed them with, so I thought it'd be worth a try. I know where you went to school at ten, if you care. Krungthep, wasn't it? Dealing with someone else's memories isn't too pleasant but –" Prae shrugs, a foreign little gesture. "No worse than anything else."

"That's what you feed them?"

"Even I run out of bad shit to flush out. This way I can make up for a lot of people – I've got excess, if there were more cocoons hatching right now I could fill them up. Maybe if we preserve the bugs. Dry them. Make chili paste."

Janthira grimaces, looking down at the fragments of carapace. She imagines Prae must've cooked and flavored them quickly, or perhaps bitten into them on the spot, crunching, swallowing. Dry legs down her throat and caught between her teeth. "What does that *do* to you?"

"Do?" Prae's expression defocuses. "Nothing. I'm not going to get any worse off knowing who cheated on their spouses. You'll be doing the grafts, right?"

"Right."

The young woman doesn't ask for permission; she attaches herself to Janthira the rest of the day, a second shadow.

Janthira collects seeds from the hothouse, checks the registrar for this year's hosts. Her next stop is the hospital, an ancient leaning building of three storeys and a disappointing lack of ghosts and dark history. Sometimes she still needs those, spindly-limbed terror in bathroom mirrors and rotting women in antique clothes. In the face of the real thing, fictional horror is strangely comforting.

Janthira joins a team of nurses while Prae stands against the wall, watching, gaze intent on the gleaming equipment. There are three doctors present counting Janthira; among them hers is the most prestigious PhD, obtained in Singapore. She used to be privately snobbish about that.

Children line up. An eight-year-old stares unblinking as Janthira rubs her arm down with alcohol, hardly flinches as Janthira presses the syringe in. Boys are more difficult, louder, frighten easily. Absent other obligations in life Janthira has always thought having a daughter might be nice, one she could train to music or art and forbid from ever trying for med school.

One of the nurses relieves her. Janthira thanks the man, goes in search of fresh air. The first lot of hosts is in the playground shared between the hospital and the school, elementary students entering their next semester with a cocoon in their arm.

She flicks a lighter on, ignites a cigarette. A low hum of air-conditioning someone has turned on at full blast against the humid heat. Electricity works, even though all their power lines connect to nowhere. The things one can get used to, learn not to question. She opens the window, wisps of tobacco streaming out to join the smell of sunshine and cut grass. Prae leans nearly halfway out, careless that they are on the second floor.

"Look," she says softly.

By the rose apple tree, its roots strewn with overripe fruits, a boy seizes up like a doll winding down.

There is no cry of pain as he falls, no sound of bones breaking as he bursts into butterflies.

ON HER WALLS the queen hangs feeds like pennants. Through them she may monitor the breaking of her soldiers, the shattering of her domain, composite enemies in soft focus as they blaze across the sky. Their edges bleed to stain the clouds; their bellies open to birth explosive shells. Beneath them towers unmake to graveyard-dust, humans to marrow-ghosts.

The feeds shudder and crease, folding in on themselves. When they straighten again the battlefield has changed.

Mandibles clack shut over muzzles. Insect limbs find purchase on plating and scythe through joints. Machine-parts twist and tremble under the pressure of their own fuel, bursting into fragments of circuitry and null space.

"You look surprised that they came through," the entity says.

The queen turns her gaze to the creature, her face expressionless. The strands of her hair rustle, briefly appear like antennae, but that may simply be faulty lighting. "I didn't imagine they would achieve embodiment this soon."

"You strike me as an individual who prefers fast results." Under the roiling haze it laughs, genteel amusement wreathed in smoke. Sunlight pierces its eye sockets. "And speaking of fast, would you like to negotiate the settlement of your account?"

They might have been haggling over an asteroid, a trade concession; the queen has always known this for a transaction. "I think," she says, "I know what you want."

"Then by implication you agree to it?"

"At this juncture, do I have a choice?"

NOTHING OF THE boy remains behind, after, except a pair of spectacles. Myopia, perhaps. By evening nobody has picked them up so Janthira does, turning the frame in her hands. The butterflies were small and uniform, stained-glass wings in primary colors spiraling toward the clouds. Absurdly she wishes she could've captured it on film, that exquisite, brief vision.

"We're going to die," Prae says, indifferently. "We were going to anyway, but if what happened to that kid is contagious it'll be that much sooner."

Janthira grips the spectacles harder. "Can't you say anything constructive?"

"*Saying* nice things isn't very useful. Doing would be something else." Prae's smile is hard. "Though I'll be fair, nobody could fault you for not having done enough, doctor."

Janthira doesn't answer.

The next day some hosts try to tear their cocoons out. One woman did it with a box cutter, struck an artery, wasn't found in time. Not the worst way to go; being vivisected by the swarm is an agony of days upon nights, blood frozen like pearls, skin flayed petal-thin. Everyone has seen the bodies, spread and bared in the streets as though the swarm means to map human anatomy. But dead is dead and the pupa doesn't outlive its host.

Before nightfall, a teacher dissolves into a roar of gnats.

Janthira finds a room to herself in the dormitories. Safety in numbers is an illusion; since the change she has come to prefer her own company to the near-exclusion of any other.

The sheets are worn and gray, the mattress tattered. She lies down and the bed creaks. Everything falls apart.

A stab of light jolts her. "Doctor," Prae murmurs. "I know you're awake."

Janthira gropes for a switch. The light bulb flickers; shadows twitch and flutter like scorched moths. "The door was locked."

"What are you afraid of? A lock won't keep out the swarm, and anyway it was dead easy to pick." Prae wipes at her mouth, brushing away flecks that might have been cicada shell. She takes hold of Janthira's hand. "Let's talk."

Janthira tries to pull away, but the young woman doesn't give. "About what?"

"There was a time when things were normal. It's funny how no one can remember when or how this started, don't you think?" Prae cranes her head back, shutting her eyes, though her grip doesn't relax. "Not that they'd listen to me; everyone thinks I'm crazy and you thoroughly sane. You're the one they rely on because you just know all about the bugs, how to grow them, what to feed them. You counted on that, didn't you, doctor?"

"What do you –"

"Memories of how all this happened and what you did, that's what the bugs must have eaten first... There *were* people there when you made the bargain, you know. Can't say I have a complete set – I've been collecting them in bits, piecing them together. The bugs were supposed to beat the swarm and everything would go back to normal." Prae leans close. "Only you didn't pay up."

Janthira eyes the door. Prae has relocked it. "How much did you see?"

"Enough." A snick of switchblade, the metal frigid against Janthira's arm. "I'm good with a knife, doctor, and you can bleed for a long time without dying. Being a surgeon I'm sure you know that." With her free hand she digs a syringe from her back pocket. "Administer it yourself, will you? And don't try to get away. Small room. I'm fast."

"You asked before what moves the bugs." Janthira licks her lips. "I do. I'm the one who guides them to fight, keep them here for a year."

"I'll take that risk. If you explode into termites maybe they'll call it a day, send the town back. If not we all die and you get to pass spectacularly. Butterflies. Bees. Think about it, that's much nicer than a corpse. Tidy. Very pretty."

The look in Prae's eyes and Janthira thinks, *Something's wrong with this girl* but something is wrong with all of them. When she takes the syringe her hand doesn't shake, steadied by the weight of inevitability. "I'm not going to apologize." She primes the needle, conscientious to the last. "The offer they made was never fair."

"Probably. But you did put your life ahead of the rest of us." The blade turns, pushes harder into Janthira's skin. "Revenge is better than nothing."

Janthira sets the syringe down, lets it roll away. The pain is a bite, the cocoon-seed entering her blood a throb. A second life inside her begins.

By MID-ROUND half the enemy force has been scourged to patches of light and imaginary numbers, equations cleaved apart by warped variables. Through the feeds the queen scents their defeat.

She checks her pawns. They have been dwindling as her combat units grew. She does not spare a moment to question and imagine; what flesh is carved to serve her city's survival is a matter best postponed for when she again has the luxury of philosophy and remorse. "I'll discuss the terms of compensation now."

"Very good. Our preferred currency is in troops."

"My armed forces will take a long time to recover, let alone be combat-ready again."

"Not those," the entity chides. "I'm hardly asking to enlist your infantry as mercenaries for distant conflicts having nothing to do with you. That would be inappropriate." Its hand opens, a revelation of wasps and locusts cast in platinum and gold. "These are metaphors that, through correct nourishment, can be actualized. I have a use for their mature forms. Cultivate them and I'll take five years' worth of results. The rest, as a courtesy, you can do with as you like."

The queen takes one of the icons. It is warm, viciously alive – a jab and her blood beads. "You must have a projected quantity."

The entity waves a hand of vapor and crackling charge. "That'll sort itself out. I'm not so discourteous as to burden my clients with logistical minutiae."

"Indeed no." She advances the round to a close.

THE CHRYSALISES TAKE a year to gestate, but as Janthira drifts in and out of fevered sleep she knows she won't have that long. The ache of an alien heat, the burn of a parasite pulse: a hundred heartbeats drumming inexorably toward birth. A low buzz in the back of her skull like flies waging war. She imagines proboscides tickling her from the inside, sipping at lymph and suckling at fat. Larvae wriggling through her bloodstream, galvanized by serotonin.

She thinks the end will be pus and gore, epidermis rupturing to release a cloud of insectoids. Or it may be neater, bodies exiting through mouth and ears, leaving her a husk. Mostly she hopes she won't feel it.

When she opens her eyes to morning, she knows it will be the last time.

The window is a halo of sunshine burning at the edges, as though in eclipse. She tastes rose apples gone to near-rot and thinks of an afterlife behind hive nerves and faceted sight. What she will be summoned to fight, if anything. How long it will last, if it ever ends.

Prae is a shadow, a sound of switchblade clicking in binary. Open or shut. One or zero.

Janthira tries to speak, finds her throat too dry or else her mouth already transformed, tongueless, to a shape meant for pollen and nectar. When she holds up her hands she can see the ceiling through them, skin stretched that thin, flesh to membrane.

The moment strikes and she knows. And maybe Prae is right that it is less messy than human death, human birth – she expected it would be like labor, the push and pull, contractions and blood and screams. This is painless pressure.

One breath in, another out, and she *opens* –

THE CITY OF cities no longer burns. Its enemies are dead, leaving imprints of their shadows and the outlines of their ruin.

In her throne the queen gazes out at nothing in particular. She has summoned her commanders and ministers, and in her lap is gathered such wealth that might have been selected from her treasury: icons of jeweled mantises and gilded cicadas, topaz scarabs and citrine flies. Each is finely made, their details captivating. Her courtiers and soldiers find that they cannot look away.

"These are seeds," she says, turning over the tokens. "For their fertilization and growth you will require no instruction. See that they are cultivated and we'll never need fear another war. A thousand nations pay us tribute now; in ten years we will have the riches of five thousand."

Perhaps as she speaks a phantom of flies passes over the feeds. As her commands pupate into action her face elongates and her irises become compound reflections – but that may be imagination or simply a trick of angles and shadow.

The windows are sealed, the halls meticulously clean. Nevertheless a moth alights on her knuckle as though begging audience. She strokes its wings slowly, through the texture divining a message, a warning: or maybe nothing at all. She tips the moth into her palm and, very precisely, crushes its thorax.

At her feet a game board lies, oxidized russet as though it has weathered centuries, the pawns long crumbled. A curl of smoke lingers over them.

But in time that, too, dissipates.

SOUTH MOUNTAIN
PAUL KEARNEY

As with all of Paul's fiction, 'South Mountain' has an authentic sense of place. This tale is steeped in history too and as a story about a band of American Civil War re-enactors this is apt. History is a game to some, an arena in which they can act out their fantasies, but as this story shows, some of those fantasies hold a great deal of truth.

THE SUN WAS settling behind the hills of West Virginia as the Chevy came powering hoarsely along highway 40 towards Frederick. It was a huge, golden evening in early fall, and the country here was a vast tableau of sunlight and shadow, darkening woods, hillsides rumpled for miles in a north-south line, lowland farms eddying around their feet.

"This is the old National Road," Pete Bristow said, one arm hanging out the car window, the other maneuvering the vehicle with small jerks and nudges of the steering wheel. His broad face was red and slick as a broiled ham. "We advanced up this in '62, after we'd pushed D H Hill's boys out of Turner and Fox's Gap. Should really be approaching the Mountain from the south-east, like we did back then. Then you'd get a better idea of the steepness of those south-facing slopes."

"Yeah, they'd be bitches to slog up on a hot day," Wilson Garrity agreed. He was in the passenger seat of the Blazer, a dark, frowning man with a gunmetal mustache, a drinker's nose and the scar of an old war on one temple. Upon the sleeves of his dark coat were stripes of paler blue.

Crammed in the rear were three other men, old and young, black and white. The trunk behind them was piled to the ceiling with knapsacks, blankets, and rifles, and the interior of the four-by-four smelled like an old locker-room.

John Avery had his face turned to the window as though trying to suck in some cleaner air from the evening passing by outside. His wool pants were sodden with sweat, and he was wondering what in the world he was doing here.

"Fewer trees back then, apparently," Bristow went on. "More farms. It's all grown over now, and there's still a lot of laurel on the heights."

"It was only a skirmish though – South Mountain," Avery said, pitching his voice to be heard over the Chevy's engine and the whistle of wind through the windows.

"Depends what you mean by a skirmish," Garrity retorted. "In one day over three and a half thousand men died or were wounded here. By those standards I guess Desert Storm was a barroom brawl."

Avery went silent. The sunset-glory of the Blue Ridge continued to pass them by.

"I take it you phoned up that guy and got his permission for us to camp out?" Bristow said casually to Garrity.

"Nope."

"What? Wilson, for crying out loud –"

"I phoned him. He wasn't home. Hell, we're not even going to pitch a goddamned tent. We'll find some secluded nook further down the mountain in the woods. He'll never know we were there."

"That's trespassing, Wilson," Phil Keyser spoke up from the back, his thin, bespectacled face pursed with annoyance. He looked like a Rockwellian schoolteacher, which is what he was.

"Long as we don't set his barn on fire or spook his cows, I can't see what harm we'll do. Jesus, it's a free country."

"It's private property, is what it is."

"Yeah, well, you want to go find his house by tramping up and down mountain roads when it's getting dark, then you go ahead. You any idea how easy it is to get lost around here? Tracks and old paths that aren't even on the map, all over the place. Least said, soonest mended. Pete, there's a hotel – or *inn*, rather – on the left here, just before the road dips. Big, stone-built place. We'll leave the car there and hike in the rest of the way."

"Whatever you say First Sergeant!" Bristow snapped.

WHEN THEY FINALLY stopped and got out of the car the world seemed to open up around them, a bloom of birdsong and hazy silence, Maryland stretching out wide and quiet to the far horizon. They stared at it as though it were some unknown country newly discovered in the gathering dusk. Garrity breathed in deeply.

"Gentlemen, welcome to America."

"God's own country," Cyrus Adams said, smiling. He might have been Keyser's older brother; whip-lean and with an evangelical light in his pale eyes.

"Come on. Let's get the gear sorted out. I want to be down the mountain a ways before dark."

They hauled on their knapsacks and blanket-rolls as the sun disappeared behind the Blue Ridge at their backs, and then set off after Garrity in single file, following a meandering track that led into the woods on their right. The veteran had a compass which he consulted regularly, and Avery thought he heard him counting his paces between bearings.

The woods closed in on them, and the light died into a blue gloom.

"Hey, Hawkeye," Bristow called out to their leader. "Don't you be getting us lost in this shit now, you hear?"

"Can it. I'm concentrating."

The path took wide loops around the contours of the mountain. In the midst of the woods they glimpsed open spaces, like long abandoned pastures, and here and there the remnants of a wooden fence was moldering in the undergrowth.

"I can see it now," Keyser muttered. "*Deliverance* in western Maryland. All we need are the bows."

"Don't forget the canoes," Bristow told him with a low cackle.

It was dark now, and through the branches overhead the first stars were glimmering fitfully. Garrity paused yet again to check his brass compass by the flare of a match.

"Haven't you got a flashlight, Wilson?" Bristow demanded. They saw the veteran's teeth shine in a grin.

"What – and ruin the historic authenticity of the moment?"

"Historic authenticity my –"

"Got it. Nearly there, ladies. Look on the bright side, it's all downhill. You'll be slogging back up it in the morning."

"How in the world can you navigate in woods these thick?" Keyser wondered aloud, an edge of petulance in his voice.

"Ask Davy Crockett up front," Bristow told him.

It was so dark now that they had to periodically reach out and touch the back of the man in front. Avery's eyes felt as though they were about to pop out of his skull, so hard were they working to utilize every mote of light. He heard Phil Keyser behind him muffle a curse as he tripped up over a root.

"Hell-damn!"

"What is it?"

"Muzzle of my rifle went into the ground. I'll have to pull it through in the morning. Wilson – how much farther?"

"Oh, about ten feet. People, we have arrived."

"Arrived where exactly?" Cyrus Adams drawled. Even he seemed a little testy.

"We're south of the site of the Wise farm, in the woods where the 6th New Hampshire arrived late in the afternoon of

September 14th, 1862, after drawing picket-duty for several hours previously along the National Road."

"Terrific," Bristow said, wheezing. "We're lost, I bet."

"The hell we are."

"Let's get a fire started," Keyser said. "Wherever we are, it's where we're going to sleep. I'm bushed. I just hope we aren't too near that farmer's house, Wilson. If he sees firelight he's liable to come out for a closer look with a twelve-gauge."

"And they don't take kindly to folks in Yankee uniforms down here," Adams added.

"Are you serious?" Avery asked the older man. "I mean getting carried away in a re-enactment is one thing, but –"

"You walk into Sharpsburg wearing Union blue, and try to get served in a bar," Garrity said with a sneer. "Now someone help me gather up some firewood. There's plenty of it around. I been tripping over the shit for the last hour."

THE FIVE OF them fumbled around in the darkness, yawning and bumping into one another. Periodically Garrity would light another match to help them get their bearings. When he was finally satisfied with the pile of firewood they had gathered, he set up a tiny pyramid of dry moss and finger-twigs and coaxed it into flame, blowing the sticks into molten wires. Then he began placing larger pieces on top, one by one, until the flames were robust enough to have a fair-sized log tossed into their midst.

The others had unrolled their bedrolls by that time and were lying with their feet to the fire like the spokes of a wheel, blinking owlishly and wrestling off their brogans. Cyrus Adams sniffed the air. "Gonna be cold tonight, maybe even a frost before morning. We'd best keep the rifles under the blankets."

Garrity brought his earthenware jug out of his knapsack, sloshed it around, and smiled. "Anyone for a snort?"

"I'll have one," Avery said unexpectedly. "Might as well try to keep the cold out."

The fire cracked and spat. Keyser had to beat out a glede which had come zinging out of the flames like a tiny meteor. Adams cut himself a villainous-looking twist of chewing tobacco and placed it inside his cheek. Garrity lit up a short-stemmed pipe. No-one spoke for a long time. They stared into the fire as though mesmerized. Pete Bristow took a swallow from Garrity's jug and bared his teeth, grimacing. Around them, the woods were silent. They could smell the rich loam, the leaf mould underfoot, all entangled with the blue fragrance of wood smoke and the sweeter riband of Garrity's pipe.

"Sometimes it feels closer, when you sleep out like this, right on the battlefield," Adams said quietly. "Feels… connected."

"I knew some guys from the 9th, camped out by Burnside's Bridge couple years back," Pete Bristow said. "They sneaked in after dark and set up a shelter-half, lit themselves a fire where the woods come up to the creek, and sat sharing a jug and singing old marching songs. They had a candle-lantern on a forked stick, and it started swaying back and forth like it was in the middle of a gale. There wasn't no wind that night though. They steadied it, went back to singing. And damned if it didn't do it again."

"What was it, a ghost?" Avery asked. He had meant to sound sarcastic, but somehow as the words came out they were merely curious. Bristow shrugged.

"Darned if I know. They thought something was there with them though, looking in on the firelight. Wasn't a bad feeling, just… strange, I guess. They didn't sleep much that night."

As a man of science, Avery felt he ought to mock, but he couldn't. Not while hunkered round a campfire on one of those battlefields. You couldn't make light of all those lives, that spilled blood. It was real. He was sitting on it.

He realized Garrity was watching him closely. "What?"

"You ain't quite a believer yet, are you John?"

"It's my first time out. I don't know what I think yet." Avery felt uncomfortable, as though Garrity were reading his mind. It was not his color, of that he was sure. Garrity disliked him merely because he could smell the skepticism in him.

"Some people think we're a bunch of quaint reactionaries dressing up like this – we've got our noses buried in the past." Garrity spat, his mustache framing a snarl.

"Well it ain't the past. It's to do with the way people think, then and now. And some people's thinking hasn't changed in a hundred years.

"You know what I'd like? I'd like to see a whole black regiment – the 54th Massachusetts or suchlike – go down to Mississippi and march through every little shitkicker burg in the state with Old Glory waving at their head. And fixed fucking bayonets, too. These Southerners forget sometimes that back then they got their asses well and truly kicked."

Phil Keyser, born in Richmond, raised his eyebrows.

"Oh hell Phil, you know the kind of Southerners I mean. Redneck jerk-offs who pine for the days of mint juleps and magnolia."

Keyser laughed, the firelight making two yellow discs of his spectacles. "What are you now Wilson, our social conscience?"

Garrity grinned. "Maybe it's the moonshine talking."

"The Johnnies aren't all like that," Pete Bristow objected. "I got good friends in rebel regiments. At least re-enactors know their history."

"And wouldn't they like to change it. What do you think, Cy – you're a West Virginian – would you have liked things to be different?"

"West Virginia was Union through and through," Adams said. He spat a hissing jet of brown saliva into the fire. "That's how it became West Virginia."

"Yeah. Bad example. Phil, what about you? You're from the Old Dominion."

Keyser took off his spectacles and rubbed them with a handkerchief thoughtfully. "The war ruined Virginia. It hasn't recovered even today. I guess if I had to change anything, I'd like the war to have ended before '63, before the Wilderness and Petersburg – before Sherman burned his way to the sea. The country would have been better off as a whole. Less bitterness, fewer lives lost."

"And what about the slaves?" Garrity asked, stealing a look at Avery.

"They would still have been freed – that much was inevitable anyway."

"I think John might see things differently."

Avery shook his head. "I'm a Pennsylvania Doctor. I know nothing of the South, and not much more about history –"

"You're black, for crying out loud. Don't tell me you don't have an opinion."

"Leave him be, Wilson," Adams cut in. "His first day as a re-enactor and you have him refighting the whole war."

"Just making conversation, Cy."

There was an awkward pause, until Avery spoke up. "Why do you do it?" he asked Garrity.

"Do what?"

"This – the re-enactor thing. You're a Vietnam vet – didn't you get enough of war over there?"

Keyser and Pete Bristow shared a glance.

"That wasn't a war," Garrity said with a fixed grin. "It was a *policing action*, don't you know?"

"Do you wish it had been more like the Civil War, honorable and above-board? Is that it?"

"Yeah, well, even the Johnnies didn't napalm too many children!" Garrity snapped. He looked away. Avery felt he had scored a point, but he didn't feel good about it.

"Some wars are worth fighting." Cyrus Adams said at last. "And it's worthwhile remembering why they were fought. That's all there is to it."

"Amen." Pete Bristow said without irony. The big man stretched, and a yawn widened his florid face.

"Time to turn in, guys. The debate is closed. Me, I need a piss." He labored to his feet and strolled out of the firelight whilst the others began wrapping themselves in their bedrolls.

"No offence." Avery said to Garrity.

"Hell, none taken. Don't mind me – I got a big mouth, is all."

Pete Bristow's voice came out of the darkness. "Hey, Wilson. Shouldn't we be able to see the lights of Middletown from here?"

"If you're facing downhill you should."

"Funny. Can't see a damn thing. The whole country is as black as a witch's tit. Not a light anywhere."

"It's late, Pete."

"Yeah, but there's no streetlights, no car headlights, nothing."

"You're probably looking the wrong direction."

"Yeah – yeah I guess. Damn, it's getting cold. I can see my breath."

"Careful your wiener doesn't shrivel up."

"Too late. Happened years ago."

"Yeah, matrimony'll do that." They heard a chuckle come out of the darkness. Bristow reappeared, buttoning up his fly, and stepped in among them to his bedroll. The fire was dying down to a saffron glow.

"We'll be shivering before morning."

"By the time you settle yourself it'll *be* morning."

"Night Wilson."

"Night John-Boy."

A LAST FLICKER of light flared up from the sinking campfire, then shrank down again. In the sky above, the stars wheeled in a silent dance, and a mist came stealing up from the bottom land to seep around the knees of the hills.

*   *   *

AVERY LAY AWAKE for a long time on the cold ground, watching the stars come and go between wreaths of cloud. His hand was resting on the barrel of his rifle-musket under the blanket – the oddest bedfellow he had ever known.

He and his wife Trish had hosted a dinner party the previous night, and his friends had greeted the news of his forthcoming weekend with incredulity and amusement. "Those Civil War eccentrics. Aren't they all a bunch of reactionary rednecks?" Bryan Parsons had asked with raised eyebrow and poised Martini. Avery had laughed along with the rest of the guests, but now that the moment of truth was near, he wondered about Bryan's words. What would they be like, these men, and how would they receive him?

John Avery was black, the only black man on the muster-list of the 6th New Hampshire. Four generations removed from the Maryland slaves who had been his ancestors, his interest in the Civil War had stemmed from his interest in them. Their slave-name had been Watts, and they had lived on a small plantation not far from Sharpsburg. They would have heard the guns of Antietam on a terrible day in September 1862, little guessing at the time that it signaled the beginning of their journey to freedom.

Avery's father had been a man not much interested in anything to do with origins. He had worked in a lumber-yard in a little one horse town in southern Pennsylvania all his life, not much less of a slave, in his son's opinion, than his ancestors had been. But then one sunny April morning Avery's father had somehow been jostled or shoved at his work, and the circular saw he had been feeding took off his right arm just below the elbow.

That had been fifteen years ago, but John Avery still remembered the shocking, bandage-wrapped stump in the hospital, his father's face gray with pain, the whisperings of relatives in the corridor. To this day, he did not know the real truth of what happened, and his father never spoke of it. But through hints and rumors down the years he gained the impression that his father's accident had been no accident. In any case, the lumber company had paid out handsomely in compensation, and the money which Avery's father received for the loss of his limb put his son through med-school, and saw to it that he never wanted for anything.

But John Avery Senior never worked again. He just dwindled into a wizened figure on a porch chair, and one day ten years after the accident he upped and died as gently and quietly as he had lived. And his son realized only then that he had never really known the man. The old father-son cliché had held true. They'd hardly ever had a proper conversation together. That gnawed at Avery, grieved him more than he could have believed. He would have given one of his own arms to talk to his old man – really talk to him – one last time.

Bizarrely enough, his father's maiming had ensured that John Avery's life had been privileged. He had had it given to him on a big fat platter, and had never encountered racial prejudice even once in his thirty-two years. Even his white friends found that incredible.

He had ceased to think much about his color or the people from whence he came, until he had found an ancient photo-album and scrap-book while clearing out the old house after his mother's death. He had sat there amid the junk and packing-cases and heaps of old newspapers and the detritus of lifetimes, and had looked back into another world.

People who were akin to him, who shared his blood, stared out at him from old, faded sepia photographs. They were stiffly uncomfortable, dressed in their Sunday best for the photographer – some of the children barefoot, even so. They were his family, and they were utterly strange to him, peering out from a lost time, their cares and worries and hopes and dreams wholly unknown.

Always in a hurry, it seemed. He had only hazy memories of his grandparents, images of big people with huge hands – his grandmother's and grandfather's almost identical. The hands of laboring folk, gnarled by decades of toil.

There had been stories on the porch, firefly evenings with hot, sugary coffee, the grounds gritting his tongue. He'd squandered it all, let the anecdotes pass him by and become lost forever. He simply hadn't been interested. His grandparents and his mother, talking over ancient history, who had been born where and married whom. Boring stories to a kid who thought only of the present, and a future which was becoming more diamond-edged and glittery with every passing year.

And it was there in that mildewed photo-album – the reminder of everything he'd tried to turn his back on, caught in time like a fly in amber.

One portrait in particular had stirred him. It was of an old, old black man whose hair and beard were white, and whose face was a crumpled, eroded ebony mask out of which two sharp eyes gleamed. The man held a meerschaum pipe in one great, work-callused fist and eyed the camera as though facing the barrels of a firing squad. Underneath the picture, there had been a caption:

Charles Watts Avery, born Hagerstown, Maryland 183-, died Hanover, Pennsylvania, July 18th, 1923.

Avery was looking at the face of his own great, great, great grandfather, a contemporary of Abraham Lincoln who had been born a slave, and who had died a free man. That was history brought home, hidden in the hues of an old photograph. His people's suffering shining out from the eyes of a man long dead. Avery found it hard to meet those eyes. They seemed somehow accusing.

What am I trying to do? he wondered to himself. *Make up for turning my back on it all?* The question disturbed him. He knew that all his life he had been plagued by a vague sense of guilt. Everything had always been there for him. Nothing had been too much of an effort. When he read of the struggles of his forebears for freedom, rights, equality, he felt oddly ashamed. The feeling had been growing in him for a long time, fuelled by the eyes of the old man in the photograph.

Avery would never be any sort of an activist – he was too inward-looking for that. He knew that in the end he was purely selfish. He liked this life of his, he loved his wife – who was white – and his two daughters. There was no need to go picking fights with the world. But when he had chanced across a re-enactment one fine day in northern Virginia, something in it had just grabbed at him. It had needled him in that tender, guilty spot. Trying on that blue uniform for the first time he had been laughing, but he would never forget the look on his wife's face. She, the Ivy League liberal New Englander, had covered her mouth with her hand, eyes wide above it.

"What? What is it?" he had demanded, still grinning. And she had embraced him, hard.

"I think I just realized I married a black man."

"Trish – now what the hell?"

"That uniform. You look like someone from another time."

"Oh for God's sake –"

"Look in the mirror."

He had. And he had seen staring back at him a black soldier in the uniform of the Union. A figure from another century. He had somehow reached across the years and touched the austere strangers in the old photographs. It was like someone walking across his grave.

AVERY WOKE WITH a start. It was still fully dark and the night was as quiet as ever. The fire was dead, nothing but the glimmer of a scarlet glow at his feet. The others were fast asleep, someone snoring gently.

It had been a dream, that was all. Avery settled himself in his blankets again. The tip of his nose was icy cold and his face was wet with dew. Dawn could not be far off.

A strange dream. He thought he had been wakened by the sound of men's voices, and the noise of them moving through the wood in the night. Odd, the tricks the sleeping mind could play upon itself.

He drifted off to sleep again. Around him the woods were hushed, as though awaiting some revelation that would come with the morning.

BIRDSONG, RUNNING THROUGH the woods like a silver ribbon. Avery breathed deep, eyes still closed. He could feel the light on his face, a hint of warmth burning through the dawn. He smelled wood smoke, and the deep, deep reek of the fecund earth. The air was sharp and clean, and he drew it into his lungs for a few moments, tasting it.

His own smell rose with it from the damp blanket, yesterday's sweat and ash. It was intimately familiar, and yet somehow strange at the same time.

Someone was watching him. He opened his eyes and lifted the visor of his kepi.

The rest were still asleep, and there was a mist clinging low upon the ground. The woods were full of light, but it was still up in the heads of the trees. Down below the last grey chill of the night still held sway.

A man sat watching him on the other side of the dead fire. He was dressed in Union blue, and held a musket across his knees. Below a battered forage cap, the man's face was lean and dark, sun-wizened, underfed. But his eyes were as bright as two frosted stones.

Not a man. He could not have been more than fifteen years old.

"I do declare," the stranger said softly. "What you doing wearing that, nigger?"

Avery sat up. Around him the others were stirring. Wilson Garrity groaned, rubbed his eyes and ran his fingers through his bristling mustache. He saw the newcomer and his eyes widened.

"What did you call me?" Avery demanded.

"You fellers get yourseln lost, or somethin'?" the stranger asked. "What outfit you with anyways?"

"6th New Hampshire," Garrity said, tossing his blanket aside. "Who the fuck are you?"

The boy looked at the stripes on Garrity's arm, and tensed. "I thought you was skedaddlers."

"You don't use that word with me," Avery said, standing up, rifle in hand.

"What word? Sergeant, I got me lost in the woods, I swear to it. I'm Jacob Carmody, 24th Pennsylvania, Wilcox's Brigade, and I ain't no deserter. Just lost, is all – I'll take an oath to it."

"Did you hear what he called me?"

"Easy, John," Garrity said, though he was frowning. The others were clambering out of their bedrolls. "Who's the new guy?" Bristow asked, yawning.

"Are you up here on your own, son?" Garrity asked, holding up a hand to Avery.

"My outfit is around here somewheres, First Sergeant. I was waiting for daylight to go and find 'em."

"I thought we were the only ones here," Phil Keyser said, setting his glasses on his nose and squinting. "This is private property."

"The Division is down the hill a ways I reckon," Carmody said. He stood up, clearly nervous. "By your leave, First Sergeant, I'll take off and try and find them."

"What division?" Bristow asked.

A distant, rolling boom sounded out, astonishing in that morning stillness, more violent than thunder. The birdsong ceased at once.

Then there was another, and another. They could almost feel the tenor of the explosions in the quivering air.

"Jesus Christ," Bristow said. "That's artillery."

"There it starts now," Carmody said. "I'd better take off. I ain't no coward – I just got lost, is all." He turned to go, and then paused a moment to spit. "I didn't know we had us niggers in this here army." And then he pelted away into the woods with his rifle at the trail, swift and agile as a deer.

"You little cracker bastard!" Avery shouted after him.

"There's no re-enactment scheduled for South Mountain," Cyrus Adams said, his pale eyes wide as pennies. "Not today or any other day."

For a moment they all froze in place, listening. The woods were silent, the sun lighting them up more brightly by the second as it rose upon the mountain.

Again, the massive salvo shook the morning. The very sunlight seemed to shudder. Avery flinched at the sound. And then, a noise like the ripping of a long piece of linen.

"That's musketry," Garrity said.

"Well hell, let's pack up and join in the fun," Pete Bristow grinned. "I guess they decided to throw something together impromptu-like. We might as well pitch in."

Avery looked at their First Sergeant. Garrity the Vietnam veteran was sweating despite the coolness of the morning, and there was something in his face he had not seen before. A wild kind of surmise.

"Yeah, pack up," Garrity rasped. "Let's go see what's going on."

Cyrus Adams smiled and looked up at the sunlit tops of the trees.

"A heck of a fine day for it, at any rate."

THE HEAT ROSE into the morning, the early mists withering away. They tramped along a track beneath the trees, heading downhill towards the sound of the guns. Avery was sweating freely now, as though his anger had uncorked a bottle. His body felt constrained by the straps of his leathers, and the collar of the wool jacket chafed his throat. He could smell the taint of a strange smoke on the air, and taste it on his tongue.

Nigger.

He thought of Wilson Garrity's vision of the previous night, and found himself fantasizing about it as he trudged along. That little bastard, as bold as you like. Right to his *face*.

The noise grew. More artillery, and the tearing rattle of musket volleys, followed by the firecracker snap of single shots. And now there was a new element.

Men shouting. A host of voices raised to rival the gunfire.

"Christ, it sounds like they have thousands of guys down there," Pete Bristow said, breathing hard.

Garrity, in the lead, said nothing. The veteran's eyes were wide and set, and he was fumbling in his cartridge box as he strode along, as though his fingers were counting the contents.

They came to the end of the trees. Before them was a snake fence, beautifully restored, and beyond that a stretch of open pastureland sloping downhill. Above them the blue sky was half-obscured by toiling clouds of grey, bitter-tasting smoke, and it rolled like fog across the grass.

A Union battle-line was stretched across the fields, banners flying. Perhaps two thousand men loading and firing while their officers, on foot and on horseback, waved sabers and encouraged them. Far off to the east, there was the glint of gold as the sun caught the barrels of a twelve pounder battery.

To the rear, other men were being dragged or were dragging themselves through the trampled grass, singly and in shattered knots. Even from here, it was possible to see the blood trails.

Avery's breath clicked in his throat. Upslope of the Union line was another, but these men were clad in earth-tones, grey and brown and butternut. They hallooed shrilly as they stood there, and above their heads waved the blood-red flags of the Confederacy, a flag Avery had detested all his life.

"This is no ordinary re-enactment. It must be a film set," Phil Keyser said, awed.

"It's the best I've ever seen," Bristow said, with a similar note of reverence in his voice.

"I wonder if they'd let us join in," Cyrus Adams said.

Garrity wiped his eyes. "Load your rifles," he said. There was a thickness to his voice. Looking at him, Avery realized with astonishment that there were tears streaming down the veteran's face.

"I'm going down there, and I'm pitching in with them. None of you have got to come with me. Avery, you especially."

"Are you kidding?" Bristow said jovially. "I just wish I had a camera."

Avery and Garrity stared at each other.

"Are you a believer now, John?" Garrity asked.

And Avery knew then what the veteran meant.

This was no re-enactment, or Hollywood epic.

Somewhere west of this mountain was a young black man called Charles Watts, who was a slave.

But in a few months, because of what was happening here, and what was about to happen along a little creek called the Antietam, he would be free.

And that is where I am, Avery thought.

An instant of pure, animal panic washed over him, cold as winter water. But it passed, and in its wake he felt the restless guilt which he had harbored all his life simply blow away.

"Let's go join them," he said to Garrity. "They need all the help they can get."

THE GAME CHANGER
LIBBY MCGUGAN

Libby's medical and science background comes into play here, giving us a story that explores the fascinating relationship between nanotechnology, the quantum world and the observer. To those patients involved in the process, drug trials must sometimes seem very much like a game, one in which the outcome can be less than favorable. However, it is a game that Adam and Natasha are willing to enter their son for, because for Max, the alternative would be unthinkable.

"I ADDED A new mission. You want to see it?" Adam Sherman handed Max the iPad. It dropped from his small hand onto the bed.

"I'll hold it for you," said Adam. "So. This one's set in a cave. You have to find and destroy the Screachers hiding in the stalactites – these pillars of rocks – see?"

"What weapons do you have?" Max's voice was weak, almost inaudible.

"What do you want?"

"Blaster."

"Okay." He scrolled through the options for Max.

Max tapped on the screen.

"Watch the birds," said Adam. "They're friendly. There. That's a Screacher behind that rock. Blast him!"

Max tapped and tapped until the Screacher glowed green

and exploded. He looked up and grinned. "I got him." Then he closed his eyes, drained with the effort.

"Yes, you did." Adam ran his fingers across Max's bare scalp, feeling the clamminess of his skin and the injustice of it. He kissed his forehead.

"Mr. Sherman? Can I have a word?" The doctor stood waiting at the door.

"Nothing? There's nothing you can do?" Adam clutched his head as he paced the room. Sunlight spilled through the window onto the two couches and the table with the box of tissues. His wife, Natasha, sat with her hands over her nose and mouth. She was trembling. The Charge Nurse sat to her left, a hand resting softly on her back.

"He's six years old," said Adam. "There must be something…"

"Even if he get's over this infection, he's too weak to survive the next cycle of chemotherapy." Dr Simpson spoke patiently.

"But what about surgery? If you did the surgery now, then tried more chemo later…"

"It's meant to be adjuvant chemotherapy. To shrink the tumours before surgery." Natasha glanced up at Adam, stuck in a place between being a doctor and a mother, of knowing the facts but having no control.

"Natasha's right. Even if he was well enough for surgery now, it wouldn't stop the cancer that's already spread. We need to help Max enjoy what's left of his life, as much as we can." The doctor held his eye, compassionately, then gave the space needed for the sentence to sink in.

Adam sat down next to Natasha and they sobbed into each other's arms.

Adam stood at the door, watching Max's small chest rise and fall too rapidly for comfort. His eyes were closed, sunken, his skin tinged pale yellow, which Natasha had explained was a side-effect of the chemo on his blood cells. Antibiotics ran from a pump into the drip in his twig-like arm. Max had always been small for his age, but he seemed tiny now. He had never complained. He cried the first time they took blood, but he didn't pull away. Beside his bed was his favourite picture: him hanging upside down, dangling from monkey bars, taken the day they went to the adventure park. He loved the rope swings and scrambling up the ladders into the trees and he kept asking to go back. His dad had said he would take him once his sore leg improved, but it turned out that it wasn't an ordinary pain. So Adam designed a game – Aztec Jungle Wars, Max had named it – so that he could go there in his bed, while he waited to get better. Only now...

Adam watched, helpless, as Natasha's tears fell onto their son's cheek.

THEY TOOK IT in turns to sleep, although Adam didn't sleep much. He found himself watching the slow drip of the fluids running into Max's veins, dewdrops loaded with antibiotics. He watched the nurses come and go, checking his temperature, giving him medicine to stop the vomiting. Max liked Maggie best. Nothing was ever a problem for her, and she always managed to make him giggle, even when it was an effort to breathe. She didn't treat him as if he was sick.

All they could do was wait. By the eighth day, Max's fever had come down and his breathing had settled to something that wasn't quite normal but was easier to watch. His eyes were brighter too and they twinkled when he showed Maggie how to blast Screachers on his game.

They scanned him again. The cancer in his leg was bigger and there was more of it in his lungs and kidneys. They could do no more. Natasha and Adam elected to tell Max in their own way at the right time.

* * *

ADAM HELD THE door for Natasha as they returned home. They stood there for a moment in the hallway, listening to the silence of things to come.

"I'll make some tea," said Natasha.

He followed her into the kitchen.

"We should aim to visit the hospice next week," she said.

He nodded, numb.

Natasha busied herself with the tea. "And I'll sort out his room for him coming home."

ADAM COULDN'T SLEEP. He sat down at his laptop, trawling the internet for the latest treatments of osteosarcoma, something he did regularly. Max had had all the conventional chemotherapy they could offer. He cross checked it with the file on the USB stick which held Max's medical records. It was reassuring in a way, but in another, he felt cheated. *How can we be sending people to Mars and not know how to cure this?* The thought ate away at him. He broadened his search to recent medical advances – stem cell research, liposomes as drug carriers, photodynamic therapy, nanotechnology. He followed the last thread. It led him to an outline of research that was being undertaken at the Institute of Medical Sciences. Here, in his own city.

"NATASHA. WAKE UP. Natasha!" It took a few minutes for her to come-to, so exhausted was she. When she did, she sat bolt upright. "What's wrong?"

"Nothing, it's fine." He knew what she was thinking. "It's alright. But I found something."

He led her downstairs and made her some tea while she read over the paper he'd printed out. The darkness was thick outside the window and he could just see the edge of the moon behind the drifting clouds. He smiled as he remembered the story Natasha told Max on a journey home one night in the car, about the man in the moon and how, if you looked hard enough, you could see him smiling. For a fortnight after that, every time they'd come to check on him before going to bed, they'd found Max at his bedroom window, peering up into the sky.

"Adam, this is not established research. It's a phase one trial with iffy results. I don't know much about nanomedicine, except that there are problems with toxicity. That's the last thing Max needs right now."

"But they reported no toxic side effects in this trial. They may not have had great results, but some people responded. And the lead researcher, Ripley, works at the Institute, right on our doorstep."

She scanned the paper again, stifling a yawn. It struck Adam then how worn out she looked.

Natasha placed the paper on the table and closed her eyes. "We have to make peace with what's going to happen, Adam."

He stared at her. She looked more beaten than he'd ever seen.

"I can't face another false hope."

He knelt down beside her and took her face in his hands. "What if it isn't?"

HE DIDN'T SLEEP for the rest of the night. By eight am, when Natasha was packing some things to take for Max, he was dressed, ready to leave. "I'll speak to Dr Ripley, and I'll call you when I'm done."

She nodded. "I'll see Mark Simpson today. See if knows he anything about it."

He watched her fold Max's favourite onesie, the red one with plastic-soled feet and a hood with ears. It was one of the most delightful sounds he knew, to hear Max padding about in his onesie on the kitchen floor. Adam held the back of Natasha's head and laid his forehead against hers. "I'll see you later."

THE INSTITUTE OF Medical Sciences was just off University Place. An old building with a stone arch leading to a small pathway lined with shrubs and bushes, it looked like it belonged in the past. Adam made his way to the smartly dressed porter manning the reception area.

"Can you tell me where I can find Dr Ripley?"

"He's based in the new wing. His secretary is down the corridor, third on the left."

Dr Ripley's secretary looked sweet, with her blonde hair and neat dress, but she was a gatekeeper. "I'm sorry. He's very busy right now."

"I don't have a lot of time. This is about my son."

She smiled. "You'll have to make an appointment, and he's fully booked until…" she scanned the computer screen in front of her, "next Tuesday."

"My son is six years old and he's dying. I need to speak to him."

Her smile faded. She scanned the screen again. "He can see you at four today."

ADAM WAITED FOR Natasha under the arch.

"So what did Mark Simpson say about it?" asked Adam.

"He thought the trials were too early to be used for routine treatment."

Adam held her hand as they walked to Dr Ripley's office, passing the secretary who smiled a little awkwardly.

Dr Ripley was in his fifties, lean, tall with greying hair and glasses, and eyes that were sharp; alive. He shook their hands, offered them a seat and listened quietly as they told him about Max.

"He has bone marrow suppression now, and haemolytic anaemia," said Natasha. "He got through the last infection, only just, but he won't tolerate another cycle of chemotherapy. There's nothing more they can do."

"We've read about your trial," said Adam. "From what we've gathered, nanomedicine uses much smaller doses, so is less toxic, and targets only the areas affected by cancer. You could help Max."

Ripley studied them over clasped hands. "Yes, that's the benefit of nanotherapy, but we're in the very early stages of research. We had no significant adverse events in our trial, but neither did we get the organ specificity we'd hoped for. It's slow progress. We're not yet at the stage of offering it as treatment."

"But can't you enroll Max into the trial?"

"The trial is finished. There's no more funding for it."

"Can't you just give him the treatment?" said Adam.

"Nano2 isn't licensed for use in children."

"Who cares about a license? Max is dying. We're not going to sue you if it doesn't work."

Ripley leaned forwards. "I would love to help you, Mr. Sherman, but I'm afraid I can't. I think you should go home and make the most of your time with Max."

Adam swallowed hard, tasting the bitterness in his mouth, trying to keep his breathing measured. He turned to Natasha. "Let's go."

MAX WAS EXCITED ABOUT coming home. They walked him slowly along the hall. His limp had become more pronounced and his breathing an effort when he moved, but it didn't stop the grin that spread across his face when he saw his bedroom. His favourite toys were laid out to greet him – his monkey, his unicorn, his Leonardo Turtle action figure, and a pile of others. He hobbled to his bed and picked up his suction construction Squigz kit.

"What are you making?" asked Adam as Max pulled it apart and began reassembling it.

"A robot."

"Nice. What's his name?"

"Morph."

"Good name. And he has three arms."

Max nodded. "So he can hold three blasters." He waved Morph around, shooting some unseen enemy, and made blaster noises with his mouth.

"How about some cookies?" asked Natasha.

Max and Adam nodded.

ADAM LOST TRACK of how long they played with Morph. An invincible superhero-robot, he rid their imaginary world of baddies and Screachers, hunting them down in the Temple in the bookcase and the Cave under the duvet. The room became the Aztec Jungle and Morph was king. They took his mission to the iPad, as he swung from the rope swings and explored underground caverns. Then they fell asleep together, Max in Adam's arms.

NATASHA WOKE ADAM gently. "We need to check his blood," she whispered. They had been given a home testing kit to check his white cells, and instructions to return to the hospital for antibiotics if they dropped any lower.

Adam extracted himself from Max gently, placing his head on the pillow. "Let's do it tomorrow. Let him sleep."

ADAM LEFT THE house at seven am. By seven-thirty he was waiting under the arch, watching as the staff trickled past to the Institute's entrance. At seven forty-eight, Ripley approached, his collar pulled up against the rain. His pace slowed as he saw Adam.

"What can I do for you, Mr. Sherman?"

"You can reconsider." He handed Ripley a USB drive. "This is a copy of Max's medical records."

Ripley took a slow breath. "Even if I wanted to, and I do, I'm not in a position to help. Anyway we have no stock left." He studied Adam's face, and Adam felt him catch a glimpse of what his world had become, of him understanding. Ripley swallowed. "I'm sorry." He tried to give the USB drive back.

"Just take a look at it," said Adam.

Ripley lowered his head and walked on.

Adam watched him disappear into the building, as rain dripped from his cheeks.

WHEN HE GOT home, Natasha and Max were eating pancakes. He ate one with them then kissed Max on the forehead.

"I got all the Cave Screachers," said Max, holding up the iPad.

"Yeah?" Adam looked impressed. "What score did you get?"

"Fifty-one thousand points."

"No way! You beat my record!"

Max grinned.

"Right. We need a rematch. I'm going to do some work and then you're on. Can't have the Gamemaster's son beat him at his own game." He got up shaking his head, as Max chuckled behind him. Natasha watched him leave the room.

FINDING THE PRODUCT was easy. It was held by a central distributer in Leeds. Adam spent the morning hacking their system. Then it was simply a case of authorizing a shipment to Dr Ripley. As a previous recipient, it would raise no questions. It would be there the following day.

*   *   *

AT SEVEN AM, Adam woke Max. "Let's go on an adventure. You can bring Morph."

Natasha came in to find Max in his coat. "What's going on?"

"I'm taking Max to see Dr Ripley."

"What? You heard what he said! And Max shouldn't be going out. He's not strong enough."

"His white count is better than it's been for ages," said Adam. "We're only going to say hello, then we'll be right back."

"Can we have pancakes when we come home?" asked Max.

"Of course," said Adam.

THEY STOOD WAITING by the archway, Max wrapped up in a duffle coat, hood and gloves, holding his robot. Adam had carried him there.

Ripley stopped when he saw them, then walked towards them slowly.

"This is Max," said Adam. "Max, say hello to Dr Ripley."

Max held up his robot. "This is Morph," he said. "He has three arms."

"I can see that." Ripley crouched down beside Max. "Nice to meet you, Morph." He shook one of Morph's arms and stood up. "Adam, we've been through this."

"You'll receive a package today," said Adam. "I've arranged for the distributer to send you some more stock."

Ripley stared at him. "How did you –"

"Never mind that. Please, Dr Ripley. I'm begging you. You're his last hope."

Ripley watched him for a long moment, then turned his gaze to Max who stood holding his dad's hand, studying a puddle. Ripley shook his head and walked on without a word. Adam felt his heart plummet. "Do you have a son?" he called after him. "What would you do?"

Ripley stopped. He stood for a moment as the rain pattered

on the hood of Max's duffle coat. Then he came back to them and spoke in a low voice. "Meet me back here at nine pm tonight. And I did have a son. That's why I do this job." They watched him walk away into the drizzle.

"Now can we get some pancakes?" said Max.

THE WINDOWS OF the Institute were dark. Only the light from the porter's desk was on. Adam, Natasha and Max waited by the arch, Max between them, holding their hands. They turned when they heard approaching footsteps. For a moment, Adam considered whether Ripley may have called the police to report his hacking efforts. *He couldn't be so heartless,* he thought. He didn't care: he had no choice.

Ripley arrived alone, looking serious. "Follow me and just smile at the porter."

ADAM CARRIED MAX and they followed him as he led them inside, striding past the reception desk. "Evening Alfred."

"Evening, Dr Ripley. A little late for you to be in?"

"Just catching up with some work and showing some friends of mine round my patch."

Alfred grinned as Max waved Morph at him. "Evening folks."

HE TOOK THEM to the control room. It was dark apart from the blue glow of the consoles beneath the glass partition that looked onto the MRI scanner. Ripley turned on the lights and warmed up the scanner and it hummed like a ship's engine. Adam set Max down in a chair and set up Aztec Jungle Wars.

"You both understand that none of this is licensed and therefore illegal?"

They nodded.

"I have no reason to suspect that Max will have any adverse reactions to Nano2, but neither can I guarantee that he won't."

"We understand," said Natasha. "But if we don't try..."

Ripley nodded. "I read through his records." He glanced at Max who was tapping furiously on the iPad, his cheeks lit by the green glow of an exploding Screacher. He looked up and grinned. "I got one."

"Well done, Max," said Adam.

"We'll use the consent material from the trial, if you don't mind." Ripley handed Natasha a sheaf of papers. "Take your time to read it over and let me know if you have any questions. I'll be back shortly."

He left the room and Natasha studied the paperwork.

RIPLEY RETURNED WITH a tray of vials.

"So you inject him with nanoparticles for the initial scan to find the hotspots," asked Natasha.

"Yes," said Ripley. "It's better than normal contrast dye. Their quantum properties make the tumours light up as Quantum Dots on the scan."

Natasha nodded. "And then you inject the treatment?"

"Yes. The nanoparticles carry cytotoxic drugs. Once they bind with the surface protein of the cancer cells, they release the drugs and destroy the surrounding tissues. Our main problem has been targeting the cancer cells. We're using the surface protein TEM7 as a marker for drug release, but so far we've had limited success in homing in on those cells."

Natasha nodded, considering. "So we just have to hope they cross paths."

Ripley nodded. "Yes, we do."

THE SCANNER HUM was much louder in here. Max stepped onto a set of scales and Ripley noted his weight and ran a checklist, then Adam lifted him onto the scanner table, and rubbed his head while he caught his breath. He held his hand as Ripley inserted a cannula into Max's arm, feeling him grip harder and seeing his mouth tighten into a straight line as the needle pierced his skin.

"Morph and Aztec Jungle Wars will be waiting for you outside when you've finished," said Adam.

"Cause they're metal," said Max in a whisper.

"That's right," said Ripley. "You don't want them flying off and sticking to the ceiling, do you?"

Max giggled.

"You can have a think about Morph's next mission," said Adam. "I want to hear about it when you come out."

"Okay."

Max put on the headphones Ripley handed him and lay down. He watched as Ripley injected the dye into his arm.

"How are you feeling?" asked Ripley.

"Fine," said Max.

"We're just next door," said Natasha. "You'll be able to hear us and we can hear you."

Max rolled his eyes. "I know, mum. I've done this before, remember?"

She smiled and kissed his forehead.

A 3D IMAGE of his body appeared on the console, turning on its axis, and as it unfolded, green fluorescent dots lit up within it like neon bulbs. If he didn't know what it signified, Adam might have thought it looked beautiful.

"It's progressed," said Natasha.

Adam squeezed her shoulder. "That's why we're here."

She nodded silently, her hand over her mouth.

"Alright," said Ripley. "Now we have a baseline, we'll be able to track his progress." He got up and went through to the scanner room.

"How are you doing Max?"

"Fine."

"Ready for the treatment?"

Max was pulling at a thread on his top. "Mmhmm."

Ripley drew up the dose of Nano2, checked it with Natasha, then injected it into Max's arm. "Might feel a little cold," he said.

Max watched him quietly as the last of the nanoparticles entered his bloodstream. He frowned then suddenly looked vacant.

"What's wrong?" said Natasha, on edge. "Max?"

A montage of anxious thoughts gatecrashed Adam's mind. *Is this a reaction? What have we done to him? What if this is it, this moment in time is our last with Max? What then? What if there's no more time?*

Max burped. "I think Morph should lead an army for his next mission," he said.

Adam and Natasha breathed a laugh and hugged him.

THEY RETURNED ONE week later. Max's breathing had become a little worse and he had needed Adam or Natasha to carry him from his bedroom to the living room as his leg was too sore to walk far.

Ripley shook his head as he studied the scan. "These markers show the distribution of nanoparticles around his body." He pointed to tiny white pinpricks, like fairy lights, sprinkled around the image of Max's body. The green glows were larger, and there were more of them. "But they're not targeting."

"What does that mean?" asked Adam.

Ripley turned to them. "It hasn't worked."

WHEN A TEAR escaped Natasha's eye as Adam lifted Max from the scanner table, he said, "What's wrong, mum?"

She sniffed and smiled. "Nothing, Max. Everything's fine." She kissed his forehead. "Let's go home."

THE ONLY LIGHT was from the streetlamp outside. It was a light that added no warmth as it sliced across the room. Adam had left Natasha and Max asleep together, driven by the pain in his gut. He got up and tried to eat something, but he couldn't. He found his way to his office and sat in the darkness where the pain became a soft rage. He turned Morph around in his hands, watching his shadow in the streetlight, then laid him down gently. He opened Aztec Jungle Wars and began to play.

He was in the Temple. Dark corridors led him deeper, linking passageways and stairways tangling themselves in an unfathomable web, drawing him further and further in. The sound of his breathing getting faster in the shadows. A Screacher screamed at him from a dusty statue and he turned his blaster on it, firing well beyond the time it had vaporised in a green haze. He paused, relishing the power and release he felt. He stopped the game and opened the program. The model was set up, the physics in place. All he needed to do was change the view.

He made the Temple walls move, in and out, in and out, closing in around him then expanding the space between things. Passageways became bronchioles; rooms became alveoli, all the time squeezing in and pulling out as he hunted the Screachers. The Cancers of the Temple; the Screachers of the Lung. He found a clump of them at the top of the cartilage stairs and blasted them until the whole bunch expanded and exploded. More of them in corners, lurking, the only indication of their presence the scream they let off when he got close to them. He burned them all, all that he could find.

He left the moving walls and stepped out towards the river. Blue became red, water became blood, birds became host cells flapping towards him, the sky became the arch of the vessel roof above. He jumped into the current of pulsing blood, tumbling along inside it, surfacing to see the tunnel walls rushing past. He let it take him onwards to the jungle.

Branches of trees meshed out above him, edging a giant crescent-shaped cliff face that dropped into a mighty waterfall. It roared and sprayed mist as it plunged into the cavern below. He turned it red and morphed the scene into the meshwork of a kidney. He grabbed hold of a rope and rappelled down the cliff face, finding clumps of Screachers sticking to the walls, and melted them as he descended. They screamed as they detached and fell past him into the abyss below.

Last was the Cave. The origin of the Screachers, the place in which they bred. He climbed through a pothole in the jungle floor and dropped into its belly. Blackness. Then, as he adjusted to the light, stalactites and stalagmites rose from the darkness in front of him, the sound of dripping water nearby. His feet squelched as he crept deeper. He knew they were in here. This was their fortress.

He made his Cave the Bone, its rock formations the trabecular web that ran through it, interlacing barriers he had to scramble over. The screams of the Screachers grew louder, rising to a deafening pitch as the rage drove him on, the hunger for destruction alive in him. He found them. A huge seething mass of amorphous parasites, draining the life and the light from everything. He turned his blaster on them and fired.

THE CURSOR BLINKED in front of him. He sat back, exhilarated, breathless, his eyes wired with victory. The room was bathed in light from the rising sun and a blackbird sang outside like today was its last. Adam saw Morph, lying still on the carpet. His world relocated, and then imploded. He sobbed like he had never done before.

* * *

HE WENT TO bed and slept. When he woke, it was ten pm. He stumbled out of their room and into Max's where he lay snoring gently, one arm around his unicorn. Adam felt his heart break.

ADAM SAT HOLDING Natasha's hand in the kitchen. "You must have needed it," she said.

"I don't want to miss a day with him." He felt her squeeze his hand. "What did he do yesterday?" he asked.

"He played on your game the whole day." Natasha snorted. "If things were normal, I'd have told him to get off it and do something else, but he was having a good time and I figured, what the hell…"

They shared a smile that hurt.

A sound made Adam turn.

"I like the new game," said Max. He was standing in his red onesie and came padding across the floor towards them, a little out of breath.

"Adam," breathed Natasha.

He turned to her, alarmed by her expression. "What is it?"

"He's not limping."

"Can I play it again today?" said Max.

They stared at him.

"Thanks," said Max and he turned and trotted from the room.

They scrambled after him.

"Max!" Natasha's shout startled him. She knelt down beside him.

"What?"

"Max, how's your leg?"

"Fine." He turned and padded into the office.

They followed him in.

"See what I got?" he beamed to Adam. "Ninety-seven-thousand points."

"That's incredible," said Adam. "What mission were you on?"

"This one," said Max, tapping the keys of the laptop.

"The Bone Game?"

"Yeah, the Bone Game."

"Oh my god."

THEY TOOK HIM to see Ripley that morning. Adam found himself pacing the control room as Ripley set things up.

"Don't get your hopes up," said Ripley as he came back through.

"Did you see him walking?" said Adam.

"Let's just see what the scan shows."

It seemed to take forever for the images to load into their 3D format, but when they did, a cluster of white particles sat just above his left knee. Green glowed brightly in other places, but there was only a faint hint of green in his leg. Ripley sat back in his chair.

Eventually he spoke. "Can you show me this game?"

"Sure." Adam set up his laptop.

Ripley studied the game. "Alright," he said after a while. "What I want you to do is upload today's scan onto your interface. Make the reward screen the scan, so the more points he gets, the more the Quantum Dots fade. Can you do that?"

"Of course." Adam couldn't stop himself from smiling.

"Get him to focus on the Lung Game. We'll rescan him after that. This could still be coincidence." Ripley looked back at the rotating image. "But I've got to admit it's one hell of a coincidence."

THEY ATE PANCAKES and a lot of popcorn and played the game all day. When Max's score crossed the hundred-thousand mark and the green dots faded from the score-man's chest, they danced round the room. When they rescanned him, a few weeks later, his lungs were clear.

"How is this happening?" asked Natasha from the control room. He had spent several weeks blasting Screachers from his kidneys. The image of Max's body spun slowly on the screen. There was no sign of any cancer.

Ripley bounced a little in his chair as he stared at the space in front of him. "Perhaps we've overlooked something fundamental."

"Like what?" asked Adam.

"We're dealing with quantum particles here. And in the quantum world, the observer is inextricably entangled with the outcome of the experiment. Max is the observer in his own game."

He looked up at Adam. "We've got work to do."

DISTINGUISHING CHARACTERISTICS

YOON HA LEE

To those not familiar with the hobby, roleplaying games can seem utterly absurd – a gathering of people in which they pretend to be fantastical characters in a fantastical realm; for what reason? Yoon explores that sense of absurdity here in a Kafkaesque tale that is perhaps the most political piece in this anthology. 'Distinguishing Characteristics' is unsettlingly weird while also being completely on-the-money when it comes to exploring themes of invasion and the loss of identity.

YOUR CHARACTER SHEET has holes in it again. You feel them like a trickle, as of snow or ashdrift, down your spine. On the backs of your hands in their mittens.

You're late for your Improvisational Tactics session, but the new government's curfew is at the Hour of the Coalhound, and for ritual reasons the session goes on all night. If you don't grab something to eat on the way, you'll be condemned to the dreary vending machine fare: sticky buns in foil wrappers that make crinkle-crunch sounds like cicada shells underfoot. Soups that taste of uninspired kelp. Dried roasted cuttlefish, their eyes punched out; the absence disturbs you more than their presence would. Where do all the eyes go?

The best food carts are on Central University Promenade. It's the sort of dull, utilitarian name the new Sthenner government has given all the streets in what used to be the Free Academic City of Poi Jiahl. Three years ago, as a newcomer from distant Mwaan, you would have appreciated the change. The Poians don't believe in naming streets. But the local convention of navigating by landmarks took surprisingly little time to adapt to: a house whose fourth-story window is never repaired, a fountain where liquor-of-euthanasia is dispensed once a year, a winehouse where you can (illegally) bet on mirror-duels. Now, however, the Sthenner Fungus-Lion banner flies everywhere the Poian Crowned Heron once did. You hate the sight of it.

To distract yourself from the flapping banner, you look back down at the food cart where you're waiting, huffing into the cold air, scarf scratching your throat. You've threatened to marry the cart. (Not the cart's owner. The cart.) It specializes in a fried pancake called *hattahk*, which comes from a neighboring country's cuisine. *Hattahk* are stuffed with brown sugar and plump dried fruits and pine nuts. Every bite oozes with a combination of warm-grit-sweet. The dough sizzles on the griddle, making holes in the surface as the bubbles pop. You lean as close to the warmth as you can without being pushy.

The owner flips the *hattahk* expertly one by one. He usually has six going at a time. Almost done, just slightly browned, the way you like it. You hand over a few coins, fumbling partly because of the mittens, partly because you're not used to Sthenner currency. The coins are shaped like octagons with square apertures so you can carry them looped on a cord, although you just have them loose in a pouch.

"Here you go," the owner says in his hoarse voice. He adds, "The two biggest ones just for you." He wraps the *hattahk* in paper.

You've never been able to tell whether they really are the biggest. They're so similar in size that you'd have to weigh them, and they never last that long. Still, you thank him, then hurry up Central University Promenade toward the winding street you think of as 'between the gallows-shrine and the shop where they sell truncated noodles' rather than Spindle Street.

The itching feeling has only gotten worse. No help for it but to get to the session as fast as you can.

YOUR CHARACTER SHEET lies before you on the table, creased in the center, greasy fingerprints down one side. You try not to squirm at the accompanying oily sensation down your ribs. Oil from the *hattahk*: you're normally neater than this, but you're terribly hungry. You haven't filled the sheet in yet. Session leaders ordinarily provide character sheets and any other paraphernalia: charts, tokens, masks with eye slits almost too narrow to see through. All you had to bring was a writing implement, which you did, a mechanical pencil that tears the paper when you write too hastily, and an eraser that's more gray than white.

The sheet should just be paper, but you always feel that unsettling connection between yourself and the one you're going to be given. You knew about the holes in advance, for instance. One of the many quirks of academy life.

There are six people in the room, like sides of a die unfurled, including the session leader. Tonight's leader comes from one of the city's oldest families. Her full name is Mweren Ahm Roia Beniyat. Most people simply call her Roia Beniyat. You've seen her in the winehouses, watching the mirror-duels with eyes as cynical as old coins and long hair in pinned-up braids, elegant in a luxurious gray coat trimmed with dark lace. The brooch at Roia Beniyat's coat was impossible to miss, a treasure of the city: gold wirework, large enough to be gaudy on anyone less poised, with beads of bone and jasper and carnelian that moved whenever she did.

No one blamed you for staring. It's the only wealth she owns, they say, besides the genteelly decaying house she inhabits. Yet people buy her drinks or dinners, or defer to her at doors.

The Sthenner governor paid her a courtesy call on his first day in the city, and citizens noted that she saw him to the door herself three hours later, smiling and quoting witticisms from Sthenner plays.

You sit almost directly across from Roia Beniyat, and your glance snags on the pen she has taken out of its understated leather case, in which there is also a matching mechanical pencil. They must be antiques: gold-toned, probably real gold down to the pen's long-tined nib, so deeply engraved that it's hard not to convince yourself that there's nothing inside, no ink or graphite, nothing but a lacuna caged.

You were a last-minute addition to the group, your presence requested because of your 'unique background.' The Poians believe outsiders, as witnesses, have unique abilities of judgment. As much as it rankled to be counted an outsider yet, your curiosity prompted you to agree. Everyone else assigned to this session is a stranger.

You devise stories for the others to make them easier to remember. You can always revise the stories as more information comes to light.

The two men to your left could be brothers, or cousins. Say they're brothers.

The taller one has a rip in the sleeve of his otherwise expensive blue satin jacket, which he hasn't taken off, and he keeps tapping his foot nervously. He doesn't want to be here. People expect him to fight because he's big and why else would he be in Improvisational Tactics, anyway. However, he's bribed an official in the hopes of getting reassigned to Propaganda. (It's easier to remember something a bit unexpected, a bit odd.)

The shorter brother's clothing is less lavish, and the brown of his knee-length coat is the exact color of pine bark, down to the odd threads of dull gold suggesting cracks through which sap bleeds. Since he's sitting next to you, it's tempting to reach out and touch the threads, see if they're sticky like the melted sugar in your *hattahk*. (Only half of one left, with the crescent bite marks forming a ragged boundary between eaten and not-eaten. You eat fast when you're hungry.) The man has a marked facial resemblance to his brother, light brown eyes in a dark face and a beak of a nose, but what draws your attention are his hands. He hasn't taken his gloves off. Scars, you decide. A little later it turns out you're right.

He's the one who likes to fight, unlike his brother. They dueled once, and never speak of what happened. You leave the result a mystery, a maggot-question in the back of your head. But he smiles at people so that people smile back – you've already noticed how brilliantly he smiles, like a knife striking a knife-edge – and they don't see the mirror-slashes on his hands, or in his heart, and the violence gaping open.

The woman to your right leans back in her chair. Her belt of pale leather has an empty holster hanging from it; you spotted it as she lowered herself into her seat. The Sthenners confiscated weapons from everyone except the city watch in the first weeks. You had expected there to be an outcry. Several Poian societies carry, as their badge, old weapons, forged bright and dark and deadly. You like to think that this woman handed hers over without complaint or comment because the Sthenners mistook the gun, rather than the cutting cold behind her eyes, as the real threat.

The last person, sitting next to Roia Beniyat, is an older woman. She can only come to winter sessions because otherwise she will melt in the sun, like the Poian story of the Gray Grandmother and her coal-eyed children. You are half-afraid that if it gets warmer in here – not that it's very warm to begin with – her entire body will slump into an ambitionless larval mass, that all that motivates her is the memory of starvation winds and birds frozen into lakes, and in a time of plenty no one will listen to her warnings of famine.

Some of these stories are true. Most of them aren't. They're full of holes, just like the sheet you were handed. Your palms itch, and you resist the urge to rub your ribs. The effect is no worse than it has been in the past, and you've never been harmed before. Just a side-effect of your studies.

FIRST THINGS FIRST (says Roia Beniyat, after everyone is seated, in a voice like gunsmoke and demolished foundries). Decide upon a name for your instantiation in the evening's world. You may choose anything you like, but the name will be shared with everyone in this room. Consider what it implies about you and your place in the scenario, which is this: a city-state has become the protectorate of a more powerful neighbor. The name need not reflect who you are, merely how you wish to be seen.

Instantiation is such a formal way of putting it. However, it's no surprise that a scion of the city's elites would speak thus. Even though you've scarcely said anything since entering the room, mainly to affirm that you're the foreign witness, you're self-conscious about your accent. You haven't thought about it in a while – the way you talk is the way you talk, and your command of the language and its idiom (so they tell you) is excellent – but you're taken back to your first days in Poi Jiahl. You'd repeat yourself to good-humored locals because they couldn't understand your questions, and listen to them repeat themselves in turn because they talked too fast for you no matter how slowly they spoke.

You write down your character's name on the character sheet in painstakingly beautiful looping cursive. The modern Poian script was hard for you to master; you like showing off your handwriting. The Sthenners have distributed all their texts in their native language, written horizontally instead of vertically, with stilted accompanying translations. So far you have resisted learning to read any but the most necessary basics.

The taller brother chooses an old-fashioned Poian name, Warau. It means *sheltering tree* and is, a lover told you once, the kind of name you would expect someone's staid older sibling to have in a drearily unsubtle play. More telling is the lack of an accompanying family name, or string of family names, to indicate alliances of blood or coin.

The shorter brother, on the other hand, picks a name-of-poetry, used by courtesans or courtiers in the old days. It is abbreviated Nyen-moirop, or Undrowned; in actuality it consists of a quatrain in turbulent syllables, which must have made declarations of love during the throes of passion an interesting challenge. There's something of a courtesan's merciless wit in his eyes, at that. You wouldn't have thought it of him. First impressions can be misleading.

The woman with the empty holster chooses a Sthenner personal name paired with a Poian family name, although she retains Poian name order, with the family name coming first: Yuo Keresthen. The others shift and murmur nonetheless.

The Poians have a name for people of mixed descent, *dragon's get*. The old stories say this is because dragons are neither fully of air or water but move in both. (The Poians are delightfully wrong about elemental mythology. Dragons are creatures of fire and metal. But you have refrained from correcting them.) In their way the Poians are a cosmopolitan people, no doubt due to the Academy's long history of accepting foreign students like yourself and the city's healthy population of immigrants. The Sthenners, more prosaic, simply say *mixed heritage*.

Context is everything, however. Given recent events, Yuo Keresthen's choice can only indicate her interest in stabbing through the evening's fabrication and stapling it to reality. It hasn't escaped you that she keeps glancing your way, smiling thinly. She must believe the Poian superstition that foreign witnesses are like lenses, focusing reality in ways impossible among themselves.

The shorter brother's eyes flick to Roia Beniyat like a knife-draw. Whatever he sees in her untroubled expression displeases him. Did he expect her to object to something so trivial?

The last is the Gray Grandmother. She stared dully, obdurately, at the sheet that was passed to her while Roia Beniyat gave everyone time to choose. In her hand the Gray Grandmother grips an ordinary wooden pencil, much chewed. Filthy habit, and you try not to look, instead taking another tiny bite of your remaining half-*hattahk* to distract yourself with the cooling crystals of sugar. Her pencil didn't move once. You imagine it growing deformed in her grasp, forming uneven depressions corresponding to the fingers, then bending like a stick of taffy, and finally no longer resembling a pencil so much as a pulped eel.

Roia Beniyat raises her eyebrows at the Gray Grandmother. "Old one," she says, as politely as required and no more, "things cannot remain as they did during your youth. Pick a name."

"I saw you dancing with the new governor the other night," the Gray Grandmother mutters. "He's pretty enough, but that was no Poian waltz. I should know; I danced them all as a girl."

"Are you here to participate or to gossip like a schoolgirl?" the session leader says archly. "If your sharpness of memory is starting to fade, I'll happily tutor you in the new dances myself."

The Gray Grandmother's face sags. She puts down the pencil, which is not distended after all, and heaves herself up. She walks out without rejoinder, and you stare after her. The woman with the empty holster coughs uncomfortably.

You go around the table to introduce your alter-selves. The brothers (close cousins) come from a family of leading industrialists. The woman with the holster is a magistrate. Roia Beniyat used her own name, and is the only one to have done so. She notes that, for the scenario's purposes, she represents the occupying power, and then the game begins.

* * *

CHANGING THE NAMES of characteristics does not alter the nature of what is measured. The Academy's character sheet chose the names of attributes by committee, with a standardized result that satisfied no one, even with the generous inclusion of fill-in-the-blank space.

It does not matter whether you call it Strength, or Force, or Ox's Blessing.

Dexterity, or Finesse, or Grace.

Wit, or Cunning, or Way of the Fox.

Trauma, or Wound, or Gash.

(All of these are poor translations from the native Poian.)

Yet people argue as though the choice of label, with their subtle distinctions, their failures of isomorphism, was a matter of great importance.

Perhaps it's not a coincidence that the main characteristic you're concerned with, this session, is *name*.

HERE'S HOW IT works (Roia Beniyat says).

The person who has lived in this city the *shortest* period of time will begin by establishing one fact that elaborates upon the situation. (That person is you. You just entered the story, after all.) After that we will go clockwise, in the direction of entropy increasing.

Proceed.

SOME STORIES EXIST independently from the paper they are written on, the stone they are chiseled into, the skin they are tattooed across. Then there are the other stories.

Here is what you need to know about paper in the former city-state of Poi Jiahl.

Papermaking has a long history in the region. Fibers of mulberry, hemp, cotton, even imported banana leaves have been used. Sometimes red strands are included for luck, or else silken petals. Many Poians care passionately about paper and will debate the virtues of different papers while sitting on benches or standing in the shade of trees, the way other people might discuss wine or automobiles or tachistoscopes. Nevertheless, the mechanics of papermaking are well-known and need not be reiterated here.

Rather, of concern is the relationship between the city's Academy and its food carts. Several generations ago, the Academy almost closed due to student protests. Accounts of the protests' cause vary from new regulations on pigeon-hunting to a botched handling of quarantine during a plague. One of the Academy's statues, commissioned some time afterward, depicts elongated dancing figures with their eyes and nostrils stitched shut and headless pigeons hatching out of their mouths.

In any case, during that time, the Academy's head council decided that it needed to offload excess paper. Not blank paper; that would have been easy. The problem was paper that had already been printed on, brochures and maps and examinations; the latter included character sheets used in the ubiquitous roleplaying scenarios. The Academy's mission is to *develop character*, although it uses a phrase from Archaic High Poian – mistranslated, it turned out, but by then the motto was so entrenched that the correction never stuck.

An enterprising gentleman, whose real name is uncertain, bought up the excess paper. Everyone expected him to pulp the lot, as he was suspected of being involved in counterfeiting and the paper was of high quality. Instead, he turned around and made deals with the food carts. Where feasible, he cajoled them into buying the paper to wrap food in, replacing the earlier practice of loaning cheap bamboo containers to customers: everything from carp-shaped pastries filled with red bean paste to riceballs wrapped in seaweed to *hattahk*. This being Poi Jiahl, different types of food became associated with different fields of study. The carp pastries, riceballs, and *hattahk* wound up with Nonrepresentational Illustration, Structural Materialism, and Improvisational Tactics, respectively.

The Academy survived this difficult period, but the arrangement stuck. People peruse the stained sheets of paper as they eat the way they would read the newspaper. In this way the Academy even educates people who are not, technically speaking, its students.

YOU KNOW A great deal about the evening and how it will end in bloodshed, if blood is measured in scribbles and translucent glass tokens rather than liters. At least, you can't see how it would end any other way.

What reassures you least is that you had understood most Poians to be, if not enthusiastic about the Sthenner occupation, resigned to it. Initially you'd thought the Gray Grandmother's objection was a function of generational conservatism, and that the others accepted the pragmatic benefits brought by the protection of the Sthenner military and bureaucratic apparatus. The Poian governing council invited the Sthenners in, after all. Say what you like about them, but the Sthenners have, in their three-odd decades of gnawing expansionism, been scrupulous about only attacking when attacked; only treading where invited. The very legalism of their interactions, however, seems to be a source of offense.

You thought you'd lived here long enough to gain some small insight into local attitudes. Poi Jiahl has survived since it gained independence from a now-defunct alliance by adroitly maneuvering through the politics of larger and more powerful states. Increasingly you realize that the Poians' outward courtesy disguises a cynicism as well-honed and distinctive as absinthe. Perhaps, if you punctured the man to your left, the woman to your right, the absinthe would leak out and drizzle to the floor, leave the room steeped in a distillation of defiance.

The curfew bell tolls. It's the same bell that has hung in the town square since you first arrived, and for an odd century before that. Yet you are convinced that the tone is deeper, wavering like sound heard through water, or something thicker and murkier than water. Is this whole session a convoluted loyalty test? You can't imagine that the Sthenner authorities would look kindly upon it if they walked in, even if Roia Beniyat is on good terms with them.

You're not the only one distracted by the bell, but the session leader taps the edge of the table with her pen, and you pay attention again.

ONE OF THE great arts of Poi Jiahl, better known than the Academy's quirky method of disposing of old examination papers, is meat-carving. Visitors are either charmed or disgusted by the practice. Animals are hunted and brought upon platters of shiver-ice to great feasts, and cut up by master chefs. The chefs then arrange their limbs, their glaring bones, their ropes of intestine, into meat-sculptures in a deliciously temporary display. It is especially popular to transform prey into predator, or predator into prey: a flock of cranes into a dragon, a tiger into startled gazelles.

Sometimes the carcasses are eaten. More often they are burned without satisfying any hunger but the hunger for spectacle.

SOME GAMES ARE cooperative and some are competitive. Typically, however, a conflict of some sort is implied, even if only against an outside force: an hourglass with its trapped grains trickling earthward, the whimsy of tumbling dice, the players' own growing boredom.

Narration proceeds clockwise, as before, with each participant owning a scene in turn. Your goal is to resolve the situation. What resolution entails must either be decided by consensus or imposed. If a consensus can be found, there is no need to invoke the conflict resolution framework.

(A description of the rules, which involve dice, tokens, masks, and the ritual consumption of a raw heron, follows. You have seen any number of peculiar rites at these sessions, which you must complete to be certified as a tactician, and even so the heron is new. It arrives borne by six masked figures wearing the emblems of the cardinal directions: North, South, East, West, and two for the up-down World Axis in the center. If you had known that you were going to be fed raw heron, you are not sure whether you would have brought more *hattahk*, to get the taste of red out of your mouth, or none, since the Academy is feeding you.)

Fixated on the heron-sculpture, the glistening meat and membranes and bones, you almost miss the most important part:

Every time you lose a conflict, you lose a part of your name.

(Everyone, even Roia Beniyat, wrote their name in pencil.)

Every time you win a conflict, you gain some of your name back. But you can never recover more of your name than you had to begin with.

THE NEW ADMINISTRATION takes no responsibility for disappointments of the following nature that may occur in the city or on the Academy campus:

Gasoline rationing.

A change in the flavor of beer.

The adjustment of concert tuning from mai-cho = 453 cycles/second to 460 cycles/second.

A shortage of lizards.

The increase of minimum sentencing for littering and graffiti from two days to two weeks.

The collection of bronze and tin spoons and chopsticks as resources for the war effort. These will be exchanged for wooden spoons and forks.

The reduction of the rainbow's colors to six from seven.

The sudden failure of children's chants to rhyme.

A profusion of fungal strands in bottles of ink, and the recommendation to switch to an approved brand of iron gall, especially for filling out official documents. The appearance of similar strands in bathtubs is not part of the same phenomenon, no matter what rumor may imply.

(The list goes on in this vein.)

You LIKE THE taste of the meat, whatever it is, better than you hoped. It's hard to remind yourself that it's not really a heron, when it *looked* like one owing to the unnamed chef's artifice. Especially since you have no idea what heron tastes like. This is good, since you've had to consume quite a bit of the meat. Conflicts come up often, and each time you are involved in one, you must eat.

The Sthenners establish a cadre for the Poians, who thereafter wear the Sthenner Fungus-Lion badge and are given limited police powers. The dragon's get Yuo Keresthen, having established this in her first move, uses her next one to join the cadre as a spy. Courtesan Nyen-moirop is her lover.

The taller brother, Warau – who is not Nyen-moirop's brother in the scenario – joins the countryside resistance. It's a coward's act. Everyone knows that the country people are irrelevant, and from his lack of involvement in the scenes that follow, he knows it too. He just wants to get the session over with.

Your motivations are simpler: you will get more out of this evening if you go where the action is, so you go where the action is. Besides, it's not as if Warau looks like he wants company.

WAYS THAT A resistance can discombobulate an occupation:

Bursting into song each time a constable rounds a corner. "My true love's lips tasted of peaches, but yours like honey wine" is the most popular. The woman with the empty holster has a good voice, the others less so. You can't tell whether the group is singing to mai-cho = 453 cycles/second, 460 cycles/second, or something else entirely; you don't have perfect pitch.

Carrying guns whose firing chambers are stuffed with embroidery floss. Alternately, cloves.

Student demonstrations during finals week. (You have to do something drably expected once in a while. It keeps them guessing.)

Incubating locust eggs in the emergency silos.

Stealing and arranging the ties of railroad tracks so they spell out a riddle when seen from above.

The obligatory seductions and assassinations. The shorter brother has a gift for narrating Nyen-moirop's escapades with just enough detail to be tantalizing but not vulgar. Mostly. You didn't want to hear about the thirteen uses Nyen-moirop has for inkwells, but at least Roia Beniyat stopped him before he listed a fourteenth.

You do all of these and they aren't enough. You keep losing tokens to Roia Beniyat with her coin eyes. She's cleverer at every turn. There is a twisting logic to her countermoves. Rather than resorting to force, she leverages the tools that you yourselves have built into the scenario. But you know it's truly lost when she spends four tokens to rename herself.

Rather, she renames herself, and she doesn't: the same name, except in Sthenner order, the given name first and the family names after, so she becomes Roia Beniyat Mweren Ahm.

"Thank you for your participation," Roia Beniyat says. "It will prove most useful in the days to come. Please use the proper order for my name going forward."

There are holes in your sheet, new ones. You squint at the partly-erased name. For a moment the world tilts. You've written yourself horizontally, not vertically, the way the Sthenners do. You sneeze at the graphite dust, as persistent as spores.

Your head aches. You shouldn't be hungry, but now that the session is over, you are suddenly ravenous. It would be improper to reach for the shredded remnants of the heron. Still, this is why you visited the best food cart on Central University Promenade, the one that sells hearty Sthenner meat-and-mushroom pies. And you have about a quarter of one left.

You've been chewing for half a minute, forever, there's no difference in the longevity of distraction, when you realize there's an odd, tasteless, fibrous intrusion in your mouth. You have been eating the paper the meat-and-mushroom pie came wrapped in. Without checking to see if anyone is watching, you hurriedly fish the sodden mass from your mouth and fling it to the table. Even so, you feel some of the fibers stuck in your throat, and your convulsive swallowing does not dislodge them.

With trembling hands you unwrap the paper. A form – a character sheet, in fact. There are faint smudged remnants of handwriting in a looping, beautiful, and unfamiliar script, barely visible over the rows of Sthenner type.

CAPTAIN ZZAP!!
SPACE HERO FROM 3000 AD
GARY NORTHFIELD

Video game violence is something of a hot topic – what effect does playing violent games have on the young? Why do so many seek fictional violence for the purposes of entertainment? Gary tackles such questions with a darkly comic three page cartoon.

DEATH POOL
MELANIE TEM

*There's a humanity and emotional depth to Melanie's fiction
that makes her one of the natural literary successors to Shirley
Jackson. Like Jackson, Tem is equipped with a sharp mind,
an acerbic wit that dissects character within a compelling
narrative framework. Here, we meet someone so damaged by
life that he can only think of living in terms of a game, but
when he chooses to play the Death Pool he quickly finds the
game no longer to his liking.*

IT TOOK HIM a while to find the house because he kept *noticing*
things. The scallop of a knee-high wall along the edge of a
yard, in and out and in and out, shadow and rounded light.
A guy offering a hug to a screaming kid who didn't want to
give up the tantrum yet, but the guy kept quietly offering.
Piano music, not very good but it sounded nice. The pavement
against his shoe against his sock against his foot. Blue-and-
white signs 'Streets' and 'Ways' and 'Circles' and 'Places' with
all the same name and none of them straight, making it harder
to find the house he was looking for but it was cool how the
signs swayed in the wind.

He hadn't expected this wind. Yesterday it had been sunny
and calm, and they'd said more of the same all week. Those
weather people didn't get it right any better than just chance.
Maybe he could get a job like that, where you were paid to
notice things and predict things but you weren't expected to

be right. He stood and watched the clouds, wishing he knew what their movements and colors and shapes meant would happen in the next few minutes or days, glad he didn't and they could just be fun to look at through the chunk of glass or hard plastic he held up to his eye, light gray and lighter gray and thicker-looking in some places than others.

Finally he found the house and rang the bell. You could never tell what would come next when you rang a doorbell or knocked on a door, and those minutes before something happened – even if it was just that nothing happened and you went away again – always bothered him, so he concentrated on the echoey sound of the bell inside. He'd have liked to press the button again just to keep hearing the music, but that might've seemed in-your-face. While he waited he held up the piece of glass or whatever it was so that it caught the light and made beauty.

The door opened. Kind of old and fat in a shirt with flowers on it, she wasn't anything like he'd pictured. She held the outside door with one hand and the inside door with the rest of her body and said to come in. Until his eyes adjusted to the dimness – or to brightness going the other way – it was stepping off into the unknown.

She introduced herself. Her voice was sort of screechy. He gave her the name he'd come up with for this game, and she laughed and that pissed him off a little. Death Pool was about prophesying and his game name was from some prophet in the Bible. He didn't know what exactly the dude had said would happen or if any of it had come to pass, but he hadn't meant it as a joke.

She shook hands like a girl. He didn't like shaking hands. Who knew what someone had been touching or what they were going to touch next.

Her house was like one he used to live in, maybe more than one of them, maybe for less than a day or for three-and-a-half years. All friendly and happy-looking but you never knew what was going to happen in it or when you'd have to leave, so sometimes you made things happen like the fire or stealing money, or you just left on your own when you were eight or nine or twelve and they'd find you and put you someplace else. Plants on the windowsill could be blooming today and dead in their pots tomorrow, so you had to notice the flowers while you could. Whatever he smelled baking now might taste great but might come out burned or not cooked all the way through so you'd catch some disease. This nice brown dog constantly wanting its ears scratched could turn on you and bite you for no reason. It'd happened.

In a place as unpredictable as this house, any house, the whole world, you had to notice beauty. The dog's ears were soft.

"Have you played before?" He hadn't, but he said he had.

They sat at the dining room table surrounded by pictures of probably her family on the walls and shelves. She handed him a list with columns for Name, Age, Death Date, and Pay Out. He didn't know why she couldn't have done this online. But some of the houseparents actually did the random computer checks they were supposed to, so for him in-person was probably better, and her fees were the cheapest he'd found, so he pretty much had to do it her way.

The blue folder with pockets and with his game name on it weirded him out a little. He bent over to read the printed piece of paper without touching it. When the dog nudged his hand again he realized he was messing with the lump in his pocket, the little bit of beauty he tried to always keep close to him. "Rule number one," he read aloud. "Don't kill 'em."

This time he laughed and she didn't. "I mean it," she said.

"Yeah," he agreed. "Okay."

"Or yourself."

"Hadn't planned on it."

"The game's pretty straightforward. Players bet on when their picks will die, and whoever guessed closest gets the pot. Minus my admin fee."

"How do we know when they –" He stopped.

"Die," she finished for him. "This game's about dying. That's the whole point."

"So how do we know when they –" Was there a rule that he had to say the word in order to play the game?

"Die. I keep track and I notify the winners. The current pick list is in the other pocket. Prices there on the right. Mostly, the older and sicker they are the less they cost, but some of the young crazies are pretty affordable, too. Depends on the odds."

A lot of the old ones, ages 70s and 80s and 90s, he didn't recognize the names of. Most of the younger ones he did. Would his chances be better if he picked somebody he'd heard of or somebody he hadn't? Two had been crossed out and he couldn't read names or dates or how old they'd been or if anybody had won. A couple were right around his own age. That was weird, and cool. He kept going back to those, tapping his finger on the names, calculating what he could afford.

"Take your time."

On another piece of paper was his own name, spelled right and everything. Not the one he'd come up with for his game persona, but his 'real' name, his 'given' name given to him by people he barely remembered. His age was right, too, as far as he knew. Both the last two columns – Death Date and Pay-Out – were blank.

She opened a green notebook, uncapped the pen that had been stuck in the spirals. "You ready?"

She'd said to take his time but now she was pressuring him. People were always pressuring him. "I – I don't know." He said that a lot, and it was true a lot more often than he said it.

She got in a pat or two on the back of his hand before he could pull away. "Remember," she told him, "you're just betting on when somebody'll die, not making it happen."

"It's weird, though," he said.

"Well, yes, probably. I think that's what makes it fun for people. That, and predicting what really can't be predicted. It's a game of illusion, really. What's in your pocket?

"Nothing."

"Put it on the table where I can see it or get out of my house."

Something terrible might happen no matter which he chose, or something good, or nothing at all either way. She watched him. He tried pulling the joint out of his pocket and laying it on the table. She barely glanced at it.

Just holding the piece of glass up between his thumb and forefinger put beauty in his mind. He expected her to try to grab it or him, but all she did was adjust her glasses and look and ask, "What is that?"

"I found it a long time ago." He couldn't remember when or where he'd found it, or a time in his life when it hadn't been reminding him to notice beautiful things.

"What, it has magic powers or something? Protects you or brings you good luck or something?"

"I like it, that's all." He liked its smoothness and its roughness, the different colors in it, its little weight. He liked the smell of it and the taste.

"Ooh," she said. "This'll be fun."

Stabbing at the paper with his middle finger, he demanded, mostly to change the subject, "Why's my name on here?"

"Just a little twist I put in for laughs, to give an extra edge. Now that I've met you I'll record a death date for you. If you don't make it or it's right on the money, I keep your fee. If you get past it, you get a rebate. A little side bet between the two of us."

"I'm only eighteen."

"Yep."

"I'm not sick or anything. I don't do stupid dangerous stuff."

"Death can happen any time to anybody."

This was seriously creepy. "How will you know? It's not like I'd be on the news or anything."

"I'll know," she said. "I always know."

He pointed. "That's not the right name."

"Sure it is," she said. "For this part. But let's settle on your picks first. See anybody you like?"

It took a while but he finally decided on the oldest on the list. He'd never heard of the dude and she didn't try to tell him who it was, just wrote the information in her spiral notebook on what he supposed was his page. "Low risk, low pay-out," she reminded him.

For a second he was confused; you'd think somebody ninety-two would be at high risk. Then he realized he was betting that the guy *would* die soon, and the risk of that *not* happening was low. "Got it," he told her.

"This one or this one," she tapped with her pen, "or even this one would more than double your money if they come in for you."

"But my chances of losing my money are bigger."

"Right. That's how it works."

Decisions sucked. No way to tell how they'd turn out. Anything he thought of to do after high school might be perfect or a disaster. The instant he ordered something from a menu he wished he'd ordered something else. He could never decide what to wear – How warm would it be in the afternoon? How cold would it be in the morning? Who would he see that day and what would he be wanting from them? – so he just wore the same clothes till somebody made him put them in the laundry and he had to remember to take the rock or glass or plastic thing out of whatever pocket it had been in; then usually he'd be too hot or too cold or dressed wrong somehow for whatever occasion he hadn't foreseen but sometimes he'd look good. From when he was little he knew that when they told you to go get a belt you couldn't know which one would hurt least or how many times they'd hit you with a wide one or a skinny one so it wasn't a real choice but if you didn't choose it would probably be worse but once in a while if you didn't go get one they wouldn't hit you at all.

Finally, he just randomly signed up for the seventeen-year-old female whose craziness was all over YouTube plus the ninety-two-year-old. The game lady gave him receipts in a plain white envelope that he'd have to think where to keep where nobody would find it but he'd know where it was when he needed it. "Okay," she said, businesslike. "Now you."

"Now me what?" he bluffed.

"Your death date."

The dog worked its head under his hand so he was petting it without really meaning to. A timer went off in the kitchen. She went to check and he heard her open and shut the oven door. When she came back she didn't sit down at the table.

"Got a date you like?"

How could you answer that?

"Okay, listen. The cake just needs a few more minutes, and I've got to get ready for my next player. So…" She wrote down what he supposed was her prediction, or just some random date because she wanted to be done with him. She put the folded paper into an envelope, sealed it, and slid it into a pocket of the other blue folder she'd made for him, the one she was going to keep. He waited for her to make a copy or write the date down again for him, but instead she filled out an invoice and laid it in front of him. He hadn't expected to spend this much. Now he'd have to wait till Friday before he could buy more weed. That was the problem with budgeting; stuff always came up that you hadn't thought about that cost money.

"How will I know?"

Behind her glasses her eyes twinkled. "Well, if I'm right –"

The end of her sentence was "you'll be dead," and he talked over it. "How will I know if you're wrong and I win money?"

"Trust me. I'll let you know."

"What if I move or change my Facebook or something? How will you find me?"

"I won't have to find you. We're connected now. I'm your new BFF." Before he could anticipate and dodge, she'd hugged him. She smelled sweet and smoky, like burning flowers.

He stood up, pushing the chair back hard. The dog yelped. He hadn't meant to hurt the dog. Before he got her door open, it occurred to him to ask, "What if you... go first?"

"I won't," she said. On his way down her front steps, he realized he'd left that last joint on her table. The pebble thing was still in his pocket, though. He was sorry not to run into her next customer to see what kind of sicko idiot would pay money to play this game. The bird in the tree in her front yard stopped singing almost before he noticed the song. The light had changed so that the scalloped wall across the street didn't have deep sharp shadow and bright round light anymore, and he didn't take time to notice how it looked now.

The wind was coming from a different direction. He got lost in all the streets and circles, missed his bus, got back to the house too late for dinner. He grabbed a banana from the bowl, firm and yellow but it was starting to go soft and brown under the peel.

He didn't die that night. He didn't sleep much either, because whenever he started to drift off fear would explode in his chest like a pistol shot and he'd catapult awake with "I'm gonna... I'm gonna... I'm gonna..." rattling in his mind, finished every time with a screechy "die!" that made him cry out. He took a shower in the middle of the night even though it was against the rules, put his clothes in the laundry and remembered to take the glassy nub out of his pocket, but he couldn't get rid of the sweet smoky smell and he couldn't lose her voice in his head screeching or whispering or singing, "You're going to die. Maybe today, maybe not."

All night long and then all day every day he searched the web to see if he'd lost his bets, but as far as he could tell both his picks were still alive.

One afternoon he was listening to Zoe Keating and starting to get sort of into her amazing music when the Death Pool lady got on the bus and sat down beside him. He'd never seen her on the bus before. He must have had the volume up too loud because apparently she could hear the cello, and he must have looked happy or blissed out or something because she tapped his shoulder and when he took out the ear bud she said, "Don't forget. You'll lose it all."

"What're you, stalking me?"

"Stalking's for amateurs. I'm just with you. Will be till the minute you –" She raised her eyebrows at him, almost like flirting.

He didn't say it out loud but the sentence got finished in his head, the way a phrase of music or a rhythm would finish itself.

He got off way before his stop. It was a long walk. When he turned Zoe Keating back on the music sounded stupid, and he thought he almost got hit by a car but he hadn't been paying attention enough to be sure.

He caught a cold. Cough, headache, chills. A couple of the other kids in the house and a weekend houseparent had the same symptoms, but he knew it might kill him. The game lady texted him, 'Feeling ok?' and he answered, 'Headache' and she answered back, 'Stroke? Tumor?' He didn't think he sent her the pictures he took of the flowering bush in the yard or the morning light through the school windows, but she tweeted, 'So? They and you will be gone soon' and he deleted the pictures as if they'd been porn.

At a party he was starting to have fun until he saw her, seriously out of place. She waved and came right up to him and yelled over the noise, "Having a good time? Not for long!" and faded back into the crowd. Wondering if anybody else was playing this game, he asked around, but nobody said they knew her.

As time went on, which it wouldn't forever, everything got blurry and far away, nothing to do with him because he was going to die and he was afraid. He couldn't have said what the weather was like or who said what to him or what was on the history test or sometimes even whether he was asleep or awake. He discovered all kinds of twinges and lumps and rumbles in his body. Eating didn't occur to him very often. He was aware of seconds and minutes going by, but they barely registered with him. When he jerked off, he didn't feel much of anything, even when there was evidence that he had come.

He was going to die any minute. He was going to die sometime, and he didn't know when or how, so what was the point of anything else?

Somebody mentioned what a nice day yesterday had been. When the game lady texted, 'Yesterday's dead and gone and so will you be so what good's a nice day?' he was glad he'd missed it. The girl he'd been sort of thinking about before he bought in on the game said hi to him in the hall and he ignored her. *Why start something that'll just end sooner or later?* the soft screechy voice in his head pointed out. He still couldn't sleep more than a few minutes at a time, kept waking up to see if he was dead yet.

At 3:17 one morning his cell rang. He answered and went on tweeting on his laptop about nothing in particular. While she was asking how the pain in his back was that he hadn't told her or anybody about, he did a quick search for any mention of his picks but found nothing.

"Just checking," she said like metal on metal. "Have a nice night," and hung up.

A day and a half later, in the middle of history class which he used to actually kind of like, she texted him, 'Still there?'

He texted back 'Think so,' and then couldn't keep his mind on all the cool stuff about the Civil War. He must've passed his death date, or it was coming up soon. The stupid fat old lady must be tracking her bet.

He went through a couple girlfriends and a couple jobs. Nothing stuck because she kept reminding him that nothing would stick forever, he'd lose everything. Catching sight of her ahead of or behind him, or just smelling her, or even just thinking about her which he did constantly, he'd quit going to their houses and the job sites. When he graduated she was the only person he knew in the audience, so he left before the ceremony started, ditching his cap and gown outside the door. She was clear across the auditorium but he heard her say, "First day of the rest of your life, huh? Might be the only day."

It'd be Monday and then Thursday, or 6:10 a.m. and then 3:46 p.m. and he'd have no impression at all of the time that had passed except of seeing or hearing or smelling her all over the place. They said on TV that there'd been a spectacular full moon but he was glad he hadn't noticed because it would be gone in a night or two anyway, or he would. "That's right," she somehow let him know.

He went to a movie with some people and sort of zoned out through the whole thing, wondering if he'd die here in this crappy theatre. He heard there was awesome music somewhere downtown but it wasn't worth the effort.

There was still nothing online about either one of his picks. He kept waiting to hear from her about them, checked his phone all the time, half-dreamed she was behind him or around the next corner or right in front of him in disguise.

Then one day – bright and chilly, he could tell – he was walking somewhere because he didn't have anything else to do, not going anywhere in particular because who knew what would be there when you got there, who knew what would happen, and he was going to die anyway. Maybe he was hungry, tired. Maybe that was a squirrel, a flower. What he knew for sure was that death was in his future, somewhere, sometime, in some form. And she was walking beside him, taking his arm, and then she wasn't. Another minute he lived with his mind and body full of death, another week, another heartbeat.

It was all over the internet when the old guy went. Turned out he'd been a big-deal musician and people said all kinds of cool stuff about him but what good did that do now? A bulk email with bcc'd names announced that there hadn't been any winners. When he didn't bother to answer she texted, 'You okay?' and he answered 'yeah' because he didn't want her showing up and anyway she knew better than he did whether he was okay. It was also all over the web when the girl pick turned eighteen and had a crazy blow-out party. Another email said there'd been a winner, but it wasn't him.

After a while things started poking through even though he didn't exactly want them to. Ice cream tasted really good one day and he was letting it melt in his mouth when he got a text, 'Might be your last ice cream' with a smiley face, and he threw the rest of the cone away without bothering to look for her. Sitting in the park, he realized he wasn't just waiting, he was noticing how the squirrels' tails fluttered and how the sunshine picked out blades of grass, and he was happy; *I'm happy*, he caught himself thinking. She caught it, too, because she was whispering in his ear, "You're going to die!" Behind a tree he threw up the happy feeling in his gut.

He'd both turned eighteen and finished high school, so he had to go live somewhere else, but how could you predict whether you'd have enough money or not, how long to sign a lease for, whether you'd be around next winter when the drafty place might be too cold? So he didn't do anything. Sooner or later they'd kick him out, if he didn't die first.

One day or night, he happened to put his hand in his pocket and the piece of glass or whatever wasn't there. How long since he'd even thought about it? His stomach clenched. He was still alive, but she was standing out of reach, the piece of glass that used to remind him of beauty now dangling lifeless from her hand.

"I win," she said. "This is how I win."

THE BONE MAN'S BRIDE
HILLARY MONAHAN

Set in a Dustbowl town in the US during the Great Depression, Hillary's story – her very first short story, in fact – oozes atmosphere and menace. A tale about the hypocrisy of desperate adults, willing their children to a game they would never play themselves. When times are tough, it is often the youngest that suffer.

EVELYN WOKE TO the preacher calling her a sinner.

The voice rang out from Mama's radio, that hulking brown thing she'd inherited from Uncle Melville on his passing from the tuberculosis. It sat in the kitchen between the vegetable bin and the laundering buckets, and Mama spent her days and nights listening to Scripture while she smoked her cigarettes. She had it turned up real loud now for Father Coughlin's program, which was her favorite because the father "Said the good words, Evie-beans. He knows the right way'a it." Sometimes, when Coughlin got particularly impassioned, Mama closed her eyes and nodded like she was hearing the Gospel from the Lord's own mouth.

Evelyn tore herself from her narrow bed, her feet striking the cold wooden planks of her floor. She put on an extra pair of socks, hoping the second pair's holes didn't align with the first's, and pulled a shawl around her thin shoulders. Mittens were the last of it, and she rubbed her hands together, the friction of the yarn returning the feeling to her fingertips.

She entered the kitchen expecting to see Mama bent over the skillet, but not today. Today Mama was wrapped in a ragged, wool coat, her breath coming out in puffy clouds that blended with the cigarette smoke pouring from her nostrils. Her nose was crusted red, her eyes cat-slit-narrowed.

"Porch. Go look," Mama said in greeting.

Evelyn's stomach dropped. She knew what she'd find even as she shuffled her way through the kitchen to push the screen door wide. It squealed on the hinge, hungry for oil, but she paid it no mind. Her pale eyes flicked to the left – empty crates, a rusted-out watering pail, a rocking chair that needed caning. She looked right and that's when she saw it. In front of the tool cabinet, dangling from the porch overhang like a wind chime, was a branch strewn with dried sinew. A half-dozen milky white rib bones bounced on the strings, the delicate arches no longer than her pinky finger.

"He's coming, Evie-beans. The Bone Man's coming to stake his claim, but don't you fret. There's fifty girls in town the proper age, most of 'em far prettier than you," Mama had said. Except here it was, the Bone Man's gift tinkling on the winter wind. He only picked three girls to play his bride game, and this was Evie's invitation.

Evelyn's heart felt thick, her mouth as dry as a dead man's eye. *It's a privilege,* the pastor said last Sunday after they sang the Psalms, *that one of you will serve our patron in the wood. You'll taste immortality with His legacy.* Evelyn didn't want a legacy. She had no interest in renown or esteem. Yet the tribute dancing before her said that her wishes didn't matter – she didn't choose because she'd been chosen. The Bone Man's will usurped her own.

She dropped her head into her hands, thick ropes of matted blonde hair tumbling over her shoulders. Mama's chair squeaked across the kitchen floor before the door hinge shrieked its rust song. Her wire-arms locked around Evelyn's middle to pull her back into a smoke-and-talcum-powder embrace. Evelyn fumbled for her hands, her mittens engulfing Mama's pale, twiggy fingers.

"I remember seeing Prudence, the last time," Evelyn rasped. "She stopped at the stream crossing to wave. There was blood all over. She never came back, Mama. None of 'em come back."

"I know, Beans, but there's still the game. You still got to win the game." Mama's lizard lips pressed a kiss to the side of her neck. "Don't lose hope. Sister McPherson says hope brightens the dark paths and cheers the lonely way."

"Sister McPherson don't do shit for me!" Evelyn whipped her head around to glower at her mother, her bottom lip quivering. "Y'all are writing vouchers my blood'll cash!"

Mama's hand slapped her hip, her pointed fingernails pinching Evie's fat through that thin, moth-eaten nightgown. "Sixteen ain't so old I won't put soap in your mouth for your swill. Now go get your good dress. They'll be waiting. And take off them mittens. You know they'll need your palm."

Mama gave her thigh another smack and disappeared into the house. Evelyn glanced out at the emaciated remains of the corn field, the crops dead and teetering in their yellow husks. She could run, but how far would she get? The fields stretched for miles. And would the town come get her? Probably, with guns and beat bats at the ready. The Bone Man's tithe was a long-standing tradition. No one shirked their duty.

Especially not a bride. The Bone Man needed his Blood Queen.

It's an honor, Evie-beans. If you're took. It's an honor, remember. Ain't all bad.

Evelyn swallowed a groan and followed inside. Mama was singing along with the hymnal on the radio, the kettle spewing coffee grits over the stovetop. At least there'd be bitter black to warm Evie's bones. She ducked into her room and peeled off her layers, mittens first, abandoning them on her pillow and rubbing her thumbs over her palms. Would they cut through the calluses or around? She didn't want to think about it as she reached into her closet for her sole finery.

The dress was papery, like a butterfly's wing. She'd forgotten how delicate it was until she stripped raw and tugged it over her head, the cotton grazing her breasts, her middle. It hugged her waist and flared around her hips, the skirt tickling her calves. It'd been fashionable once, some years ago, but it was thin along the seams, the threads fraying near the folded flaps of the neckline.

She tottered to the kitchen only to see the ash plummet from the tip of Mama's cigarette.

"M'cold, Ma," she said.

Her mother glanced at her and frowned. "Put on some woolens and pinch them cheeks. Don't want you all milquetoast. The coffee'll help. I'll get the rouge. Splash'a sweet water. It'll be fine." She was talking to herself more than Evelyn as she darted to her bedroom, the doorway covered by a tattered Confederate flag. Wasn't the most patriotic thing in the world, but lean times meant all their haloes sported more tarnish than usual.

Mama emerged with a string of dipped pearls, a handkerchief, and cologne she'd watered down so many times, it barely smelled of roses anymore. "Get your shawl on. Game's at the church. Can't keep the Bone Man waiting." Evelyn's feet stalled, suddenly heavier than old delta silt. She didn't want to get her shawl – didn't matter that she had goosepimples breaking out all over her skin or that her teeth chattered. She couldn't make herself go.

Mama grabbed her by the ear and dragged her across the floor, Evie's feet skidding through old bacon grease before she was thrown into her room. "C'mon Evie-beans. Leggings and slippers. We gotta go."

Evie did as she was told despite the lead in her limbs. When Mama shoved a tin cup of coffee in her hands, she drank, the hot liquid scalding her tongue. Mama stole it away before Evie finished so she could pat Evie's cheeks with rouge. Sweet water followed, the spritz so cold Evie flinched, but Mama kept right on fussing. And when she was done fussing, she hauled her out into the crisp morning air, pausing only to retrieve the bone token from the porch.

They made their way past the half-collapsed fence and the pull-tractor that hadn't moved in five planting seasons. Gravel crunched beneath their shoes. The drive was overgrown, edges lined with the clutching fingers of hip-tall grass glistening with frost. The radio preacher's voice died to a tinny echo as they crested the road only to find themselves shuffling alongside another family with an equally-as-terrified girl stumbling at their heels.

Abby Taylor. Seventeen, dark hair, dark eyes. Evie'd taken lessons with her years ago, from Pastor Thomas's wife. Mrs. Taylor taught piano while Mr. Taylor worked the stock room at Anderson's Dry Goods. Evie and Abby had been friendly for a time, but they'd drifted apart when Abby started seeing the Jenner boy. And then the Little boy, and the Chilton boy after that.

By the carved bone effigy in Abby's hands, it seemed the Bone Man didn't mind a little bit of harlotry.

They exchanged terrified stares, their mothers pulling them down Main Street and toward the clapboard church. Most days, sunrise brought the din of commencing business – doorstops swept, shelves restocked, and chickens squawking as their nests were robbed. But not today. Today, the town stood stalwart before their storefronts, their chapped, red faces empty as they watched. Evelyn knew them all by name, but whenever she met one of their gazes, they looked away, their cold forms huddling in beside their loved ones.

There but for the grace of God, they thought.

"Hypocrites. SINNERS!" Evelyn shrieked, her voice caught by the morning wind and carried far and deep – beneath the carts, down the alleyways, and up to the second floor terraces.

She tore from her mother's grasp to spin, a waif in rippling clothes on a stretch of dusty street. "'Here is my servant whom I have chosen that you may know and believe and understand that I am he. Before me no god was formed, nor shall there be any after.' Isaiah. I KNOW MY ISAIAH!"

Her mother's hand snapped out, her fingers plunging into the nest of Evelyn's hair. The pain was immediate. Dragged through town now on her mother's fleshy tether, her feet scuffling and kicking up grit.

Up the church steps, the Taylor family quiet and demure by contrast. Mama shoved Evie through the double doors, tossing her daughter into the back pew. The backs of Evie's knees struck the worn wood and she sat. She'd come here every Sunday since she was born but never before had it seemed so stark. White walls, gray floors, the altar a spindly, repurposed dining table with a single relic. Pastor Thomas stood behind it now in his faded black clothes, his gray beard long enough to touch the middle buttons of his shirt. He was talking to Miranda Shepherd's father, Hal, who leaned over his cane and clutched his prayer book. His hair was oil black with silver at the tips, Brylcreem flattening it to his skull.

Miranda Shepherd was curled into her mother's shoulder, the two of them weeping, their entangled red hair resembling a fire bush. Evie understood their tears even before she saw the bone figurine clutched in Miranda's fist. She was a nice girl – the kind who gave canned beans to the vagrants that came off the rails looking for a better life. They wouldn't find it here – the town kept its Dustbowl bounty to itself, selfish as they were, the fortune they'd bargained for too precious to share – but at least Miranda gave them a meal.

A girl like that didn't deserve a thing like this.

But then, none of them did.

The pastor looked between the families, his frown cutting trenches in his leathery skin. He gestured toward the little room Mama once called the sacristy, though the pastor later told her that was a Catholic term, and there weren't any damned Irish around here. But that room, sacristy or not, was one of the few mysteries left in these parts. The preacher went in, the preacher came out before and after Sunday services, but she'd never witnessed what was tucked away behind that door.

Mama dug her eagle talons into Evelyn's shoulder and jerked her to her feet. Evie tried to shrug her off, but Mama's grip was ironclad as she pulled her into her side, her arm snaking around her waist. They walked the narrow aisle together, the pews bumping against their hips, the wood beneath their feet groaning under their combined weight.

"C'mon, Beans. It's just a game, a'right? Nothing to fear now," Mama whispered, forcing the bone chime into her daughter's hand before steering her toward the pastor. The Taylors waited at the front of the church on the left, Abby's head fallen forward. Her parents looked straight ahead, expressions vacant save for the pinched line of their lips. The Shepherds were on the right, Mrs. Shepherd's snivels dying when Mr. Shepherd cuffed her ear.

"No use in blubbering over the tithe. You live on the land, you pay for it. Jesus sacrificed for us, remember that now," he said, his cane thwacking his daughter in the shin. "Up, Randa, an' stop that cryin' or I'll give you somethin' to cry on."

"For God so loved the world, that he gave his only Son, that whoever believes in him should not perish but have eternal life. Amen,'" the pastor said, the tips of his fingers pressed together in blessing. Evie stared at his back as he moved toward the side room. Speaking the word of the Lord after a man struck his wife in a holy house seemed wrong.

The Shepherds were first to go in, the patriarch smacking at his wife and daughter's legs with his cane so they'd move *faster, faster*. He got Randa behind the knee once, nearly collapsing her to the floor, but her mama reached out to catch her before she tumbled, pulling her head into her warm bosom. The Taylors went next, their processional grimmer than when

Marty Oudekirk drowned in the creek last year. That left Evie and her mama, the two of them moving as one unit thanks to Mama's hold.

"No frettin'. An' when ya don't win, you'll be marked free'a him." Mama leaned in close to press another kiss to Evie's cheek, but Evie ducked and Mama swiped at empty air. Her rebellion earned her another pinch to her soft stomach roll.

They stumbled into the side room like a three-legged beast. It was tinier than expected, the walls close-in and tall, stretching for the steeple with a slanted roof. There was only one window, a square that did little to cast light, but a stool in the corner had candles on it to supplement, a half dozen flames flickering above pools of molten wax. The walls and floor were white here, too, only brighter, like someone had bleached the paint. Along the top, strung on twine and held in place by rusty nails, was a long line of bone tokens similar to the one Evie found on the porch. Some of them had gone yellow with age while others were as crisp as the fresh paint behind them.

In the middle of the floor was a milk crate with a burlap sack leaning against its side. They'd cut the crate down and sanded the edges smooth. It was natural wood, save for the slats along the bottom which had been painted red with an X. Evie hissed. She knew what came next. By Abby's whimper and Miranda's sharp intake of breath, they knew, too. Evie took an unwitting step back, but Mama grabbed her by the scruff and someone else slammed the door closed. They were all trapped now, squished into this tiny room like sardines in a can.

Pastor Thomas lifted his hand as he often did on Sundays when he wanted the congregation to pay particular attention to his words. It was this man holding this stance that had taught Evelyn about Daniel in the lion's den and Jesus's bloody sweat in the gardens of Gethsemane. But here, now, he was on about something else, something darker and more foreboding.

"And lo, the Bone Man that did bless this land granted us his grace, and we the flock to his shepherd give unto him the third day of the third month of the third year a queen of flesh. She is the field to furrow, the fertile valley, her communion with her master bonded in blood and chosen by bone."

No false idols, Evelyn thought, her muscles tensing and demanding she flee. Mama must have sensed the encroaching panic. She lined Evie's body with her own, her front pressed to Evie's back, her arm sliding along the underside of her daughter's arm and manacling her wrist with her thumb and forefinger. Evie didn't quite know why until Pastor Thomas reached into his coat to produce a knife. It wasn't long, no more than three inches, but the rusty edge and the glinting tip promised menace.

"No!" Evie's outburst sent the other two girls to scrambling, a pulse of terror filling the tiny, stark room. The girls' frantic pleas bounced off the walls, echoing up toward that tall, slanted ceiling.

The pastor came at Evie first – Mama'd given her hand up for the knife, after all, or maybe it was because Evie had triggered the fuss – and his fingers wrapped around hers, pinching them together so tight the tips went red. She tried to wrench away, but he wrenched back, pulling her arm out from her body so hard, she thought it'd rip from her socket.

"Hold still, girl," he snapped as he slashed the blade down. He splayed her from thumb to pinky, over the soft pads, through the callus just below her ring finger. She screeched, blood welling in the gash before she ripped away from him, thrusting Mama into the wall in her panic. Sanguine droplets splashed across the too-white paint on the floor.

"Damn it, Evie. C'mon, baby. Don't be like that." Mama slid a hand around her throat and up under her jaw, pulling her head back as the pastor swiped at her for his second pass. He couldn't quite get a grip thanks to the blood smearing Evie's fingers – she was as slippery as a spring toad in creek mud.

"Stop this nonsense," he barked, his fingers digging into her forearm. She wailed as the knife came down for a second time, bisecting the plump flesh of her middle finger and splitting what the carnival reader had called her heart line. It cut across the first welt to form the cross, marking her as the game's bloody property.

"All done," Mama crooned into her hair. Evie pulled her hand to her chest, smearing her skin and the neckline of her dress with hot copper. She crouched, feeling like a hunted animal, and Mama sank with her, pulling her back against her slender body, her spider-like fingers stroking across her daughter's forehead.

It was madness to take comfort from the very person who'd held her under the knife, but that's what Evelyn did, so scared that she sobbed into Mama's perfumed neck. She was almost loud enough to drown out the screams of first Abby, then Miranda, both girls crying out as their hands were desecrated. The floor had a scarlet stain, the walls dribbled with red tribute, but the pastor remained unmoved, just swiping the sullied blade of his knife against his trouser leg to clean it.

He reached for the burlap sack next, plunging his hand into the scratchy depths to retrieve an animal skull. It fit inside his hand, all boiled and bleached clean of its meat, the empty gaps of its eyes pointed in Evie's direction. He offered it to her but she refused. Mama was the one who plucked it from him, her fingertip gliding over the smooth brow.

"Cat, I think," she whispered, as if the others couldn't hear. "Too long front-to-back to be a squirrel. Cats are good luck." Evie didn't want to look at it, and she cast her gaze away, but Mama shook out Evie's injured hand, splaying her fingers and forcing the skull into the cradle of her palm. "You hold this, Beans. He'll tell you what to do."

Evie stared at the macabre thing, wondering if this had been the same skull used three years ago when Prudence had won the game. Had her blood smeared the skull? Had this been what she'd thrown when they cast the bones? Or was this some other hapless creature that had lost its life in the name of the Bone Man?

The pastor circled the room, equipping all three girls with skulls. Evie glanced over at Abby, who stood tall in the corner, her hair hanging past her face to hide her features away. Her arms were limp by her sides, a pool of blood formed on the floor beneath her left hand. Rivulets ran over the skull she grasped, one particularly thick river slithering from the corner of the eye socket like a tear.

Miranda fared no better. There was blood all over the front of her blouse like she'd used it to staunch the bleeding. She was nestled against her mother, trembling, the skull clutched between her hands and tucked against her neck. She rocked back and forth, her lips moving in voiceless prayer. Her father stood at her back, a severe, scowling shadow whose dark brows knit so close together, there was no space between.

"You will cast your skulls into the box at the same time. It must strike one of the sides to count. If it does not, we cut the other palm and do it again," the pastor said.

"How do we know who's won?" There was no inflection to the question, which was appropriate considering it came from Mrs. Taylor. The Taylors were caricatures of their former selves. Or maybe more like golems sculpted from clay. They were sightless, soundless. Emotionless. Even with their daughter on the precipice of the sacrificial altar, their weathered faces remained stoic.

"The closest to the crosshatch gets two points. The next closest, one, the furthest out, none. If the skull lands on its side, a point. If it lands neck down, two. If it lands upside down, three points." The pastor retreated until his back was pressed to the wall. Evie hadn't followed his explanation, but she wasn't going to ask him to repeat it. It was almost better not to know. "Give me your tokens, please."

Evie'd almost forgotten she had hers clutched in her good hand. She'd gripped it so hard, the rib bones had dug arcs in the meaty part of her palm. She offered it to the pastor, happy to be free of it, but her eyes strayed to the other tokens tied along the ceiling. Did all of them get pinned there or just the winner's? Was that a string of bride prizes?

The pastor held the bone invitations to his chest, motioning the girls closer to the crate with his other hand. "Come now." When none of them moved, Mr. Shepherd smacked his cane against the wall, the clatter ricocheting up to the ceiling. That had Miranda and Abby scuttling close, though Evie took another moment, her heart thumping inside her chest faster than a hummingbird's wing.

"Go on, Beanie. I love you," Mama said, gently shoving her toward the box. Evie dropped to her knees, her body hot despite the draft wafting up through the floorboards.

"On three, you cast. No cheating or I cut you until you do proper by our patron." Evie's arm trembled as she lifted her skull. Abby and Miranda mirrored her, the three of them positioned like points of a triangle. Evie thought she might be sick. Her stomach roiled and her breath came in short pants.

"One."

Her fingers spasmed around the skull.

"Two."

Her shoulders hunched.

"Three!"

The skulls flew and struck the box from all angles, rattling and rolling across the crate. It was hard to follow which one was which until they settled. Only then did Evie see her skull was different than the other two. One was shorter and squatter, maybe a raccoon, while the other was smallish and sleek, making Evie think of a rat.

Evie stared as her cat skull teetered into place. It wasn't closest to the middle – that was the raccoon skull – so she knew that was good. What she couldn't remember was how the positions were scored. The other two skulls were on their sides, which was some points, but Evie's had landed upended, on the rounded top portion.

It wasn't until Mr. Taylor jerked open the door and thrust his daughter outside that Evelyn's skin began to itch.

"What's it mean?" she demanded. The only answers were Mama's plaintive groan and Mr. Shepherd shoving the now-sobbing Miranda toward the body of the church proper. "Wait, hold on! What's it –"

"Four points," the pastor said, motioning at the skull. "One for being second closest to the middle, three for being upended. Miranda was three – on her side and in the middle. Abby was two. You are the Bone Man's Bride, Evelyn Beecher."

"No, I ain't!" But no one heard her. The door slammed shut and the hands came at her from all directions. The Taylors grabbed for her, the Shepherds. Even kind Mrs. Shepherd who'd held her weeping daughter close swooped in to haul Evie into the center of the room. The crate was thrust aside as fingers tugged at Evie's shawl, ripping it away. Another pair of fingers – nimble and feminine, Mrs. Taylor's – unbuttoned the front of Evie's dress, exposing her skin to the eyes of the looming gathered.

"WAIT!" Evie screamed. A hand shoved her head forward, pointing her nose at the floor. Others settled on her shoulders and squeezed. Her mouth opened, she panted like a dog, but they were blind to her terror, fingers adroitly rolling her dress past her shoulders. Her breasts weren't bared, but nearly, and she felt the heat of embarrassment creeping along her face.

"No. No, wait," Mama called, the only one not crowding in like a hyena over fresh dead. But there was no waiting. There was only people gripping, holding, and stripping. Evie sobbed as the pastor murmured above her, the cadence of his words indicating prayer. Abby and Miranda's bone tokens dropped to the floor. His heel came down to crush them to bits and dust.

Only Evie's would survive. Only Evie's would dangle on the wall.

"Mama, help me!" But Mama couldn't help. There were too many others seeing to it that the Bone Man got his due. Tears rained down Evie's cheeks as Mr. Shepherd's hand clenched on the back of her neck. She knew it was him by the gleaming polish on his shoes, by the rubbery tip of his walking stick.

Rustling and movement above her, Evie unable to see anything except shattered bones and feet. There was a fluttering by her eye and the burlap sack dropped as the pastor pulled something else from its depths, but what it was, she couldn't say.

"And so she that is his mate is given her mantle, a proper queen born of blood to serve her lord husband," the pastor said. Mr. Shepherd's shiny shoes moved aside and Pastor Thomas's replaced them before the shredding started along her upper back. Something hard and cold scoured her skin, raking and peeling the layers away to expose the meaty bits just below the surface. It was agony unlike anything Evie'd felt before and her screams bled one into another as he ravaged her from shoulder to shoulder and down to the middle of her back. Blood saturated her dress and rained along her sides, drenching her from the waist-up, sticky and thick and oh-so-hot.

"S'enough!" Mama cried, but they kept at it, giving the wound a second punishing pass. Evie was slumped on the floor by the time they were through, boneless, her woolens slurping at the puddle of blood congealing by her knees. There were spatters on the wall, spatters on the witnesses and their clutching hands. Evie'd screamed so much, spittle pooled at the corners of her lips and dribbled down her chin to gob her bared chest.

"Bring her to the creek," the pastor said. A pumice stone thudded against the wooden floor before her, its pebbled surface covered in blood and ragged flesh. The same hands that had stripped her dressed her, tugging the drenched cloth of Evie's dress back into place. She'd screamed when they undressed her and she screamed now, too – this time because her gaping wounds were so raw, even the feather-light kiss of threadbare cotton was excruciating.

She was buttoned up and hoisted, hands looping under her arms, another set taking hold of her feet.

"Mama?" she called, nigh on delirious as they opened the door and carried her through the church, past Abby and Miranda who erupted in hysterical squeals upon seeing her. Mama flew to Evie's side, her thin, bird-like face mottled with tears, the whites of her eyes the color of vine-ripe tomatoes.

"Never forget I love you, Evie-Beans," she whimpered, stuffing the pocket of Evie's dress with the pearls and the handkerchief. "You're gonna please him fine. I'm proud'a you, a'right? So proud."

Mama leaned in to kiss the side of her head but the pastor thrust her away as they exited the church, marching their newest offering down the steps and towards the creek. Evie whimpered with every jostle, her back throbbing, her nerves shooting electric jolts through her tormented body. It was so cold out, her tears froze on her cheeks and her snot froze inside her nose. Her head lolled back and she stared at the sky above, wishing for sun or clouds but only getting bleak, endless gray.

By the time they got past the town line, an entourage followed just as it had three years ago when Evie'd seen Prudence for the last time. The pastor was the Pied Piper to somber, dead-eyed rats. He stopped next to the foot bridge – which was really just a couple of clapboards nailed over longboards – and raised his hand.

"She goes alone from here," he said.

It was strange how the grips gentled. They didn't drop her like a sack of turnips, but tipped her upright and steadied her when she wobbled on her feet. She was faint and tired and the world spun real good, like that time she'd ridden the tilt-a-whirl at the fair. Everything was topsy-turvy and wrong, and she blinked to clear her vision, but it did no good.

"Mama?" she called. She nearly slumped but more hands reached out to steady her. *Hands here, hands there, hands near and everywhere.* Mama didn't answer.

"Mama!" she yelled again, only louder, but it was quiet save for the mocking caw of a nearby crow. Evie's eyes stung, more tears threatening to spill over her cheeks as her panic returned. She wanted her mother. She didn't want to go over that bridge and into those woods, but that wasn't a choice now. There hadn't been a choice from the moment she'd won the game.

"Go with the grace of God," the pastor said. "You are our salvation."

Evie swung her gaze his way. For just a moment, some of her fire returned and she spat at him, spraying him in a wash that took him in the eye, the cheek, and across his beard. He flinched away from her, his hands grazing his forehead and then his lips in a blessing.

"'Idolaters shall have their part in the lake which burneth with fire and brimstone: which is the second death,'" she hissed before stumbling toward the bridge and away from her leering audience. She nearly fell when she hit the opposite bank, her steps uneven on account of blood loss and the throbbing in her temples.

She didn't know where she was going, though she recalled Prudence bumbling between the trees and beyond the overgrown brush before disappearing from their lives forever. The vague hope that Prudence yet lived niggled at her. Maybe there was a way out. Maybe there was a place free of blood and bone and old bargains somewhere past the woods. Her pace quickened at the thought, her steps lurching and ugly, strain compounding behind her eyes. Nearing a tree at the forest's edge, she lifted her hand to steady herself, ignoring the blood on the back of her hand sloughing off in dried, rusty flakes.

A few more steps and she was inside, the wood's embrace shielding her from the town's eyes. Afraid, yes – beyond anything she could have imagined – but she was also determined. The Bone Man could be near, but maybe he wasn't, and she walked on, feeling woozy and disoriented. With no sun to guide her, it all looked the same after a few minutes, and she feared as she passed yet another leaf-barren tree that she was treading circles.

"Should have followed the creek," she whispered, a shiver wracking her spine. The woods around her creaked and moaned through a winter wind. The cold shredded through her clothes and made her gasp, and she stumbled to a thick trunk covered in dried lichen. She slid down onto her knees, allowing herself a respite before trudging ahead. She wrapped her arms around her middle to hold her warmth close.

She never heard him come. Hands settled on her shoulders, a delicate weight so unlike the punishing grips inside the church. But that didn't mean she didn't scream. Her cry echoed through the vast, Spartan landscape, sending the birds in the treetops aflight. Her fingernails raked over the tree trunk as she tried to stand, but there was a groan and a tut behind her and then a body lined her back, his front oh-so-warm. It should have hurt more than it did, but he treated her as a fragile thing, careful not to brush against her strained, pained flesh any more than necessary.

An arm went around her waist, a nose pressed against her hair. Evie's eyes went huge and she warbled in fear, but the thing behind her – the man? – only grazed the top of her head with a caress. A cheek, maybe, or perhaps it was his chin. It was hard to tell.

"Please," she whispered, not sure who she was addressing, not sure what she was even asking. There was a grunt followed by a sigh, and his second hand came up to glide over the bare flesh above her dress. She dared to look down. It was such a normal-looking arm, all masculine and peachy with a brush of dark fur until she got to the wrist.

There, threaded in a loose circle, was a bracelet of sorts, chunks of meat still clinging to the freshly-threaded bones.

HONOURABLE MENTION
TADE THOMPSON

Desperation can drive one to play a game otherwise thought far too risky. Here, Tito, penniless and down on his luck, plays ayo, or Sentry as this variation is called. This is a game of endurance, of sleep deprivation. Fortunately Tito has a guide. Tade has produced a brilliant horror story about a desperate man willing to pay a terrible price.

THE FOURTH ONE was called Tito. He was keen to point out that the second syllable of his name was a high note, unlike the famous member of the Jackson Family. Iona said she would bear it in mind but in truth she did not care. To her Tito represented twelve hundred pounds for half an hour's work.

Tito sat on the couch clad in Betty Boop boxers. She mused that he may not have grasped the cultural significance of the old cartoon.

"Cough," she said, and felt the transmitted impulse as she palpated his hernia orifices. He had the good manners to turn his head away. No hernias, but a grape cluster of lymph nodes on both sides. Not unusual in West African males.

He was like the others: early twenties, in good physical condition, recent arrival from West Africa. Nigeria mostly, but often Ghana or Benin. Sometimes she found round worms in their faeces and dewormed them, but most of the time she certified them healthy. They were all desperate to demonstrate that. They ran faster on the treadmill or breathed especially deep when she listened to their chests. They didn't always make it through. Once Iona had picked up a heart murmur from childhood rheumatic fever and turned a candidate back. She had on occasion found drugs or over-the-counter stimulants and diet pills in or on a candidate. This had become a nightmare of rage, recriminations and tears and she'd had to call security. Now there was a panic button within reach and an attack alarm on her key ring, since the time a few years back when a player had tried to rape her.

Tito had no heart murmur or illegal substance on his person. He also had no deodorant and the acrid masculinity of his sweat filled the examination room.

"Everything is new here," said Tito.

"Not everything," said Iona, peering into his ear, trying to get the light to bounce off the eardrum. "My equipment is good, but not new."

"I meant the rooms, Dr Clarke. The paint, plaster and curtains."

He was right. The entire venue was always given a fresh coat of paint, but Iona had ceased to notice. Tito wanted to chat. Why would he want to chat with a stranger who had stripped him nigh naked and prodded his groin looking for lumps?

She gave him a sample bottle. "Fill this to the line."

Tito glanced at the men's room and seemed nervous. "Can't I do it here? I'll turn my back."

Iona shrugged. Some of these immigrants had no modesty or sense of propriety. One came into her examining room once and just stripped naked without being asked. It had ceased to bother her. Maybe Tito wasn't used to a water closet system. She resolved to never again shake the hand of a candidate. She wrote her notes while he pissed into the universal container. She already knew there would be no anomaly.

*　　*　　*

TITO EMERGED FROM the doctor's office into the atrium of Independence Hall where a smiling, suited usher stood like a manikin. Straight ahead the toilets lay in wait and to his right was the way out, guarded and locked, although one could see through the screen door to the entrance and car park. Girls hung around the glass, peering in. They were not allowed in the venue per se but that did not stop them from trying to enter. They wore the most revealing outfits or walked and preened in a way that you could not ignore. They dressed to catch the eyes of the contestants, of course, in glitter and piled hair and a scarcity of fabric coupled with abundance of skin. They had to divine who would be successful and entice that one. Never mind that this had never worked, that no winner had ever gone with any of these hopeful young ladies.

Tito looked at them with lust, but tore his eyes and mind away and turned left to enter the short corridor that took him to the gaming hall.

It was like walking into a wall of hot air. There were four rectangular gaming tables. Spectators were already seated on two curved and tiered rows of benches. The room had the hum of constant low level conversation, the auditory equivalent of that snowy static between television channels. Beneath that funky jazz music smoothed the edges, and Tito wondered why they didn't play something more traditionally Nigerian. They had obviously lost authenticity. Only three gamers were present when the usher led Tito to the table that held his name tag. There were two bottles of water and two plastic cups on each table. Beside the water a packet of digestive biscuits stood on end.

The sponsors sat on the front row. They were wealthy Nigerians, nouveau riche but not the brain-drained middle class professionals. They were the underworlders, the interstitial types. Fraud? Perhaps. Drugs? Almost certainly. These were the ones who decided to give back to the community that spawned them. They were all male, and about half wore dark glasses. Tito didn't look too closely at them – staring was rude and these were not the kind of people you wanted to offend.

The overhead lights were bright, lighting up the ceiling like the noon sun. Tito supposed that would help keep them awake.

The table held a wooden ayo board. It was a hinged diptych of carved oak with two rows of six wells which each contained four seeds.

Tito was itching to start but had to remind himself this was not a test of skill, but endurance. He flexed and extended his fingers. There wasn't much of a crowd as the event was by invitation only, although the uninvited collected outside like water in a cistern. No information is airtight in the Nigerian community.

The music died and the MC tapped the microphone four times. His name was Peter Akeke and he was well-known in Thamesmead, fancied himself a local leader. He attended weddings and naming ceremonies. He was wearing a suit – ill-fitting, brown, new. He had a round head with an uncertain scattering of hair, and a bulging belly. His complexion was uneven, blotchy yellow and light brown with darker areas around the lips and ears. He was a bleacher, lightening his skin with dodgy products. He was ridiculous but ubiquitous, the community living in tacit agreement that he was funny and necessary while also knowing that he was a naked emperor.

"Good evening, ladies and gentlemen!" He breathed into the microphone between words, making it sound like the prelude to a tropical storm. "We are gathered here today because of one small village west of the Niger River. Centuries ago it was harried by larger city states. Having very few young men to form an army and no fortifications its survival depended on early warning systems. Sentries. When the night watch sounded the alarm the villagers knew to run and hide in predetermined places. The selection of appropriate sentries was of the utmost importance. Aside from physical fitness, candidates had to be able to stay awake for long periods during the night. What started as a life-or-death selection process for them has persisted down the centuries as a game for us." He wiped his face with a purple handkerchief. Who carried those anymore?

"Ayo is a game played worldwide. The Igbo call it *ncho*. Some call it *oware*, but this is semantics. We are here to play Sentry. Eight players, four tables. Each contestant plays *ayo* until there is only one left awake. The last man standing is Sentry and gets the grand prize donated by our wonderful benefactors who shall remain unnamed. Round of applause for them, please."

There was a lacklustre response and the front row shifted about on their seats with embarrassment. Tito was not surprised. People in their lines of work did not usually wish to draw attention to themselves. Akeke stopped looking at them and took in the rest of the crowd with a sweeping gesture.

"The grand prize this year…"

Tito held his breath. He focused on the moist tongue and the open lips of Akeke. He hated the man for the delay, the artificial suspense, but he would kiss those lips if only they would spew the right thing out.

"… One hundred and fifty thousand pounds!"

A YEAR EARLIER Tito stood on an overpass watching traffic flow into and out of Thamesmead. His loose necktie flapped in the wind. He didn't understand Thamesmead. It had no monuments, no history, no psychic imprint of ancestors. It was early evening in the summer. Tito's friend Kola passed him a lit cigarette which he dragged on and returned. The wind snatched the smoke right out of his lungs. He'd known Kola since childhood, back in Lagos where they'd spent alternate Tuesday afternoons watching Fantastic Four cartoons at each other's houses. Kola had been in London for close to a decade, Tito just under a year.

"Remember when we used to steal cigarettes from Mama Tosin?" asked Tito.

"I never stole anything. You'd steal them and we'd smoke them in the garage," said Kola. They both laughed, but there was the taint of the unsaid between them. "What did they say?"

Tito shrugged. "The usual. You're overqualified for this job, why did you leave Nigeria, how are you going to cope, we don't think customers will understand your accent."

"I told you you should have thrown some 'innit' in there."

"I'm not going to get the job," said Tito. He removed the tie altogether and wanted to throw it into the stream of cars that he would never own, but the truth was he needed it for the next round of interviews. "This country is shit."

"It isn't, *ore*," said Kola. "You just need to know how to work it."

"You mean work in it."

"Be patient."

"Patience won't pay the landlord." Tito took the last pull on the cigarette and flicked it away.

Quietly, Kola said, "You could always play Sentry."

"What's Sentry?"

Tito's opponent shook hands. "Moses Awe."

"Tito Ebunorisha," said Tito.

Moses was a big, lumbering man with an abundance of facial hair and a smile. He wore an old tee shirt that barely contained his muscles. The protocol on talking during bouts was unclear. It was not forbidden, but Tito had been told to avoid it.

A digital clock counted down and when it hit zero, they started.

Playing *ayo* is straight forward.

Each player started off with four seeds in each of their six pits. The first player would empty one pit and sow a seed in each subsequent pit in a counter-clockwise direction, including the opposing player's pits. If the last seed fell in a pit causing a total of two or three seeds in the opponent's house they were captured. Since there were only forty-eight seeds the first player to capture twenty-five would win. The strategy was in counting and anticipating where both yours and your opponent's last seed would fall. Moses was clearly a serious player because Tito could see him counting. Didn't matter. Winning at *ayo* did not mean winning at Sentry.

Tito was a middling player and sowed without capturing for two rounds, setting up a bigger harvest. He was thirsty and looked at the frosty plastic of the water bottle. There was a certain inevitability about drinking. Drink the water, empty the bottle, fill the bladder, empty the bladder. Tito glanced nervously at the hallway that led to the toilet. He resisted the urge to drink.

Buzzers sounded from some of the other tables as games were won and lost. Tito himself lost the first round.

Didn't matter. He was still awake.

TITO AND KOLA climbed the stairs to the next level and found themselves on a walkway that linked several of the blocks of flats, all painted the same dull grey or dirty light blue, all without ground-floor flats. Difficult to tell in the yellow glow of the street lights. They passed rows of identical doors till Kola pointed out the one they were looking for.

"Remember, don't mention his experience. You're here as a supplicant, looking for guidance," said Kola. He had said this over a dozen times already.

"Why didn't you seek his guidance?" asked Tito. He was slightly out of breath, tired from a day of loading goods in a warehouse, unskilled cash-in-hand work.

"I didn't know," said Kola. "Besides, it wouldn't have made a difference. I was disqualified. Good luck."

Tito bumped fists with him and knocked at the door while his friend's footfalls faded away. The door sprung open and a woman stood there. She had a head scarf tied carelessly and a frown etched into the features of a face that might have been beautiful otherwise. Barefoot, in faded dungarees, she was taller than Tito, and wiry. She looked to be in her mid-forties.

"Yes?"

"I'm looking for your husband," said Tito. "Mr Kanako."

"No, you're looking for me. People just assume I'm a man," said Kanako. "Come in."

There was a musty smell to the place, but it looked clean and neat. No shelves, but books piled together in random parts of the front room. A television was on, displaying the face of Robert DeNiro frozen in the act of eating a boiled egg. Kanako sat on a comfortable chair and picked up the remote control, as if threatening to continue her show if Tito did not entertain her enough. She put her legs on a footstool and he noticed the skin of her left sole was gnarled.

Tito handed her the gifts he had brought: schnapps, a bag of kola nuts and two bags of plantain chips, all of which he had had to travel to the Brixton Market to get. Kanako accepted them without comment. She cracked and unscrewed the lid of the schnapps and took a grateful pull. Her Adam's apple bobbed up and down and when she came up for air a quarter of the schnapps had gone.

She exhaled and the furrows formed by her wrinkles became shallower. "You want to know how to win at Sentry."

"Yes," said Tito. "I don't have any money now –"

"I know you don't. Otherwise you wouldn't be playing, would you?"

"I will pay you when I win."

She laughed, a sound like the grinding of maize in a hand-operated mill. "I've never heard that before."

*   *   *

Moses won the first four games and aside from scratching his head every few minutes, Tito could not see any sign of fatigue. If anything, winning appeared to boost the other man's wakefulness. Tito, on the other hand, already felt a low-level struggle with his eyelids.

And his bladder was full. There was no doubt about it, no avoiding the Gents. He raised his right hand and an usher came to his table and took a photograph of the gameplay in case of a dispute. Moses winked at him. Tito fucking hated people who winked.

He slipped into the men's room quickly and closed the door. It was your standard artless public toilet. Three stalls, six urinals, a couple of sinks, the smell of either urine or ammonia-laced cleaning products. Dripping water somewhere, and a hiss, forceful flow through a pipe, ubiquitous to such places. It was like being at a riverbank without the river.

Tito found it difficult to breathe. He forced his feet to move towards the stalls and he checked each one. When he established privacy he reached inside his pocket and placed a small statuette on the white porcelain of the sink. It was an ugly little thing, and showed a humanoid creature carved from wood in a forced squat. The eyes, ears and mouth were outsized and the head was in such an awkward position that the chin was close to the feet. It looked like someone taking a shit.

Tito turned on the tap and caught some water in his cupped hands, then poured it on the fetish. Important not to put it under flowing water. Insulting. Don't want to incur wrath.

He turned away from the malignant thing and rushed to the urinals. He unzipped quickly and voided, closing his eyes with the pleasure. He would have sighed if he hadn't been interrupted by the clicking behind him. He did not dare look and the stream of piss dried up. He gulped air, but did not have enough.

The hand on his arm was hot, dry, hard as wood, and unpleasant. Each movement was punctuated with clicks and snaps. Tito did not look. He knew what was coming. A creak like an old door opening, then dozens of needles of pain in his arm, accompanied by rending of muscle. He almost opened his mouth. Almost.

The creaking and clicking segued into snapping in a horrific medley and he felt warm fluid drip down his arm. Fuck. It was chewing. Chewing what it bit out of Tito's arm.

"Open your mouth. Eat." The voice was gravelly, produced by two nightmares rubbing against each other.

Tito obeyed and it was like bark: bitter, impossible to chew. Yet he chewed, and he swallowed. Bad as it was, he felt the pain in his arm subside and electricity flood into his brain. He was awake and alive.

Afterwards, he washed it down with water and wiped his mouth on the back of his hand. He saw a shadow in the reflection – something near the ceiling. He spun, but there was nothing there. He pocketed the fetish and left.

"You're a house slave, aren't you?" said Kanako. "*Omo odo.*"

"How do you know?" said Tito. "Does it matter if I am?"

"No, not really."

"I... I'm told you won at Sentry."

"Maybe. So what? You want to know how I won?"

"Yes."

"There is a price."

"How much?"

Kanako laughed. "It's not money, you yam head. There are other things in life. Like life itself."

"What do I have to do?" asked Tito.

"Have you ever heard the saying: 'The better man may win; but the winner is bound to be the worse man'?"

"No, I haven't." Tito hated proverbs. His father had been full of them. Not his father. His master.

"Now you have. Expect to understand the full meaning of it." She drank more of the schnapps, coughed and rose. She held her side as if her ribs were injured. "When you do, remember that it was you who approached me."

"Are you in pain?" asked Tito.

Kanako shook her head. "Why do you want to play?"

"I want the prize."

"I know you want the prize. What I'm asking is why you need the money."

Tito thought about his life, about cleaning toilets in his master's house for as long as he could remember, about eating leftovers after his host family had gorged themselves, about sneaking into the rooms of the children and reading their books when they were out, about a lifetime of wearing cast-offs, about not being a real person but a kind of living stress-ball whipping-post to be used whenever his master and mistress were unable to cope with their moral poverty; Tito thought of these things and said, "I just want the money."

MOSES YAWNED A few times in quick succession. His concentration was slipping too. He had opportunities to block Tito's wins by emptying the right pits, but he didn't, and lost four games. It was four-thirty a.m. on the first day. The crowd had simmered down. They could come and go, or catch it streaming over the net on websites with secret URLs, but the middle of the night was the middle of the night. A number of seats were empty and about half held sleeping patrons. This was not unusual.

Moses miscounted his seeds and laid out a series of five consecutive pits with two seeds in them, but only one seed in the last. Tito followed up by sowing in each of the pits, ending up with a total of thirty seeds. So sleepy was Moses that he had started playing another pit before realising that the game was lost.

Tito won the next five games without effort. Moses struggled with his eyelids and went to the toilet once. The rules allowed you to splash water on your face, but you could not drink stimulants. When he returned and sat Tito caught a whiff of disinfectant. He had a strange vision of Moses drinking cleaning products in desperation and he laughed.

"Something funny?" asked Moses.

Tito shook his head.

"Where are you from?"

"I'd rather not talk, if that's okay with you." Conversation could be a joint strategy to stay awake until other tables had given up, but Tito knew Moses needed it more.

They both laid out the seeds for a new game, but before they could start an usher came up to Tito.

"You've been selected for review," said the usher.

DR CLARKE CHECKED Tito's pupils for reactivity.

"Turn your eyes to the left," she said. "Uh-huh, now the right. Thanks."

Tito felt her proximity and found it uncomfortable. Her perfume, the quiet fall of her breath on the hairs of his face, the shifting of fabric, the sheer femaleness of her disturbed him. He had to distract himself from the stirring it began in him. He remembered that this person disqualified his friend for some reason.

"How shall I win, doctor?" asked Tito.

She sighed and stepped away from him, back to her seat. Zero flirting from her side, but she was a woman and he had not been with one for an age. He shifted his thighs.

"You need a guide," she said.

"You mean a teacher. I've already consulted a previous winner."

"No, a guide is different. Long-distance runners focus on something else to get them through the race. You need some mental locus that will take you out of the task. Do you have a girlfriend?"

He shook his head.

"Boyfriend?"

"No!"

"Relax, I didn't mean anything by it. There's nothing wrong with it and some of the players that come through here have told me –"

"I am not a homosexual, doctor."

"Fine. What I'm saying... okay, listen. My granddad was in the war. He was an intelligence officer in a destroyer off the coast of Portsmouth and they got hit by a U-boat torpedo. They all abandoned ship and he had this big, top secret malarkey attached to his wrist. Shore was two hundred, two fifty metres away and he was not a great swimmer, but he started swimming. The case kept dragging him down and he jettisoned that after some minutes. As he swam he heard the screams of the dying all around. His arms started to go stiff and land was too far. He saw beside him a dog, a retriever, swimming alongside. The dog had been a mascot, he could not remember who it belonged to, but the lads liked it, called it Thug. As he made for land, for life, he kept checking on Thug, who kept up. Together, exhausted and wet, they made it. Thug died right there on the pebbles, just gave up, and my grandfather said he cried more than he ever had. He said Thug saved his life."

"And this animal was his guide?" said Tito.

"Exactly." Dr Clarke checked her monitor. "There are no drugs in your system, Mr Ebunorisha. You can go. Good luck to you."

THIS TIME THE fetish seemed to be taking a gouge out of Tito's back. The tearing seemed to catch on something before it continued. Oh, God, it hurt.

"Turn," said the voice. "Eat. Quickly."

Tito broke a tooth on the first bite, an incisor. Pain lanced upwards through his head and his eyes opened. He squeezed them shut instantly, but a grey-brown image fixed itself in his memory. He ate, and the dental pain disappeared. His bladder was so full, he could feel it pushing against his lower belly. The gap in his back muscles filled out and it no longer hurt.

And wakefulness. Blazing, bright wakefulness coursing through every cell of his body.

FIFTY HOURS OF continual gameplay.

Akeke was back, talking about lack of sleep. He spoke about some dolphins who sleep one cerebral hemisphere at a time, giving the illusion of staying awake perpetually.

Moses was bleeding from the mouth. He had taken to biting himself in order to stay awake. Interesting, as such strategies go, but not effective. He had bitten the tip of his tongue and his inner cheek. His eyes were barely open and his jaw was slack. His hand was poised over a pit but the seeds in his hand had dropped. He did not notice. Tito saw him as a perfect artefact of the moment, a representation.

A dark shape slithered across the ceiling and Tito looked up, and screamed. The sound woke Moses. "What?" he asked, staring around.

"Lack of sleep can cause hallucinations," said Akeke.

There was nothing on the ceiling.

Tito's bladder swelled, and demanded to be relieved. Again. In addition he had a constant, low-grade headache right behind his forehead, like a psychic aftertaste. His body was numb in the parts the fetish had eaten away. It felt like they were not his own. Some parts were entirely without sensation while others tingled, itched, or had pins and needles. He sowed five seeds and took six from Moses' house, then, with great reluctance, he asked to go to the Gents.

* * *

"IF YOU WON, how come you still live here?" asked Tito.

Kanako laughed. "Everybody asks me that sooner or later." Her words were slurred now, edges of consonants taken off by the spirit.

"Well?"

"I spent it."

"All of it?"

"You'll come to understand, young one," said Kanako. "Tell me, can you stand pain?"

Tito remembered being whipped by his father, twelve lashes of the *koboko* on his back for a minor infraction. Welts, weals, broken skin, blood on his shirt. Not his father, his master. He always mixed them up. One day, when he was fifteen, he resolved not to cry and held his peace until the twenty-fifth lash.

"Yes, I can stand pain."

"Good. Good."

Kanako produced a small carved mahogany statuette. Ugly.

"Never hold it with your left hand, never place anything on it, never place it in flowing water. Cup your hands, get the water and wet it from there. Then close your eyes. There will be pain, but no matter what, keep your eyes closed. Do you understand?"

Tito picked it up and brought it close to his face. It had a slight stink.

"What is it called?"

"Does it matter? Do not let it get thirsty but do not drown it."

"How will I get it in there?"

"They do not mind good luck charms. You will have frequent medical examinations and drug testing, but as long as you don't have a coffee sweet or an amphetamine lollypop you can bring whatever you want in. They'll search you for weapons or anything that can be used as a weapon."

"People bring weapons?"

"Strange things happen when people can't sleep. Perceptions can be distorted, judgements impaired."

*   *   *

THE LIGHTS WERE too bright.

Tito could feel all his nerves light up, from the tips of his fingers, back to his spine, up to his brain. If there was a power failure he would glow in the dark with the eyes being the focus of blazing beams of illumination. His eyes might as well be propped open with struts, and he saw everything. He had no inclination to blink and the eyeballs dried out, so he kept drinking, even though... bladder, toilet, fear.

He played *ayo* automatically now, brain completely disengaged. He won game after game until Moses collapsed. A cheer went out from the stands, but Tito was not interested. On the other tables, which he had ignored till now, three other players remained. The ushers took Moses away and brought the player-in-waiting to Tito. A short, dark, skinny boy called Jide who plunged into harvesting Tito's seeds. He was clearly good at *ayo* and counted the pits with ease. You could gauge the skill of players by how quickly they conceded hopeless games. This player could predict the outcome of a game after ten turns. He won every game. Which meant nothing because he yawned twice a minute, while Tito was all things bright and wonderful.

Shadows flitted across the ceiling. Tito was used to them now, vague, indistinct shapes, suggestions of dark movement that loved his peripheral vision but shunned his direct gaze.

Tito played, but pictured his father – no, his master. Dying. He had suffered a stroke the week before. He dribbled from the right side of his mouth and could not shut one eye. He could barely grunt, although he seemed to understand what was said to him.

This was his deathbed. The doctor had told the family to say goodbye. His beautiful, well-fed progeny paraded and kissed him. At the end, Tito, the house slave, *omo odo*, came to pay his final respects. Tito leaned in and whispered, "I fucked your daughter, you prick." This was not true, but Tito wanted the man to suffer as he plummeted to hell.

The master tried to move and frown but his brain had disconnected from his muscles. His eyeballs would burst if they could. This was the most sublime moment of Tito's life.

The facts were Tito had not given his master the required blood pressure pills for over a month. The old man had popped a blood vessel and fallen. By then Tito had a passport, a visa and a ticket. The body was not cold before he was London-bound on a fake identity.

He won the game. Jide lost basic finger coordination, he was so drowsy. He let Tito lay out the seeds again.

THERE WAS NO more pain, no more bitterness. Even biting the fetish was easier and brought forth warm blood. The flesh was more yielding and was that a wince? Did the fetish feel pain? It wasn't bark anymore.

"I think you should look at me," said the fetish. "Just this once."

Tito remembered Kanako's warning, but he had grown fearless where the fetish was concerned. Familiarity. He opened his eyes.

"Interesting," he said. But had he said it?

They both stood in front of the mirror. Tito's lips moved, and he heard the sound, but it did not come from his own vocal cords. The fetish was grey, with brown skin covered in flaps of bark like wooden scales, head smooth like it had been sanded, coarse gouged-out facial features, taller than Tito and thicker of limb.

But whose limb? Tito spoke, but his voice was gravelly. He moved, and the fetish copied it.

"You still do not understand," said the fetish. In the mirror Tito's hand turned the tap on, scooped water and splashed it on the fetish's head.

Tito felt the impact of the water like a flood, drenching his whole body, sweeping him away. He was in a river of fluoridated water, an ocean. He struggled, kicked, broke surface.

The toilet was gone. He was in a place of trees that grew in the shapes of buildings, a sky filled with mauve blood-clouds, of other man-shaped beings that moved slowly and lacked definition. Tito clung to a small island made of fractured shin bones and marvelled. He was afraid but his heart was slow and started to beat in his back. He wore no clothes and his hands were craggy, misshapen.

The creatures sometimes stopped, came to him and licked his fingers with hot, dry tongues, otherwise they left him alone. When he screamed they ran, but always returned after a year or so...

H̲E WAS DIFFERENT.

Iona could see that his bearing was more erect. He maintained eye-contact a lot longer. He even smelled less earthy. He was winning, for there was no sleep in him. His alertness was in sharp contrast to his opponent, whom the doctor had already examined.

"You found one," she said.

"Found what?" Tito asked.

"A guide."

"I don't understand."

"Our chat. Something to get you through the contest."

"Oh. Yes, I remember."

He did not sound like he remembered, but then he'd been awake for all this time while Iona had been home to refresh herself every day. Some memory lapse was inevitable.

He put a small statuette on the desk. It was filthy and damp.

"That's it. My guide."

"You'll mention it in your victory speech?"

"Oh, I've not won yet."

"You will."

"If I do, can I ask you out for a drink?"

"Sorry, I'm married."

"Pity." He stood. "I'll be sure to give the guide an honourable mention. Thank you, Dr Clarke."

He left.

The doctor briefly pondered his attitude, then drove him out of her mind. Over the next hour she packed her equipment, and only when she was about to leave did she realise he had left the wooden statue behind.

Forgotten? A gift?

Iona dropped it in her handbag and signed her payment invoice.

She never thought about Tito Ebunorisha again.

LOSER
REBECCA LEVENE

Games can very much act as power fantasies – one only has to look at online RPGs with their emphasis on levelling-up and acquiring awards. What happens, however, when those fantasies become actualised? And what of those who take losing far too personally? Rebecca's 'Loser' in many ways asks us to sympathise with him, but when we truly realise what's going on, what game is being played, we may find such pathos difficult to stomach.

You remember when we first met. I know you do, we've talked about it so often we've worn the memory threadbare. Or... I suppose I should say, you remember when you first saw me. We were seven, I think. Eight? Still at primary school, still kids, still half-made, half-human really: only a sketch of what we'd become.

Those ugly white square cottages, the day after you moved into them and your parents came across the lane to introduce themselves to mine. You were there, hanging back, and I was too, but you saw me in that pink flowery dress I'd been given for my birthday. You saw me and you thought: I want to *be* her. You told me that, years later. You didn't want to be me, though, not really. You just didn't want to be you.

No, god, don't die. Don't die. Not now, not yet.

You remember – you know you remember. That was the first time you saw me, but it wasn't the first time *I* saw *you*. I'd heard the removal van the day before, the workmen shouting, swearing when they dropped something in a tinkling crash. Your mother's best china, you told me later. I didn't know that then. But I wanted to know who you were, our new next-door neighbours, the strangers in a world that was too familiar.

Easy, easy now. Look at me, just concentrate on my voice. Imagine me creeping along our secret path, the tunnel through the nettles that was only mine then, before I showed it to you. I stood in their criss-cross shadows, rubbing the sting from my arms as I watched you walk into your house for the first time.

Well, you weren't really walking – your father was dragging you, one meaty fist tight around your scrawny white arm. I heard the words and I didn't understand them, not then, but I knew they were bad. I knew this man hated you and that you were afraid of him. I didn't guess that he was your father. It wouldn't have seemed possible. Fathers were kind and funny and cuddly and they never, ever hurt you. You taught me different, though, didn't you? You and your family.

A month later, I let you try the dress on. You lifted your T-shirt over your head and I saw your chest, the white puckered little scars, the bruises. You were so thin, so delicate. You're... god, you still are. Look at you now. I'm trying, I'm trying to keep you alive, but that blood is leaking out of the same chest, the same person.

I had lots of friends, and you only had me. I think that should have worried me, but it didn't. I liked the fact that you were only mine. I talked to you in school, when no one else wanted to. Kids – little predators, right? They sense weakness. They sensed yours, but I protected you. *I* protected *you*.

Except I remember the day I didn't protect you – the day I couldn't. I came over to your house, through the nettle tunnel, which was both of ours by then. You didn't see me. You were playing swingball with your father. He was batting at the ball and swaying, drunk enough that I could smell the fumes from where I crouched. My parents smelled like that at Christmas and sometimes on dad's birthday, and it made my dad walk crooked and laugh too much and too loud – and at first your father was laughing and you were as well.

You were so happy it baffled me. I could sense the danger, the threat in every line of his body, the violence huddled inside every laugh and I didn't understand why you couldn't sense it too. But I think now you didn't want to. Your father was *playing* with you, and that was enough. And maybe it would have been, if you hadn't managed that lucky shot. You hit that stupid ball and it swung back round and hit your father on his head, then on and round and round and round until the pole was wrapped in string and you cheered. Of course you did – you were a little boy and you'd beaten your father for the first time.

And then he beat you. I knew I should go and get help, do something, but all I did was watch. There's a sound flesh makes when it's hit so hard the skin breaks like an overripe peach. I could hear it even over the noise you made. You didn't scream. I suppose he'd taught you not to do that a long time ago. You whimpered, and the bat cut down again, and there went your arm – *snap*. And then he hit your head and I saw you go limp, but he just kept on hitting you and that's when I turned and ran away.

You didn't come to school for a fortnight after that – a fall off your bike, the sick note said – and when you did there was a cast on your arm. I was the only one who signed it. And then, I remember it was a Tuesday, because we had double English and Mrs. Williams had her back to us to write out the spellings on the board, the chalk squeaking, little white puffs of dust with each letter. And the school secretary walked in and looked at you; I saw her face and I *knew*.

So you had another fortnight off school. They couldn't have your father's funeral immediately – there had to be an autopsy first. *Suspicious death*. Only it turned out no one was suspicious enough, because who could possibly believe a 10-year-old would arrange an accident like that? Tripping over a tennis ball and smashing his head on a concrete wall.

He didn't die immediately, your mum told me that once. He bled out, and he could have got help before he did, but he was too drunk to do it. And so he lay there on the dirty utility room floor, muck around his head, a spreading slick of his own blood. Maybe a rat ran past him. I always imagine that it did. There were rats in that room, big black ugly ones that had no fear of people. I imagine a rat running past, your father's glazed eyes tracking it and the little red footprints it left behind. I imagine that the tennis ball was right in front of him, and he watched that too as he died.

The tennis ball was a nice touch, something only you and I would understand. And your life was better after that. Your mum remarried a total arsehole, but he kept his fists to himself. You sneaked over to mine when you could, and you'd try on my clothes and let me play with your Action Man with the eagle eyes and one leg missing. You could actually have been happy, if only you hadn't needed to go to school.

Children are little shits, they really are. They're selfish little shits when they're young and can't imagine the world through anyone else's eyes. And they're cruel little shits the moment they figure out what makes other people tick. As soon as they work out how to hurt you, they do, and you were so terribly easy to hurt.

There were a hundred incidents, a thousand days through all those long years that someone made that little bit more miserable for you. But there's one... I know you know the one I mean. You don't have to say anything – you shouldn't try. Sit back and hold the towel against the wound. We have to slow the bleeding down. Just hold on, OK? I have to understand how you could have done it, and why.

School. Yes. There was John Boyle, who used to throw things at you on the bus: peanuts and little chunks of bread he tore out of his sandwich and rolled up balls of paper. Every time he did it he'd shout out a score – "15, 307, 598" – and you'd smile, as if you were in on the joke. There was Carena Crick, who pretended she fancied you and then showed the note you wrote to all her friends, because no one ever said cruelty had to be original. Neil Dunn beat you up by the bike shed and Sarv Singh stole your bike.

And in the end it wasn't any of those who mattered. It was Henry. Henry Lott, who ran the chess club. It was me who suggested we join, remember? I used to play with my dad when I was little. Silly games, just messing around: he'd neigh whenever his knight moved and make the sign of the cross over his bishops and always let me win. Maybe I thought the school club would be like that. Mostly I thought it would keep you out of the playground for at least one lunchtime.

But I hadn't expected that you'd been so bad at it. It wasn't just that you didn't know the rules, or that you had trouble remembering them. You had trouble remembering a lot of things. That horrible old witch Mrs Jenkins used to joke that you'd been dropped on your head as a baby, though even she might not have said it if she'd known. Your father started when you were very young.

And so you couldn't remember the rules, and even when you could, you didn't know how to use them. It was fine when you were playing me. I'd make horse noises like dad used to and you'd laugh and everything was OK, except for Henry Lott. He *hated* that, couldn't bear anyone not taking the game as seriously as he did. One day he challenged you to a match. I could have told him it was a stupid idea. I nearly did, but... I don't know. I suppose a part of me hoped you might win, and teach him a lesson.

Of course you didn't. I can see it so clearly. That shabby classroom with the Escher prints on the wall and the smell of overworn clothes and underwashed bodies. The blackboard smeared with chalk, nothing ever entirely erased. The squeak your shoes made on the linoleum floor and the headachy flicker of the strip lights overhead. And Henry Lott's face, his smug, round face as he beat you in two moves.

"That's called the Fool's Mate," he said. He had a nasal voice and a way of turning up his top lip even when he wasn't sneering, but right then he definitely was. "It's the quickest possible way to lose at chess, only no one ever actually does, because no one else is stupid enough."

You laughed. You always laughed, this thin appeasing sound that only made them despise you more.

"You're not even clever," Henry said wonderingly. "I mean, I'm a nerd, but you're just a loser."

You stopped laughing then and your expression... Henry thought you were going to cry and turned away, but I knew anger when I saw it. Your dad didn't teach you much, but he taught you that.

It was nine days before they found Henry's body. It was pretty ripe by then. We all knew about it because it was a sixth-former who found it. He told his mates what he'd seen and the whole school repeated what he'd said. "Like, *crawling* with maggots. And the fucking smell." He'd screamed and thrown up, though that wasn't part of his story. But the cops who came to the scene, they had kids at the school, so pretty soon everyone knew everything.

Everything except who did it. They never did find that out. Death by misadventure, the coroner said, because his body was at the bottom of one of Framlingham Castle's walls and everyone knew he'd gone there for that term's history project, and everyone knew he'd gone there alone, because Henry Lotts didn't have any friends. But he did have an enemy, didn't he? An enemy he'd beaten at chess, and although the king is taken by the black queen in Fool's Mate, it's hard to find any black queens out in the world, and a rook seemed close enough.

We drifted apart after school, when I went to university and then medical school and then my first rotation at Barts, and you went... nowhere. I saw you every time I came home. We never separated entirely; there was always some line, mooring us together. We were bound by what had happened, though perhaps you didn't realise it then.

And it kept on happening. Not too frequently. Not so frequently that anyone became suspicious, but the pattern was clear if you knew where to look for it, like a string of digits plucked from the endless length of pi, only seeming to be random.

It happened the year I graduated, the year you got promoted to assistant manager. You were so proud of that extra bloody star on your uniform. You remember how I teased you about it and you laughed, the way you always did, but I could tell you didn't really think it was funny. And maybe it wasn't. You worked hard to get that job, harder than I ever did on any night shift.

You joined the company football team that year. You'd never played, not even a lunchtime kickaround, and I'm not sure what you were thinking. That it might be a way to fit in, I suppose. I could have told you it wouldn't work. I came to watch you once, though you didn't see me, but I saw *him*. I never knew what he whispered in your ear after you missed that penalty, but I saw your face. And a week later he was gone, kicked to death. The papers said it was one of the most brutal attacks anyone had ever seen – the victim's face had been mutilated by metal spikes.

I thought about that a lot, the spikes piercing lip and cheek and eyelid, popping the eyes with a mucousy squish. The closed coffin, because who'd want that to be their last memory? The pain as it happened, and the fear. I couldn't get those things out of my head.

It was ten years before the next one, found hanging in a tangled mess of string, strangled. I guess he shouldn't have mocked you during that corporate team-building exercise. And then two years after that, five weeks ago, there was Matt.

It's OK, just... breathe. Just keep breathing. It's almost done.

The bond between us had grown so loose. It was a thread, a wisp, a Christmas card and a birthday email, a stray thought. You would have let it go entirely, I think. No, no it's all right, you don't need to say anything. I know it hurts. You might have let it go but I found that I couldn't, and so I called you up on no-day-in-particular, and you invited me over for dinner.

God, your flat is horrible. Piles of plates in the kitchen, crusted with food. Shit crusted in your loo. Do you ever clean it? You leave the window open for the feral cats and they climb in and out and piss on the carpet as they please. Old takeaway containers everywhere. It's as if you need the outside of you to look like the inside: an unsalvageable mess.

You can't cook: your mum never taught you and you never learnt since. But you'd been to Marks & Spencer and bought humus and little sliced-up carrots and their gastropub lasagne. I know how much you earn. I knew you couldn't afford it and so when you invited me to go round your friend Gavin's the next week, to join you for a game, I said yes. I knew what you were doing: showing me off. But I didn't really mind. It wasn't like either of us thought I was going to leave my husband for you, that I'd abandon my kids and go and live in your cat-piss-stinking studio flat.

The game was some role-playing thing – not *Dungeons & Dragons*, I've heard of that – something cod-Victorian with all these air balloons and brass guns and clockwork robots. That was your character: a wind-up man. I can see why he appealed to you. When he broke, he hired an engineer to mend himself, poking about in his innards with all his little tools and this big single magnifying glass on his eye, so it looked like he was peering through a fish bowl. That's how the guy running the game described it. Matt had a tricky turn of phrase, a strange imagination. But I don't think he could have imagined what that character meant to you. He was a version of yourself you could fix.

But there's no one who can mend you, is there? Not now, not with so much blood. And not before, when the missing connections, the short circuits and the blown fuses were all in your mind.

The evening was fun, I suppose, an escape everyone in that room needed: Gavin, the banker who loved his money and hated the job that gave it to him. Julia, struggling with a PhD it was clear she'd never finish and had long ago forgotten why she ever wanted to. And Matt.

I could tell he thought he was better than everyone else there. He was good looking in that blond kind of way that you know is going to be balding and flushed and jowly in ten years' time. Matt was writing a book, that's why he did this – he said he was play-testing the world, as if rules were all that mattered. As if his imagination was somehow in competition with us, and he wanted his imagination to win.

You'd been playing this game for months and the evening I came was the climax, the big action finale it had all been building towards. Matt was vibrating with excitement, almost humming with it, but it wasn't a pleasant kind of energy. As soon as we started playing, I knew he had something nasty planned. Gavin could sense it too. It was strange, the way his twitchiness in the real world translated into the unease of his character, the endless rolls with those strange multi-faceted dice. *Can I hear anything? No. What about now? Nothing? I'm using my swordstick to search for traps. You don't find any.*

But there was a trap. The whole game was a trap, a device to lure you in with a promise of making you feel good about yourself, letting you experience power in this fantasy world that you didn't have in the real one. But the only one with any real power was Matt, and in the end he used it to destroy you all.

I was the first to die: a fall of stones through the ceiling that crushed my adventurer to death. "Doesn't she get a saving throw?" you asked. It's funny, really, the way you always looked out for me, when you're the one who so desperately needs to be taken care of.

I didn't get a saving throw, and neither did Gavin, when a swarm of scorpions stung him to death. And then it was your turn. You were wise to him by then. You knew he was out to get you and you played it safe, but the game was rigged, the dice loaded, and you were never meant to make it out alive.

I can't remember what he called the creature that killed you, but I remember what it did. It was this jellyfish human hybrid – I think Matt was riffing on *The Island of Doctor Moreau* – and it spat acid in your face. He described in gruesome detail how it ate through your flesh and you looked stunned for a moment, and then you burst into tears.

Everyone was so embarrassed. Julia looked away and Gavin looked at you without looking, trying to pretend he couldn't see the tears streaming down your face. Even Matt seemed uncomfortable, but he smiled his way through it. He just smiled and smiled as he said, "No, but you see, that's the point of the game – the point of the story. It *has* no point, there can *be* no ultimate victor." I think he thought it was profound.

I laughed at him, but no one else found it funny. You didn't. You didn't have many things you cared about in your life, and he'd taken one of them and ground it into dust and smiled while he did it. And so of course he had to be next.

Listen, listen, it's nearly over, it's nearly the end. I just need to see it, I need to picture it, as if you and I are there together. As if we're both equally responsible, equally guilty. I think… I think this is how it is.

We go home that night and we think about what happened. It buzzes in our brain like a hornet so that we can't sit still, certainly can't sleep. We watch some TV, gritty-eyed in front of *Silent Witness*, *Newsnight*, *CSI* and then *CSI* again, and another, an endless stream of murder through the night. Sometimes we pace, quietly. Sound travels and we don't want anyone to know about our wakefulness. This isn't a feeling to be shared.

It's building in us, an old friend by now, and it has a focus. It's Matt's smile. That awful, smug *smile*. It changes in our mind, grows, widens until it's the whole of his face and the whole of our vision. We can remember, we can see the chip in his front tooth, browned with tea, and the glint of fillings at the back. The flakes of dried skin on his lips and the little red graze in one corner that's the embryo of a cold sore. We can see it all, and we want to *erase* it.

We know where he lives; we've been there before. And we know how to do this; we've done it before. It's better and safer in his house. We usually prefer to make it look like an accident or a random crime, but this time we don't have the patience to wait. We're too angry. We're going to do this tomorrow night.

We pass through the day like a sleepwalker, the people all around us just meaningless fragments of dream. We smile and nod when we need to, hide what's going on inside us. We're good at this: it's the one thing we truly excel at.

The minutes of the evening drag their heels, passing more slowly than they ever have before. There's more *Silent Witness*, more *CSI*. And then the world is finally asleep and we can wake up.

Matt lives alone in the top floor flat of a shabby Victorian terrace near Elephant and Castle. Even now, in the dead hours of the night, the streets aren't empty and we keep our hoody pulled low as we walk up to his front door. Its red paint is flaking, nothing like the colour of blood. Getting through it is easy. We took an evening class in locksmithing a few years back. It was dangerous, a loose thread someone might one day pull and begin to unravel it all, but it was worth it. We have everything we need in a rucksack on our back.

Inside it's stained dark carpet, browning paint on the walls, narrow and dark. This is the worst moment, when someone might come out of one of those cheap wooden doors, crooked on their hinges. But no one does, and then we're at his front door. A simple swipe with an old credit card and we're inside.

We don't turn on the hall light. We stand, patient and silent until our eyes have adjusted, until the sliver of sickly yellow streetlight through the sitting-room curtain is enough. We memorised the layout of the flat when we were here. A long, laminate floored corridor, tip-toes for that, and then an open-plan sitting room and carpeted stairs leading up – the third one creaks, careful there – past the open door to the bathroom and there's the bedroom.

We turn the handle very, very gently and ease in. It takes everything in us to stop again, to wait until each dark lump has resolved into a recognisable shape: wardrobe, chest of drawers, coat stand, bed, Matt.

It made us laugh, the first time we realised chloroform really is the best way to knock someone out. We drench the rag and then turn our head away as we press it against Matt's nose and mouth, keep pressing until we know it's done its job. He never wakes up, never gets an inkling of what's coming.

It's hard work, dragging his unconscious body to the bathtub. We're sweating and gasping by the time it's done and our heart is pounding, too. It took longer than we expected and there's a danger he'll come round.

We forgot the plug. There's a nervous second as we push against the weight of his body, heave it aside and then it's in and we can start running the water. But the cold of it shocks him and we see his eyes flutter, the spark of returning consciousness, and now we have to hurry, hurry but this can't be hurried, pulling out the ampule, filling the syringe, finding a vein – oh, why can we never find a vein when we need it? And then the needle's in and we've depressed the plunger and his eyes are open but he can't do anything. He can't move, can barely breathe, just enough to keep him alive as the pancuronium surges through his blood.

Pancuronium. It's one of the cocktail of drugs that makes up the lethal injection. It's the reason executions sometimes go hideously wrong, because it isn't an anaesthetic, it isn't a painkiller, it doesn't stop you sensing or feeling anything that's being done to you. It just stops you moving, or crying out, or letting anyone know how you're suffering. But that's OK. We *know* what Matt will be feeling.

We wait, now, until we're quite sure he's conscious again. This is the bit we mean to enjoy, and we can't enjoy it without an audience. We watch his eyes, watch him watching us until we're sure he really sees us. Then we start to pour in the acid.

We don't know any chemistry but we did our research. It's strong, but dilute. It will kill him – that's crucial – but it will do it slowly.

At first, it doesn't even seem to be working. And then there's a faint reddening, like the lightest suntan. We watch his eyes, watch, watch, try to see inside them to the pain he can't express as the first layer of skin goes and then the second.

A few minutes later and it's eating into the greasy fat beneath the skin, a few more and it's into the muscles themselves, chewing them up like a glutton at a feast. The liquid in the bath is now as much Matt as it is water, a viscous bubbling red. It's Matt soup. But he's still alive. A person can live without skin and fat and muscle, at least for a little while.

And then the acid finds his organs and that's when it has to be over. His eyes are beginning to glaze and we want to make the most of his last few moments of life, so we press against the top of his head carefully, with two fingers, pressing it under the liquid so the acid can have its turn at his face. His skin peels and his eyes go so fast it's almost like two little vitreous explosions, and then we can see the white of his skeleton, his skull and femur and all the delicate little bones of his ear before they're melted too. And then it's over.

And you went home. *You*, not me, it has to be you – don't try to say anything, you know you can't speak, not with your vocal cords cut. You went home and then two days later we met up, when the murder was all over the news, and you looked me in the eye and you knew. I saw you looking at me all week, watching with that awful expression. Watching me with fearful eyes. You knew that I knew – this is what I'll tell the police. And so you decided to kill me too. And what I did to you, it was only self-defence.

You have to see I did it all for you. All these years, all those people – I was trying to protect you, to show them that you weren't a loser, or that if you were you had a winner on your side. But now you've made me kill you – you *forced* me to do it, and that wasn't fair. It's only right that you take the blame. It's long past time you did something for me.

You're almost ready now, I can see it in your eyes. I'll stay with you till the end. I wouldn't leave you to die alone, you know I'd never do that to you. But when you're gone, I'll call the police, and I'll tell them how I put it all together – the way I've just told you. I've left certain mementoes I collected over the years in your flat, but I don't think they'll need those to convince them it was you. After all, who *wouldn't* turn into a killer after the life you've led?

It always should have been you. I never understood why it was me.

TWO SIT DOWN, ONE STANDS UP
IVO STOURTON

Ivo's story introduces us to a rather unusual game of Russian Roulette, a game with only one conclusion, though the reader may well be surprised as to what that conclusion is. As ever, Ivo writes brilliantly about power and privilege, and the fine line between the human and inhuman.

FOR A COUPLE of seconds before there is a him to understand that he is seeing the light, there is just the light. Then there is him and the light is above him because he is lying in his chair and looking up at the ceiling. He pushes himself up with the heels of his hands against the wide leather arms of the chair, dimpled with deep buttons. Directly opposite him there is a mirror, where the man pushing himself up in his chair is starting to look around the circle of the table.

He is still groggy, but even in his confusion it feels wrong that the man in the mirror should be looking around as he stares directly at him. The man should be staring back. He looks down at the table in front of him and sees the gun, and then it comes to him in an icy plunge into consciousness. He is playing the game again, and the man in the mirror is not in the mirror, and is not a man. It is in a chair exactly like his own, but not the same one, and it looks exactly like him, but it is not him. It is a thing.

The gun is a heavy, old-fashioned revolver with six empty chambers. The waiter standing silently beside the table has the bullet in his pocket. The gun has yet to be loaded or the cylinder spun. Once the bullet is in the closed cylinder it will be invisible. The barrel of the empty gun points outwards towards the shadows where a ring of figures is gathering. They are becoming popular, his games. He heard someone talking about one a few weeks ago when he came into the club's bathroom. Two men standing at the urinals in their dinner jackets, and the attendant standing by the door with his silver plate for money, and his silver backed clothes brush, and his colognes.

The man at the urinal on the left was just saying "... his eyes, it was the most extraordinary thing, his *eyes* were sweating..." and the attendant coughed discreetly. The two men looked around and carried on talking about someone quite different with absolute fluency, and the attendant smiled at him as if he was an old friend just this moment come home. It was the smile that told him they had been talking about him. He knows what it means, when your games become popular.

The only face he can make out in the room is his own. The ring of figures around him is mostly indistinct. The men are wearing dinner jackets. It is not a requirement of the club, but people often come after attending other, more formal functions. In his seated position his head is at the level of their waists, and he does not look up to see their faces. The low light from the lamp is cut off midway up their chests by the green glass shade hanging over the table. Above the line of light they tower into darkness. The women (less of them, and thin where the men are fat) wear evening dresses, and there is the odd glint of jewellery in the shadow, and the smell of perfume on skin and wine in mouths.

In the darkness above shoulder height burn the coals of cigarettes and cigars. The smoke makes his eyes sting. The room, one of twenty or so game rooms in the basement, is quite small, and the air has already become close with the bodies of the watchers. They are murmuring now, he can hear hushed giggling and the clink of two glasses. Some of them he will know personally, through school or University or work. Some of them he will recognise by sight from the club. One or two might even be famous, and he will know them from TV or magazines – the club attracts that kind of person. Others will be strangers, but for this intimacy. There will come a moment, very soon, when they will start to go quiet.

The first thing he feels, looking at the gun, is an overwhelming surge of rage. He recognises this feeling. He first experienced it almost exactly two years previously, when he had played the game four or five times. Prior to that, it was without precedent. Prior to that the closest he had ever experienced was when he cheated on his first wife. He woke up in the morning with the other woman, and he knew that he had ruined his marriage, and he knew also that he had known this would happen before he had slept with her, and he had done it anyway. In the first few moments of wakefulness, he had hated that earlier version of himself more bitterly than any other person he had ever met. The sheer arrogance of his yesterday self, setting up for him this horrific awakening in a hotel room with a view over the whole glittering sprawl of Dubai (he had been there on a business trip), smelling of booze beside the body of a junior colleague.

Likewise looking at the gun, he hates the man who walked into the club and paid for a game. He hates the man who reclined on the couch behind the velvet curtain in the lobby and let the coatroom girl slip the spike of the sedative into his pale wrist. The coat girls were all trained nurses, the manager had once told him. "Count back from ten to one please, Sir." Ten, nine, eyes closing on eight, seven… and then the light from the low hanging lamp in the game room. He promised himself after the last game that he would never play again. That had been only six months ago, and looking at the gun he makes the same promise again. It gives him a feeling of hopelessness, to promise for the second time that he will never do something again, knowing he is absolutely sincere, knowing that last time he was absolutely sincere. It makes him feel discontinuous, as if he was not one man passing through a single lifetime, but a series of billions of individuals, each sealed from the next within the envelope of a millisecond, each one of them faithless to the one before.

He has, he realises, the means to leave a message for his future selves, to pass down to them some proof of the urgent need to keep his promise. He digs his nails into his palm hard enough to leave marks. This time is really the last. After the game is over, he will look at the marks to remind himself of his sincerity. If there is an after the game for him. The thought pops up unbidden, and he slaps it back down. Of course there will be! He will walk away from the table. How can it be otherwise?

The hush falls. There is no signal, no command. There is only the collective instinct of the crowd. They feel it is about to begin, and so it begins.

"Are you quite conscious, Sirs?" the waiter asks. "Mr Roberts? Mr Roberts?"

He nods his head. It does exactly the same, and the two of them give involuntary and parallel glances of distaste at this coincidence. It is the first acknowledgement between man and machine.

"You will be Player 1, Mr Roberts."

Player 1. It is either a temporary title, or the only name he will ever have. A mere designation or a christening. Player 1.

"And you, Mr Roberts, will be Player 2."

The waiter is expert with the gun. He puts the bullet in, and snaps the cylinder back in place with one hand the way you break a rabbit's neck. The sound of the cylinder spinning. The gun is always so much heavier than he imagines it will be. And colder. The adrenalin makes it hard to judge his muscle strength, and when he first takes the stock from the waiter he almost drops it. His hand dips at the wrist and the muzzle taps the table, the sound muffled by the white linen cloth. You can put the gun in your mouth, for the oddly comforting click of the teeth. Or you can set the cold ring against your temple.

Normally the gun doesn't go off the first round, because then you don't get your money's worth. It takes time for the game to have its effect on the mind of the players, and for the tension to build among the spectators. The random placement of the bullet is an illusion, there is nothing in the world so tightly controlled, so exactly known (by management, at least) as the round of the game when the gun will fire. But they can't have it so the gun never goes off first time, or people would know not to be afraid in the first round. So it does go off sometimes, the first time one of the players pulls the trigger. The club refunds you the cost of your game, when the gun goes off in the first round.

As Player 1 holds the gun, he doesn't hate himself anymore. Instead he remembers being in love as a teenager. It is a strange thing he has found in his life that as the consequences of his romantic decisions have increased, so their emotional significance has eroded. When he was nineteen he could love by throwing all of himself, all of his happiness at the feet of another human being. If she spurned him, he felt as if he would die. He could work himself almost into a frenzy watching the screen of a telephone or computer, waiting for a communication from someone he was pursuing. But really those dalliances were nothing, nothing in the grand scheme of things. He cannot remember some of the names of the girls to whom he has said "I love you", and meant it. Later the marriages, the children, those were much more serious things. And yet he barely felt them. It is different at the table. At the table with the gun in his hand, he feels everything.

The girl he remembers as he lifts it to his head was the first really pretty girl who ever took notice of him. They worked the late shift together at a DVD rental store in London. It was an old-fashioned place, on the outs even forty years ago. The owner hadn't placed any orders for the next season's releases. The empty boxes were all face out on the shelves, and the DVDs themselves were stashed out of sight in a corridor behind the tills. A guy came up to the counter with a film, and she went back to find it, and he did the same for another customer, and he kissed her in the dusty corridor with DVDs on one side and boxes of pre-puff popcorn on the other. They kissed and fumbled for five minutes. In the end the guy he was serving banged the counter and shouted, "Come on, before it comes out on TV!" He had to shuffle out to serve the customer with his erection stashed under his belt. He remembers thinking, what's in it for her? They dated for a month after that. Her gift to him was the wondrous realisation that sex is not simply something a girl withholds in exchange for emotional involvement, it can be something she actively desires. He drops the gun and breathes deeply. He is shaking as the memory makes its way through him. He senses the discreet presence of the waiter move ever so slightly closer.

Could that memory really exist, if he was not himself, if he was merely a machine equipped with his memories? Does it even really think it is him, Player 2, the machine sitting opposite? Perhaps that is something the club just tells you so that you keep paying your membership fees. That is what the club told him, when he joined – *you won't be able to tell the difference. You will play the game, and each of you will think, and look, and act like the real Mr Roberts. Each of you will believe you are the real Mr Roberts. One of you will be right, and one of you will be wrong. And the one of you that is right will walk away*. That's what they had told him, but perhaps the machine is someone else entirely, with entirely different thoughts and memories. Or perhaps it doesn't think at all. It looks like it thinks, it is sweating now. But how would you ever be sure? It could be the perfect scam. Come to that, how can you even be sure the people you know, your colleagues, your family, your friends, really think? Firmly, Player 1 pursues these doubts.

He knows he is raising these issues to comfort himself, and for a while they do. He gets as far as feeling indignation with the club for its shameless manipulation of its clientele. Riding this wave of indignation, he lifts the gun quickly back to his temple and pulls the trigger.

Someone in the crowd gasps. The machine opposite him exhales, and smiles at him. It nods twice in succession, Player 2, the not-Mr Roberts, as if agreeing with something he is unaware he has said. He wants to simply point the gun at it and pull the trigger as many times as it takes. But the waiter lifts the pistol neatly from his hand, and sets it down in front of his opponent.

As he watches Player 2 watch the gun, he sets aside the crutch of his artificial cynicism.

Player 2 is an exact physical reproduction of himself. With the detachment which comes with extreme stress, he notices that from the look of it he is putting on weight at the jaw. You never can see yourself from that angle normally, turned to the side with your chin dropped to your chest, but he can look at Player 2. There is a bit more flesh under that blue-black stubble than there is in his mental image of himself. Maybe they shouldn't be playing the game at all. Maybe they should go for a jog together. The thought makes him giggle, and it looks at him. As their eyes meet, he acknowledges the reality of the situation, or at least, the intellectual truth of the proposition with which he is faced.

Player 2 is also an exact mental reproduction of himself. It believes it is a man. Player 2 believes it is the same man as he is. It is as sincere in its own belief as he is in his. Player 2 remembers getting up that morning, remembers the difficult conference call in the office, the one that Player 1 and only he attended. It remembers how hard he fought not to come down here, not to play the game again. It remembers how, after all the fighting, when he was finally in the chair waiting for the needle, he felt like he could wait forever. Strange how having accepted that he was going to do the thing, the burning need to do it vanished.

Until the game ends with the bullet, there is no way of knowing which one of them is right. If it tries to tear at its flesh, to peel off the organic layers looking for the metal beneath, the waiter and security will be on it and it will be strapped down with only one finger free to pull the trigger. If it tries to stand, it will be pushed back down into the chair – the weight of the robot's body feels different from that of a man's, and apparently you can tell that way, just by standing, which of you is real. That was house rule 1: *Two sit down, one stands up*.

With no way of knowing, he has to admit that he could be the robot. It could be that the time he has spent at this table is his lifetime. He was born with the knowledge of the green shaded lamp in the bronze fitting above him, and he will die when the bullet enters his brain in a few moments' time. No, not his brain, his processor. Or it could be that this is just a game, no more than ten minutes out of a life that has already run for more than fifty years, and hopefully has another thirty left to go. Although he acknowledges this as an intellectual fact, he does not yet truly feel it. Player 2 closes its eyes and puts the barrel of the gun in its mouth. Player 1 tenses up, and feels something close to compassion for his doppelganger. No time for thought, as the gun slips between the teeth. Even though the trigger is still inches from its face, closing its lips around the muzzle alters the acoustics when it pulls. There is the impotent click of the hammer. A smile spreads over its face. It is safe now for the whole of its opponent's turn. That might as well be an eternity.

The waiter puts the gun back in front of him. The barrel gleams wet where saliva from Player 2's mouth catches the light. Right now, just for this moment, there are two views at this table. There is the machine's view of him, and his view of the machine. Some time in the next five minutes, one of those views will cease to exist. It could be he is wrong. It could be that he, Player 1, is the machine, and it is his view that will cease to exist. The man, the man he thinks he is, will watch him put a bullet in his head. The man's view will continue, and his will cease to exist. For the first time he not only knows but believes it, and in that moment of terror and revelation the true nature of the game makes itself known to him.

The gun on the white tablecloth. A bullet somewhere in the four remaining cylinders. He wants to live more fiercely than he can ever remember. He wants more life. All of his problems, all of the things that plague him, the case at work that is consuming him, the fight with his second wife over the apartment in London, the bald spot that is growing, his daughter's boyfriend who smirks at him (and sometimes he can hear them. He can hear them from his own bedroom) at one moment they surround him, pawing at his flesh, and in the next he feels himself ascending, drawn up, drawn up away from them on this irresistible surge of life, until they are nothing, indistinguishable dots beneath him, which is what they always were of course! And he is free, free to feel only this raging desire for life.

He cannot escape from here. The ring of eager bodies will not let him out. The gun is his only way out. He wants so much to be free. He is primed for joy. He begins to make the private bargains with God, the offerings God receives from infrequent visitors – soldiers waiting to go over the top, and businessmen in the doctor's waiting room, with their test results already sitting in a little manila envelope. He promises God he will go to church, he will be a better man, silly things like brushing his teeth if he can be spared. Brushing his teeth! He stifles another giggle with his hands, and one of the women in the circle turns and pushes out through the ring of bodies. With her gone, it closes eagerly. At the climax of his terror and ecstasy, there is a moment of complete peace and radiant self-knowledge. Of course, he is himself. Player 1 is Mr Roberts. All the angels of certainty are around him. Faith's steadying hand is on his shoulder. He can picture himself dying, but he cannot picture the absence of himself picturing his death. In the end, it is a failure of the imagination which gives him strength. He puts the gun to his temple, smiles in triumph at his opponent, and pulls the trigger.

The explosion in the confined room makes the watchers jump. Some of them realise they have been holding their breath. There is even a nervous laugh. Spontaneous applause break out. His games really are becoming very good.

The body of Player 1 slumps in the chair. Its legs tremble violently as the ruined central processor fires random signals. The bullet stops dead eight inches from the barrel of the gun as it is programmed to do, but this is well beyond the confines of Player 1's skullcasing. A small trickle of blue fluorocarbon coolant emerges from the wound. The machines can never be allowed to reach a heat higher than body temperature, otherwise they or the human player may realise which one is which before the game is over. It is quite a feat of engineering, to manage this in the hot little game rooms.

Mr Roberts, Player 2, gets up from the table. He was right all along, of course. The other was the machine. But just for a moment there, just for a moment when it smiled at him, he thought it might know he was wrong. It looked as if just for a moment, it knew it was real, and he was the fake. In that moment Player 2 had confronted his mortality, and felt nothing but that supreme lust for life. It's still in him as he gets up from the table, and prepares to go to the nightclub upstairs. In the wake of the adrenalin surge, Mr Roberts feels peace. Someone claps him on the back, and he loves this person for touching him. Just after he gets up from the table, things matter again. They will go on mattering, he knows, for weeks, maybe months. There will be significance in everything, in the taste of food, the feeling of being touched, in the papers on his desk. The world will look the way it does after the first drink on a summer's evening when you are twenty with money in your pocket, and your first job is just-for-now. And when they stop mattering... well, no need to think about that now. Don't spoil it, he tells himself. It cost you enough, don't spoil it for God's sake.

The other guests filter out, and the waiter waits in respectful silence. As he is about to leave the room, Mr Roberts takes one last look at the machine. There is always for him a morbid fascination in seeing the image of his own face lying quite lifeless in the light from the lamp. He wonders about the degree of fidelity with which the machine's expression reflects what will be his own features in death. The eyes are slightly open, and the mouth lolls in the way he has learned to expect from films, but this could be merely the convention in movies rather than accurate observation from life. Or death. He has never seen a real dead body except on the news, dusty on the side of the road. At least his own lips won't be flecked with blue. The way Player 1 has slumped in the chair, one of his wrists is turned outwards, and Player 2 notices that there are four livid crescent marks in the palm, slowly fading to white as the system responsible for subcutaneous pigmentation starts to shut down. He wonders what the machine was trying to achieve by making the marks.

He picks up the lifeless hand. Without the coolant, the temperature of the flesh is already starting to rise. The livid little marks fade almost to nothing. It is strange to see something entirely of himself do something so inscrutable. Although perhaps no more strange than some of the other self-destructive things he has done in his life. Beside his euphoria, he feels a moment almost of envy for the machine, for the peace it has found in non-existence. Although perhaps, in that split second of consciousness after the trigger had been pulled and before the bullet had destroyed the processor, it experienced a moment of anguish beyond human understanding. If the thought had time to register, it must have known not only that it was about to cease to exist, but that it had never really existed, not before the moment it was called to life ten minutes previously beneath the light.

He lets the wrist fall and sway beside the chair. He tells the waiter not to have the machine repaired. There is no reason any more to keep a likeness of him in storage, he won't be back to play the game again. The waiter nods sadly.

"Just so, Sir. We shall be very sorry to lose your custom. Would you object, Sir, to the machine being repaired in any event? We like to keep a blank of all our members on file just as a matter of policy. And it can be helpful to you if you would like to have some tailoring done, and you haven't the time for the fitting yourself. We can get him out without any programming, and the tailor can use him for measurements. Have you put your tailor in touch with us?"

"Yes, yes, it's Lyalls just on Jermyn Street."

"They're very good, aren't they, Sir?"

"Yes they are."

"And of course Sir won't be charged for the repairs, not unless he should decide that after all, one more time..."

"That won't be necessary."

"All the same. It is club policy. And the tailoring, for convenience."

"Yes. Yes, fine repair it, why not," he says, wanting to leave the hot room. "But I'll never pay for it! You tell that to Marco, when you see him upstairs. Drinks and membership fees, that's all you'll have out of me from now on! And of course, something for yourselves."

He gives the waiter three hundred pounds. This man who would have held him down had he tried to escape.

"Thank you, Sir. Very generous."

And off Mr Roberts heads upstairs to the club, no longer Player 2 but a man again, and he takes one of the hostesses from the dancefloor home with him, and he doesn't even need stimulants to keep her entertained until the early hours of

Saturday, when he releases her with panda eyes and tottering heels into the mist of an October morning in Notting Hill. He doesn't worry about what he did with the girl as he lies in his bed staring at the ceiling, trying to remember what time he is to pick up his daughter from his former home. He thinks what a relief it is, to have resolved never to play the game again.

READY OR NOT
GARY MCMAHON

Hiding is the theme of Gary McMahon's story of a twisted childhood and a traditional children's game becoming something much darker. There's a loss of innocence here, and a yearning for home that can never be satisfied. As always there's a strange, dark poetry in Gary's bleak prose that makes for compelling reading.

THE CAFÉ IS quiet when I walk in. A handful of customers sit drinking coffee, enjoying an early lunch, or waiting for something more interesting to happen. I haven't been here in twenty years, but little has changed. The same scarred wooden floor, the same dirty-white walls, and the same sad, disinterested faces staring down at possibly the same cheap plates and coffee cups.

Sitting at a table by the window, I open the cheaply laminated menu. I haven't even seen food since yesterday afternoon; my belly thinks my throat has been cut.

"What can I get you?" The waitress hovers at the side of the table, barely even noticing me. She absently scratches her left cheek. Her eyes are pale blue, rather beautiful, but she doesn't look as if anyone has told her that for a long time.

"I'll have a ham and cheese sandwich, wholemeal bread. Coffee. Black." I put down the menu and look out of the window, averting my face in case she decides to study it too closely. A group of kids huddle at the corner. They look around nine or ten.

"Be back in a tick," says the waitress as she moves slowly away across the room.

I think I might have recognised her. It's the eyes. That colour. Her name is Martha or Mildred or Mary – it used to be, anyway. She wasn't part of my childhood group, but I think we dated for a while when we were at school. I remember her lips tasted like bubble gum.

Outside, traffic is light. I can see the main street from where I am sitting. The place is situated a few yards along a side street, just off the beaten track.

"There you go." She sets down the plate with my sandwich, pours coffee from a glass pot. I glance up at her, nod; she notices me properly for the first time. "Do I know you?"

I shake my head. Give a standard answer. "I'm not from around here. Just passing through."

She smiles sadly. Her eyes go vague and glassy again; she is tuning me out, dismissing me. "Enjoy your meal." She walks away and I feel less tense. I sip my coffee, glance out of the window. The kids scatter like scared birds. But one of them remains there, on the corner, with her face turned to the wall of an old bank. She has her hands up covering her eyes. I know she is counting while the others run away to hide. It's a game we played all the time when we were that age, one that never goes out of fashion. Hide and Seek. The same game we were playing when it happened.

I turn away, bite into my sandwich. It doesn't taste of anything real, just dust and old memories. Deep down inside me, I feel something move, but I can't put a label on what it is. Nor do I want to examine the feeling too closely, in case I recognise it. In case it recognises me.

The waitress – Martha? Mary? Fuck knows; it doesn't matter anyway – is chatting with the cook, who's come through from the kitchen while things are quiet. She keeps checking the room, seeing if anyone wants anything, but her posture is relaxed. When I'm done, I leave a five-pound note and some loose change on the table and walk out. It's more than the order cost, but I don't want to risk asking for the bill to give her another close look at me. Twenty-five years ago my photo was splashed all over the local paper because I was there when it happened. I look different now, but that doesn't mean a thing. Some events mark you forever.

Walking towards the hotel, I tug my rucksack higher on my shoulder. I travel light. I always travel light. I cross the main road at the traffic lights and slip down another side street, where the budget hotel is located. My car is parked on a back street; I hope I can find it again when it's time to leave. But I can worry about that later, once my business here is over.

The hotel is small and bright yet cheerless. There is no atmosphere, as if the place has been vacuum-packed. I walk across the small lobby and wait at the reception desk while a tall woman with jet black hair finishes sorting through some paperwork.

"Can I help you?" She looks up. Her eyes are small and bright. Her cheeks are ruddy.

"I have a reservation under the name of Elliot." I haven't used my real name. Twenty years is a long time to be away, but there might just be someone who still knows my surname. The past is never dead. It just lies down and takes a nap, waiting for something to wake it up.

The woman checks her computer monitor, tapping away at the keyboard. "Ah, yes. Mr Elliot. Welcome to the Humbird Inn. Just one night, isn't it?"

"That's correct." I slide the rucksack off my shoulder and place it on the floor between my feet. Glancing around, I note the fire exit, the lifts, and the door leading to the stairs. There is a vending machine opposite the lifts, and an old man with a stooped back is examining the chocolate bars behind the glass.

"That'll be room number 214," says the receptionist. She hands me a key card, smiling. "It's on the second floor."

I head across to the lifts. The old man is still trying to decide which snack to purchase. Hitting the button to summon the lift, I start to relax.

The lift doors open and I step inside. I press the button for the second floor and wait. The lift smells stale, as if someone has left wet clothes in there to dry. When the doors open again, I step out and turn right, following the signs to my room.

The corridor is monotonous. Every door is identical, aside from the number. I find my room and use the key card to open the door. The room shares a template with every other one in the country: narrow wardrobe on the left and bathroom door on the right. I walk inside and throw my rucksack on the double bed. The room is bigger than I'd expected, and the large window lets in plenty of light. I've slept in worse places.

I don't bother unpacking my bag. There isn't enough in there to bother: a change of clothing, some toiletries, and a paperback book. On second thoughts, I take out the shower gel, toothbrush and toothpaste and carry them into the bathroom. When I switch on the light, the extractor fan starts to hum. I turn on the shower. The spray of water is impressively powerful. I remove my clothes and step under the jet of hot water, closing my eyes as I scrub away the grit of the road.

Fifteen minutes later I'm lying on the bed wrapped in a towel, watching a documentary about killer whales on television. There are no satellite channels; just the freebies. I watch as an orca swims gracefully up through the sea, heading towards the surface, where several seals are cavorting. I take no pleasure when the whale strikes, killing one of the seals.

As I watch, I feel my eyes closing. I haven't slept well all week; my mind was too active making plans for this trip. Tiredness creeps up on me, taking me by surprise.

When I open my eyes again it's dark. The curtains are closed. I know this is a dream because when I fell asleep the curtains were open. I've always been good at spotting the minor details. It's how I manage to get through life, to blend into the background while making the most of situations.

Glancing over at the hotel room door, I see that it's open. The corridor is dim, but not completely dark. Somewhere there is a light on. I get to my feet and cross the room, the towel slipping from around my waist. I pad naked out into the corridor. The lights above my head are off, but farther along a single bulb burns. Right at the end, where the corridor branches off to the left and the right, a short figure stands with its face turned to the wall. I begin to walk towards the figure, and see that it is holding its hands up over its eyes, like the girl I saw earlier that day.

It's difficult to discern if the figure is male or female. It's just a human shape, clad in shadows. As I draw closer, I can hear a whispery voice counting down from one hundred. Oddly, the counting seems to speed up as I approach, and just before I draw level with the figure, I hear the voice clearly, "*Coming, ready or not.*" The words are spoken in a whisper; low and breathy, almost a series of exhalations rather than proper words.

Slowly, the figure begins to turn around. I stop walking, my legs stiffening, my hands clenching into fists. The figure keeps turning; it seems to take ages, as if time has slowed down. Just before the figure's face comes into view, I wake up on the bed in my hotel room, sweating and gasping for breath.

"No," I whisper. Then, more loudly, "No!"

I sit up and stare at myself in the mirror on the wall. I look afraid, but I feel nothing, not even tired. I am in control. It was a dream, that's all, a silly little nightmare. None of it was real. I glance at the door. It's closed.

I go to the window and look out onto the street. The sky is darkening. Grey clouds hang heavy and sombre, promising rain. The street is busy with foot traffic, and, beyond it, the main road through the town is clogged with vehicles. I've slept longer than I expected.

I'm not sure what called me back here, other than the desire to mark this occasion in some way, but since arriving in town I've felt on edge. I'm successful. I've broken away from this shitty little town and made something of myself. Yet part of me was left behind. I can't say what it is I lost here, but I know I either want to claim it back or bury it for good.

Unbelievably, I'm hungry again. The hotel is too small to have its own restaurant, but the receptionist recommends a Chinese place a few minutes' walk away. I leave the hotel, her rapidly sketched map in hand, and head west. The streetlights have come on.

I walk through streets at once depressingly familiar and unutterably alien. Buildings I knew when I was younger have been demolished and replaced with others that are similar but not quite the same. Old shops have closed down and reopened as something else. The landscape has altered; a lot of essential markers have been shifted or removed entirely. The geography I remember is that of the heart, and those emotional roads and byways have fallen into disrepair. They are ragged and potholed; their boundaries have been erased and dirt has encroached, making them vague and unwelcoming.

I find the Chinese restaurant easily and slip inside. The waiters and waitresses are quick and polite; their smiles look painted on. I order a chicken chow mein and wait for it to arrive, sipping at a bottle of cold beer. Early diners speak in hushed tones. Light, vaguely ethnic music drifts through hidden speakers. The place is nice but unspectacular. I could be anywhere, at any time. I might even be in the past, but for the minor details.

I WAS FIFTEEN by the time I left town and headed for the bright lights of London, to make my fortune. This restaurant – like so many other establishments I'd seen today – was not here. I couldn't recall what had once stood in its place.

But before that, as kids, we'd run wild through these streets. Not causing trouble, not breaking any laws, just playing the fool, being a child.

Even when the first of the children went missing, our parents never stopped us from playing outside unsupervised. They just gave us curfews and new rules to obey. Nothing was off limits; it was just that we had to be more careful, mindful of who might be around.

By the time the third, and then the fourth, child was taken, things had changed. We were no longer allowed out after school. People started to lock their doors when they were at home, even during daylight. Nobody found any bodies. Murder was never mentioned in public, but everyone knew it was there, beyond the veil, watching us with cold and seedy eyes.

Fear gripped the town. People waited to see who would be next. And then the disappearances stopped. Months went by without another disappearance. The rules were relaxed. The streets and parks once more rang with the sound of children playing.

Perhaps that was our mistake – thinking it was over, that something had run its natural course and everything had gone back to normal.

That was when Lucy was taken.

She was the last. No one else disappeared after that. Nobody was apprehended for the crimes. Finally, it was finished, and the rest of the parents could breathe a guilty sigh of relief. But it could never be over for the loved ones left behind. They continued to live with it, long after the darkness had passed on by. They were changed by what had come to pass, left with scars and contusions that were not visible to the naked eye. They turned their attention inward, trying to smother the pain.

And the biggest ache of all was caused by never knowing what had happened to their sons and daughters.

* * *

THE CHOW MEIN is good, but not great. Like everything else around here, it's functional. It serves a purpose, and is then forgotten. I eat the food mechanically, wondering once again why I came here after all this time.

"Excuse me."

I look up, startled. A man is standing at the side of my table, motionless, as if he is caught somewhere between fight and flight. I raise my eyebrows but do not speak.

"My God… it is. It's you. Tony Fowler. I didn't recognise you at first… you've changed so much."

Contact lenses, a little botox, a good cosmetic surgeon who fixed a couple of scars from childhood mishaps. Nothing too drastic; just enough to help me blend in, be forgettable.

"How are you?"

I glance around. The restaurant has grown busier during the time it has taken me to get half way through my main course. I don't want to make a scene. I consider simply denying who I am, playing dumb, but I can see by the man's face that he will not take no for an answer.

"Hello, Ron." His name comes to me easily, along with an image of who he once was: a shy, quiet young boy I'd allowed to be my friend. There is nothing special about him, never has been. He is just a walk-on character in the story of my life. "It's been a while."

"Mind if I sit down?" He grabs an empty seat from a nearby table and sits without waiting for me to respond. He has changed, too, overcompensating with this brash personality when he was once so introverted.

"Sure," I say, setting down my chopsticks. "How've you been?"

"Oh, not bad. Nothing ever changes around here. I see you're doing well for yourself." He points at my suit, or the watch on my wrist. Neither of these is particularly expensive, but they aren't cheap either.

"I have my own business. I'm a financial consultant. Things are okay." I smile.

Ron's face turns serious. He leans over the table. I can see his bad teeth; the way the parting in his hair barely conceals the onset of male pattern baldness. "It's been twenty-five years, hasn't it? Twenty-five years to the day." He shakes his head slowly. "A quarter of a century. Some of us never forget."

"Indeed," I say, noncommittally.

"Is that why you're here? To pay your respects?"

"In a manner of speaking," I say. I see him as a small boy, one of the runners and hiders; never the one to count and then go looking for the rest. The games he played were simple because he wasn't capable of much more. He tagged along, never outstaying his welcome, usually the first one to be found.

"I still think about them. I think about *her* – little Lucy." His smile is sad now. "The rest of the town seems to have forgotten, but those of us who knew them keep the fires burning."

"That's good," I say. "We should never forget." But isn't that why I'm here, to ensure that I do forget, to help put it all behind me and move on to the next phase of my life?

"I don't even let my kids play Hide and Seek. I can't bear it... don't even like to see other kids playing that damned game." He shrugs, and I feel sorry for him. Like so many others, he was imprisoned here by what happened all that time ago. Five kids were taken, their bodies never found, and the mystery bound an entire generation to this godforsaken town.

"You were so brave to move away. I wish I could have done the same." He opens his hands, as if bearing gifts. I am disturbed because it seems as if he is reading my thoughts.

"I might have moved on, but she's still here." I leave it there, trying to be enigmatic. I don't want to say much more to this tired-out little man. He is a reflection of what I might have been had I stayed behind, a memory that never happened. "Listen, I have to go..." I signal to a passing waiter, who nods and darts off to fetch my bill. "But it was nice seeing you like this."

"Here... here's my number. Give me a call. We could get together for a drink?" He looks desperate. I wonder if everyone else who was around at the time refuses to talk about what happened, and he just wants to relive old memories. Perhaps the pressure has been building up inside him for too long, and what he sees in me is an outlet for his own darkness.

I take the business card, slip it into my pocket, and nod. "I'm here for a few days," I lie. "I'll give you a call."

When he shakes my hand, he grips it too tightly, as if he is afraid I might snatch it away. When he leans in close I realise he's been drinking heavily. His breath smells of whisky. His skin is slick and shiny. He stands and walks off in the direction of the front door. I have no idea who he was with, but they seem to have left him behind. Perhaps they were glad to be rid of him. I know I am.

The waiter brings me the bill and I pay in cash. I don't want to leave any trace of myself behind. The money has passed through so many hands, and will pass through so many more, that my scent will soon be washed away.

THE NIGHT IT happened there was a bunch of us playing out by the old railway station, the one that had never been in use, even during my childhood. We played chase and football, and then as the shadows lengthened someone – I think it might even have been that younger version of Ron – suggested we play Hide and Seek.

I have no idea how I ended up being 'It' – the one who hides his eyes with his hands, counts backwards from a hundred, and then goes off to find the rest, searching for their hiding places. There's a good chance I volunteered. Even at that age, I enjoyed being the loner.

So I stood with my face to the wall, covered my eyes with the palms of my hands, and counted out loud. I heard scampering footsteps, rustling undergrowth, stones rattling across the ground. I smelled perfume as someone passed close by me. A few of the girls had started wearing their mothers' perfume and makeup, but I couldn't single out a particular scent. It was dull and floral; sat heavy in the nostrils.

After I'd finished my count, I uncovered my eyes and spun around. "Coming, ready or not!" It was the standard call, the words every school kid knows by heart. It meant that the hunter was ready, he was coming, and you'd better be well-hidden or you'd get caught out. Nobody wanted to be the first one found.

I've asked myself so many times if I saw anything: a quick darting movement, a thin dark figure moving with the grace and agility of an animal, a shadow slightly darker than the rest. The police and the newspaper reporters were keen for me to have seen something out of the ordinary, but I just couldn't bring myself to say that I had.

The truth is, I still don't know. I might have seen one of those things, or all of them. I might have glimpsed a blank white face with a gaping mouth that seemed more like an absence, or it might just have been my own twisted reflection seen in the shattered glass fragments stuck in a broken window frame in the station wall. Reality is a slippery beast. We try to catch hold of it, but it twists and turns like a snake, and slides out of our grip. It was no different for me. I was eleven years old, life still felt like one long game, and I wanted to be the winner.

"Coming, ready or not!" I shouted again, and my voice whipped back at me through the dimness, sounding deep and unfamiliar, as if it belonged to someone else. Perhaps it did. What if right then, in that moment, I became another person – the person whose potential had always been inside me, waiting to get out. In some ways, I've spent every waking moment of my life since trying to be that person again.

The air was sharp. I could smell every scent. The lingering odour of that floral perfume, the bitter sap from the trees, the dry, cloying stench of rotting vegetation, even a waft of excrement from a small hole in the wall where I assumed rats must nest.

The ground felt firm beneath my feet as I walked away from the old station building and into the trees. I pushed through, ripping out tall weeds and shielding my bare arms from stinging nettles as I went deeper. Up ahead, something shifted in the dense bushes. I didn't have a torch but the ambient light from distant street lamps and the low, pale moon lit my way. I think even then, I was only looking for one person. Let the rest of them hide away where they couldn't be seen – I only had eyes for her, for Lucy.

WHEN I LEAVE the Chinese restaurant I head immediately to the old train station, just outside the town boundary. I cannot think of a good excuse to delay it any longer. It's a short walk, but it seemed much longer back in the day.

I'm pleased the building is still here, and nobody has tried to demolish it or use the land to build something that doesn't belong. Then again, I'd probably have heard about it if they had done.

I walk to the wall where our childhood game began, and I turn to face the grimy stonework. Out of a sense of symmetry rather than sentimentality – to bring things round full circle – I close my eyes, cover my face with my hands, and count down from one hundred.

"Coming, ready or not," I whisper as I turn to face the world I left behind.

I know the place. Memory has not dulled the route; the passage of time has erased no trails. I go straight there, without any problem. Even the weeping willow looks unchanged. To the right of the tree, not far from the rusted train tracks, there is a pile of building rubble that is so old it looks like a permanent structure: bricks, timber, beams and columns, old doors and window frames. It seems improbable, but nobody has disturbed the area for decades.

I walk over and start to pull away some of the ancient rubble, clearing a space. It's difficult to believe that not a single soul has been here and tried to clean it up – but if this place was truly abandoned, they'd be more inclined to use their time and energy elsewhere. All that work at the centre of town, demolishing the old buildings and putting up new ones. People are too busy moving forward to look backwards.

Before long I've cleared enough away that I can see the timber door, the one laid across a shallow depression in the earth. It has been covered for so long that the wood is rotten. Black insects scurry away when I disturb their nest. I slide my fingers under the crumbling wood and start to shift it sideways, just enough to allow me to see inside the ditch that lies beneath.

Lucy was never any good at hiding. I'd found her easily, when all was said and done.

She was cowering under the droopy remains of a weeping willow, her feet pulled up under her and her arms wrapped around her midriff. She was beautiful, but not in a conventional way. She had coke-bottle glasses and tousled hair. Her nose was too big for the rest of her face and there were braces on her teeth.

But she was my first, and firsts are always the best.

Lucy didn't even speak when she realised I'd found her. She just blinked up at me through those thick lenses, shifting her weight, glad to be able to move without fear of discovery. A small, sad smile crossed her face.

I remembered the features I'd seen in the broken tooth-like fragments of glass on my way here: that yawning maw, the tiny, dark eyes, the white cheeks. It was me, and yet it wasn't me. It was something that I could become. I'd been given a glimpse of the future, and it excited me.

I stepped forward, bent down under the willow's dangling branches, and I went to her. She reached out, as if to embrace me, and I slipped my hands around her neck. I'd known this was coming – I'd felt it approaching like a distant train on rickety tracks, or a slow-advancing drumbeat – yet still its suddenness took me by surprise. There was no black-out, no blurred perception, but a moment of exquisite clarity as I began to squeeze her throat.

She struggled, but not as much as I'd expected. Still she didn't cry out, or scream, or even try to speak. It took a long time and it took no time at all. Time had fractured, like that reflection in the glass. Everything bent and bowed before the glory of this moment.

I STARE DOWN into the hollow under the boards, feeling like I've truly found Lucy at last. She was the first. Even then, I knew she wouldn't be the last. I'd taken advantage of some long-ago mystery abductor, using the smokescreen of his four victims to cover my own tracks. He stopped doing whatever it was he did, but for me it was just the beginning: the start of something that will never end.

I've killed nineteen women since then, but none of them has moved me even half as much as Lucy did that night. No matter how hard I try, I can never quite recapture the essence of that first perfect time.

The years have not been kind to her. I see a shocking glimpse of white bone, a pair of glasses with thick lenses, and something metallic that might once have been dental braces, and then I pause.

"Thank you," I say, without a trace of irony. There isn't much else to say. I've spent twenty years trying to find her in other people, and here she is, right here, in the same place she's always been: waiting right where I'd hidden her. But she was never really hiding from me. Not hiding, but waiting.

Silence sits down beside me. Not even the breeze stirs.

When I turn around, there is no vengeful phantom awaiting me, nor is there a nightmare vision stepping clumsily out from under the willow tree. The air is cool. The smells are fresh. The night is limitless in its ability to obscure things from those of us who choose not to see. The glimpses I've had since arriving in town, the small shards of her, the tiny little visions, were not her ghost. They were the memory of what I did trying to get out.

I cover over the remains and walk away from the scene, experiencing nothing that can be described as a human emotion. *Feeling* is for other people. All that interests me is the game, and how long I can continue to play before I am caught.

Concentrating hard, I send my energy soaring towards all the others out there, the countless women in bars and late-night diners, the street-corner prostitutes and runaways who have long been my playmates... because I am coming.

Ready or not, I am coming to find you.

THE MONOGAMY OF WILD BEASTS
ROBERT SHEARMAN

The games we play with each other's emotions and desires are often incomprehensible, and sometimes incomprehensibly cruel. That's not to say that what follows is a bitter tale; Robert is a master of darkly funny prose, surrealistic pieces that sound just as brilliant read aloud as they read on the page. There is a bitter-sweetness here, in a story that gives us hope on one hand, but also shows us how cruel we can be in the games that we play.

WE AGREED IT was the dog's turn to die. We'd been saving up a proper no-nonsense mammal for quite a while. Recently we'd been executing the lower lifeforms, if you regard invertebrates as lower lifeforms, and mostly I do – and it's hard to take much pleasure in killing an invertebrate, you can't get much excitement when even the beast in question doesn't seem to care. Strictly speaking, we weren't due to use up another mammal for weeks yet, not when we had a million species of insect to wade through. But Debra had been looking a little bored, and when she gets bored she gets irritable, and Brett and I may have our differences but we know that isn't good for either of us.

It really wasn't hard to pick which dog. The bitch had already made her choice. Still, we followed normal procedure. The three of us went down below deck for inspection. Sure enough, there was that one dog, right out on his own, ostracised from the other two. He seemed resigned to his fate. He knew he'd lost, he wasn't even trying any more. It's a shame, I had always rather liked him, I had high hopes in the early months he'd be able to turn the situation around – he was older than his competitor, true, but he seemed more charming and more refined somehow, when he was courting the bitch he showed an old world courtesy, he didn't just stick his nose up her backside. What can I say? I've always had a soft spot for the underdog. But the sad truth is the underdog rarely wins through – and here he was now, the very definition of underdog, he was Underdog Incarnate – he lay on his belly, head on his paws, he barely bothered to look up when we opened the cage door. Frankly, this was going to be a mercy killing. Frankly, we were doing him a favour. I picked him up in my arms, I wanted to be the one, I knew I would be gentler than the others. The other dogs, they didn't even give him the dignity of a farewell bark. They were too busy fucking, that cocky little poodle was playing the stud and doing some sort of victory lap on the bitch, he was giving the bitch a right good seeing to.

Now, how to kill it? Because we'd had a lot of fun with the killings at the beginning of the voyage. We'd decapitated them, we'd kicked them to death, any beasts with identifiable necks we'd hung from the yardarm. It was up to Debra, of course, it was *always* up to Debra – but I felt quite strongly that we should treat the dog with some respect. I didn't want there to be any actual blood shed – there was no need for that, we could be better than that. Debra began to argue, of course, at even the hint she wouldn't get her way her hands bunched up into angry fists. And then, I don't know why, Brett stuck up for me. Brett said that maybe we didn't have to be quite so cruel for a change. Debra sulked, but Brett was smart, I'll give him that – he suggested it'd be even more *fun* making the dog's death a funeral, a burial at sea. It'd turn it into a ceremony. We might get a few more minutes out of it that way.

I admit, I wondered what his game was. But maybe there was no game to it. Maybe he was fond of the dog. Or maybe he remembered what we'd done to the gazelle, and how it had taken hours to expire, and what awful plaintive sounds it made as it did so – yes, it was quite a good party, and at the end Debra for a laugh stabbed it in the throat and we all danced in the spray of its arterial blood – a good party, but the next morning I couldn't help but think it had demeaned us all rather.

We'd chuck the dog overboard. Better yet, Debra would be the one who could do the actual chucking, that would cheer her up. She said, "I'm going to chuck it hard too, if I chuck it at the right angle it'll hit the water like it's fucking concrete!" She was well-behaved that evening. Normally when we kill a mammal she wants something extra from it, she wants to put it on the spit, she wants to turn it into sausages (even though God has expressly forbidden us to eat of any creature that can lick its own bollocks) – or she wants us to shave off its fur, she says she can knit herself a fur scarf or something, and she never touches the fur, we've got a spare cabin full of monkey skin and elephant hide and she's done nothing with it and it just sits there rotting. But she was in a good mood, she didn't even mind when I let the dog sit with us whilst we ate. I kept feeding it scraps of manna underneath the table. Debra said, "I don't know why you're bothering, it'll be dead soon!" and I said it was my manna, I could do what I liked with it. I stroked the dog, he nuzzled my hand. I decided I loved the dog, and I'd give him a name, I'd name him Buster.

And soon we could put it off no longer, the sun was starting to set, and there'd be no fun in drowning Buster if we couldn't see his death throes. The four of us stood up on the top deck – me, Brett, Debra, and, of course, Buster – and we stared out across the unending ocean, out at the horizon, out at the wide expanse of sky. It would have been beautiful had it not been all so blue.

Debra had Buster in her arms, but to be fair to her, not too tightly, she wasn't hurting him yet – maybe she was falling in love with the dog as well? "Who's going to do the final words?" I asked; "My turn," said Brett, and it's usually his turn, but I don't begrudge him, he does it better than me. "O Father," he said, "into thy hands we commend this spirit," – "Holy fuck!" said Debra, because the dog had wriggled free, he jumped down from her arms, he jumped overboard all by himself.

It was almost elegant, the way he fell – paws stretched forward, head tilted down, he looked like a champion diver, he hit the water clean and there was barely a splash. "Fuck and balls!" said Debra, and we had to tell her it wasn't as if the dog had escaped, he was still going to drown, what did it matter? The dog had committed suicide, and that was as legitimate a means of death as any other. "He'll still suffer, babe," said Brett, "he'll suffer so bad." I hoped Brett wasn't right about that, but I wasn't going to contradict – I quite like Brett sometimes, in spite of everything. I wonder if he quite likes me?

And Buster broke to the surface – soaked through, buffeted by the surf, still so very much alive. Debra had a great idea. Debra said we should drop something on its head. Debra thought that might be fun. So for half an hour we all threw stuff at the dog bobbing about in the ocean beneath us, whatever we could grab – crockery from the galley, loose rigging, loose mast, entire handfuls of monkey skin and elephant hide. I wasn't really trying to hit the dog, and I don't think Brett was either. Debra had no luck, "Keep still, you fucking shit!" she'd scream as yet another of her missiles fell short, but the dog wasn't dodging anything, he never even flinched, he just paddled away amiably in the foam. Debra was furious, she said we should start over, go fetch another dog, chuck that overboard as well – Brett and I talked her down, we saved the dog from extinction.

She got bored after a while, and went inside. "You're sure that dog is going to die?" she asked us.

"Yes, Debra," I said.

"Yes, babe."

"All right then."

Brett and I stayed out a bit longer, watching him. "He doesn't give in, does he?" said Brett, and he sounded admiring. "Life will always find a way."

For all its efforts, though, the dog was getting tired, and even if it managed to stay afloat it wouldn't be able to keep pace with the ark much longer.

"What if it's still alive down there in the morning?" I said. "What if it's still swimming after us?"

"I don't know," said Brett. "But I'm not going to be the one who tells Debra."

The next morning, though, I looked out of my cabin porthole, and I could see no sign of Buster, and I felt sad.

Brett said to me later that day, "God doesn't understand why we didn't execute it properly. He liked that time with the gazelle, he liked how we danced in the blood." Brett's the only one who can talk to God directly, and give him his due, he doesn't lord it over the rest of us much, but it can make him a bit of an arsehole. And sometimes, I don't know, I wonder if he makes some of it up.

BLACK VULTURES MATE for life. I know, who'd have thought? They're such thuggish bastards, I wouldn't expect them to have any tender feelings. But it turns out they're quite the romantics. The male leaps onto his lover, and you'd imagine he might crush her, but he does it so tenderly, and they both croon a bit, and I like to think that they croon of love. It was easy to weed out the unwanted black vulture, that was one of the first creatures we disposed of. We weren't so brutal in those days, even Debra approached the killings with clinical detachment.

We took the reject and broke off its wings so it couldn't escape, then Debra held it down and told me to bludgeon it with my bare hands, and I did so, I pounded it until its skull shattered. It wasn't easy for me, because I'm really a very gentle fellow. We plucked the vulture and we grilled it. It tasted good.

I've been compiling for my own amusement a list of the wild beasts in our care that practise monogamy. There are quite a few. Prairie voles are monogamous, there's one. Swans. Penguins. Some types of osprey, and sandhill cranes, and the American blue goose. But most of the animals, they're sex-crazed lunatics, they don't show any instinct for commitment. Or, as far as I can see, much discernment either: even as a human it's clear to me which of the two male ferrets is the attractive one, but the female takes it from both sides, she doesn't care, she gets serviced by both the debonair ferret and his boggle-eyed brother. And maybe that's a kinder thing – maybe in the ferret world it doesn't matter whether you're ugly, you can still be guaranteed a bit of action. I don't know. I still want to say to them all – stop! Just for a moment! Don't you know why you're here? Don't you know you're emissaries of God? This isn't just sex, it's the evolutionary future of your species! The creatures of the world, be they arthropod or annelid, mollusc or marsupial or your common or garden member of the mammal family, so long as they're getting some they don't mind where it's coming from. It's a little disheartening. When the time comes to deal with the ferrets it'll be random, we'll just kill the male who's not actually shagging at the time we show up – the female won't have decided with which of her mates she'll repopulate the planet, quite literally, she won't give a fuck.

I keep all my observations in a notebook. Brett asked me why. I said I was engaged in scientific research, and he nodded politely enough, but I don't think he believed that for a moment. So I said I just *liked* it, it was something to do. He asked if he could see the notebook. I handed it over. He flicked through the pages, he paused to admire the drawings I'd sketched, he gave particular attention to the one I'd made of the orangutan gangbang.

"It's nice to have a hobby," he said. "I used to have hobbies."

Quite why God had chosen Brett Taylor to be his prophet was beyond me. To be fair, it was beyond Brett too, he told me he was certain there must have been better candidates to safeguard mankind's future. Brett was not an inspiring figure. He was a man of few words, and none of them illuminating. When I first met him he'd had a straggly beard and a pot belly paunch; over the last few months on the ark the paunch had gone, but the sun had bleached his beard and now it had strange blond stripes running down it, it looked rather silly.

God told Brett the evils of the world would be purged by flood. All mankind would drown. All the beasts that crawl upon the ground, they would drown, and yea, the ones that flew in the air, they would drown. Even the fish would drown, God didn't know how to do that yet, but he was God, he would work it out. Life on Earth would be stopped dead, so that life on Earth could begin anew, cleaner and purer than before. He commanded Brett to build an ark, and to put on board a representative of each and every species – and then the species could all mate, and the progeny of the ark would be the inheritors of the world. Brett thought for a bit and did the maths and told God that if mating was what it was all about he'd need to take two of every creature. God thought for a bit too, and said Brett had better make it three. He didn't want the mothers of all future life having to put up with some random jerk just because there was literally no one else they could make babies with. In fact, thinking about it, maybe that had been the problem with the world in the first place. No, take aboard three of each creature, one female and two males. Give the female time to pick her favourite, then put the extra male over the side.

Brett thought that since he was already married to Debra, that additional male rule needn't apply to humans. Debra said that was unfair. If the female of every other species had the responsibility of selecting a mate, she mustn't shirk it. She must accept the same task, however onerous. In fact, she insisted on it.

I answered the ad they put in the paper. Not many did; I don't know why.

I'm surprised I got the job. I am not a very handsome man, but I know from experience there are women out there who find me tolerable enough to shag. If I had been Brett I would have selected someone who would have been easier competition for him – someone old, or fat, or smelly. Perhaps Brett felt that would be cheating, he did not want to incur the wrath of God. Or perhaps he did not want the wrath of Debra. At my interview she had me strip naked, then turn about, then wiggle my parts at her to see how they bounced; she prodded at my body appraisingly with a stick. "Yes," she said, "he'll do." She licked her lips.

I'm under no illusion that in this game Brett must be considered the favourite. Whatever else, Brett is still the husband. Debra might be bored of Brett, I don't know, and I suppose I have the little advantage of being fresh meat. But we're talking posterity here, not a one night stand – posterity takes skill. And Brett has form, he's had years of practice in the saddle. He has learned his way around her bad moods, and Debra is a creature of bad moods, entire weeks go by when she seems determined to make every single thing an irritant. And yet, against all the odds, I have seen Brett head off quarrels at the pass, with a dexterity sometimes that makes me want to applaud. What I have going for me, I think, is youth and a pert bottom. I don't think, in the end, that it'll be enough.

Any day now. And we could be sitting around the breakfast table, and we'll raise the matter of which animal we're going to judge today. And they could say, the humans, it's the turn of the humans, it's *my* turn. Any day now, maybe tomorrow. I don't think that they'll let me die easily. The human is a precious thing, it's the only animal that can fully articulate how much pain it's suffering. They'll have something special in mind. Debra still licks her lips when she sees me, sometimes I catch her out of the corner of my eye when she thinks I'm not looking. I doubt it's for the pertness of my body, it's anticipation of how hard my body might break.

Brett need only say God wants the human question settled. Choose a day he's bound to win – I would do it, if I were in his shoes, this competition would have ended long ago. I wonder why he doesn't. I think, maybe, he likes to have someone to talk to. God and Debra aside, I expect he gets lonely.

He said, "Can I look at your notebook again?" This time he stared at my sketch of the black vultures copulating. Nudging at each other's privates with their beaks, eyes only for their life partners. I wondered if Brett felt a pang of nostalgia for simpler times. I wondered if he and Debra had ever had a love like that.

"May I borrow this?" he asked, rather shyly. "The picture. I don't know. In the bedroom, it might add some extra spice." And of course I should have refused, we're in a fight to the death, him and I. But he didn't ask me as a competitor, he asked me as a fellow human being, and there aren't many of those left nowadays.

"Sure," I said. "Knock yourselves out."

LAST NIGHT DEBRA came to me.

She hadn't shown any interest in me for nearly a month – or, not sexual interest, at any rate. Time was she'd be knocking at my door most nights of the week – we'd make love, and then we'd step out onto the deck, the waters were still rising in those days, it was strangely beautiful as we watched the highest buildings and the mountaintops submerged. But that was a long time ago, and obviously it wasn't a good sign. But still, I'd been mostly relieved: the game would soon be over, there was no need to worry much more. Brett had won, and good luck to him, and maybe he'd deserved it.

Even so, I wasn't surprised to hear her knock last night. It had been an exciting day. A mountain gorilla had got out of its cage and had broken through to the Barbary apes. We caught him fucking the female Barbary ape, it was almost funny, the female didn't know which way to look, and the two males stood around looking embarrassed. Inter-species mating is expressly forbidden. There had to be punishments. The womb of the Barbary ape female would be tainted now, we set fire to her. We made her gorilla lover watch her burn, and how he squealed. Then we set fire to him too. This left us with two spare Barbary ape males, what to do with them? Clearly they couldn't produce offspring by themselves, they were useless now. We burned them both, but we did it quickly, we didn't want them to think any of this was their fault. There was a smell of roast ape on the deck for hours, rich and meaty but somewhat overcooked, and the salt sea breeze only flavoured it.

The Barbary ape is extinct now, and that's unfortunate, but extinction turns Debra on, and I knew that night one man wouldn't be enough for her.

I opened the door. She was already naked, all of her bits hanging everywhere. "Won't you come in?" I said.

"Thank you."

"Shall I take my clothes off?"

"Please." It was odd how, even after all this time, we could still be so politely formal to each other. Only in our sexual encounters did I ever see this side of Debra, as someone vulnerable, someone who still feared rejection. And that was lucky, perhaps, because it was only in this milder, kinder form that I could ever get aroused for her.

We had sex. It was all right.

Afterwards she just lay there spread-eagled on my bed, arms and legs splayed so wide that I couldn't lie there too without touching her.

"It seems like such a burden sometimes," she said. "Knowing that the spark of future mankind will come from my womb."

I agreed in a non-committal way. I hadn't been anywhere near Debra's womb that night; she never wanted to risk pregnancy, not until she'd made her decision. She said that carrying either one of our children would give an unfair advantage.

"If I were your mother," she said. "What would you think of me?"

"If you were my mother?"

"Yes."

"I don't know."

In the daylight not knowing things would make Debra angry. Here, now, in the dark stillness of my bed, she seemed to muse on my reply with respectful consideration.

"If I'm going to be the mother to *everybody*," she said. "If the whole world one day looks back to me, what can they think? Every human impulse, every little achievement or failure, it'll come from what I pass on to them. And what's inside me, I can't control it, it just seems to get more savage each day. I don't know what I am any more. I don't know. And any little drop of goodness in me will have to be squeezed out and divvied up. What if there just isn't enough good to go round?"

She shut up then, she seemed to wait for a response. I still didn't have one. I was tired, and the lingering smell of ape meat was making me nauseous. I shrugged in a manner I hoped she would find sympathetic.

We lay there in the darkness for quite a while. I wouldn't be able to sleep like that. I wondered when she'd go back to her own bed. I heard her start to cry. I didn't know how to comfort her. I stroked her hair, maybe that would be enough.

"You're kind," she said.

"Well, I don't know about that."

"No, you're kind."

I didn't dare argue.

"Let's fuck again," she said. "You can enter me this time, if you like. Maybe the human race begins here and now, with a little bit of kindness." She seemed so shy.

I climbed on top of Debra. She was not to my taste. She had skin everywhere, clumped together in heavy folds, she had skin growing in places skin should never have ventured. One breast was bigger than the other, it was sort of lopsided, I could never look at it during the act for fear it would put me off. On her shoulder was a little tattoo of an animal, it might have been a lizard. And there was an odour, a sort of porcine odour – I had first assumed it was from any animals she'd spent the day with, now I knew it never faded, I knew it was something from within her.

But she was still the most beautiful woman in the world.

Even though I was tired, the second bout of sex was better than the first. Maybe that little kindness helped after all. I shot some seed inside her. God speed, I thought, happy travels! And then, when it was all over, I kissed her on the lips, and she actually kissed back, and we'd never kissed before, and her lips were softer than I'd imagined, the kiss felt warm and sweet.

"Thank you," she said.

"Thank you," I replied.

"Well then," she said.

"Well."

"I wish I loved you," she said. "Or even liked you a bit. That would have made everything so much easier."

"That," I agreed, "would have been nice."

As she left the room the moonlight caught her and she looked rather sad and rather old. And she was holding her belly with both hands, she was so careful, and I imagined my poor sperm splashing around inside.

Exhausted, and yet I couldn't sleep.

I got up, went out onto the deck. The moon had disappeared back behind the clouds, or maybe it had gone altogether, who knew? Maybe it had just given up at long last and thrown itself into the sea.

It was so dark I couldn't see the water beneath me, or how far I would have to fall. For all I could tell, the water was right there at my feet. It would be like wading in. It might even be warm.

And I knew I wasn't going to jump, just as I never jumped, but I knew too that I might, I might.

Somewhere out on the horizon I heard a sound. I leaned forward to hear, but steady, steady, I gripped onto the railing, still I didn't want to fall. I listened hard. Nothing, of course – nothing – but no, maybe, there again? What, a dog barking. A dog. Somewhere, out there, in the distance.

What had I named him? That dog? I couldn't remember.

I couldn't tell whether the dog was inviting me into the water, or telling me to stay safe.

All right, I thought. All right, all right. If I hear the dog bark a third time. If I'm not imagining it after all. Then. Then I won't kill myself.

I waited for a long time.

Come on, I thought. Come on, this is important.

I began to resent the dog. And after I'd tried so hard to ensure it didn't suffer. Bastard.

The moon reappeared, it hadn't drowned itself after all.

I gave up, went back to my cabin, I went to sleep.

THE VERY NEXT night, and there's another knock at my door. And Debra has ignored me all day, with a coldness that's worse than normal – did I do something wrong last night? Was it the kiss? (Was it the sperm?) I can't imagine why she'd be back at my cabin now, and as I open up I'm a little scared and also a little excited.

It isn't Debra, it's Brett, and that's odd, because Brett *never* comes to my cabin, it's like an unspoken rule. He's been crying, I think he's been crying, he's shivering.

"Do you want to come in?" I ask.

He shakes his head. He opens his mouth, head still shaking, he shakes some words out. "She's dead. Oh God, I think she's dead, I think I've killed her."

"What are you talking about?" I ask, although it is perfectly obvious what he's talking about – and I think maybe I can calm him down, but he's grabbing at my hand with his, he's pulling me, and his hand has got blood on it.

He takes me to his cabin. "She's inside," he says, and I'm the one who has to open the door, and that seems a little unfair, I only do it because I like him so much.

There's Debra, on the floor, in a heap, naked. "What did you do to her?" I ask – he tells me it was only a little smack, just a tap on the head really, but there's a big gash on her forehead and there's blood everywhere.

"She told me she'd made her choice. And it wasn't going to be me. And it wasn't going to be you. I want us to die out, she said. I don't want either of you. And if I have babies, I'll keep the girls. But the rest I'll throw overboard, I'll gut them, I'll hang them – she was going to kill our sons! Just so no one can mate any more. Just so it all ends here."

"What do you want me to do?" I ask. And it's meant to come out all harsh and sarcastic, what do you want *me* to do? But I get the inflection wrong, it sounds like I actually want to help, *what* do you want me to do? Ah, balls.

"I've ruined everything," says Brett. "And God is going to be *so* annoyed." And he laughs, and he's still shivering, and I see now he's not so much shivering with shock, he's just excited.

I've dealt with uglier carcasses than Debra's, there was that walrus for one, but she's so still and I don't like to touch her. "Give me a hand," I say. "We'll throw her overboard."

He takes her feet, and that leaves me no choice but to go for the head. As I cradle it, the eyes stutter open. She looks at me, she recognises me. "Help," she whispers, and it's so faint, and it's so scared. "Not me. Him. Then we can be together."

And I realise suddenly that the rules of the game have changed, that now I'm the judge. I thank her for that. I thank her for that power, and the sense that for the first time in months I can shape my own destiny – and that's all I want, I don't care about the destiny of the human race, the hell with the lot of them. I actually thank her, and she smiles.

"Hold her down," I say to Brett, and he does, and I hit Debra hard with my fists, over and over again until I hear something snap, and she stops moving, and none of this is easy for me because I'm really a very gentle fellow.

Debra is heavy and wet with blood, and dragging her onto the deck is hard work and unpleasant. Heaving her up to the railings is something we barely have the strength for, her limbs flap everywhere, and we drop her three times and never over the side. And by now Brett isn't just laughing, there's tears, and I know exactly how he feels.

We've got the body in position now, and it sits drunkenly on the top bar of the railings. "Do you want to do the final words?" I ask, and Brett says no, no, please, no, you do it. I say, "O Father, into thy hands we commend this spirit," and then we give her just a little nudge, and let go, and over she goes, and she manages nearly a full somersault before she hits the water.

The moon is big and brazen tonight, we can see everything. And there's no splash, what we get instead is a dull thud – and Debra doesn't go under the waves at all, it looks as if the sea is rejecting her. "Oh God," says Brett, "oh God!" – and I can't tell whether he's actually trying to start a conversation with the Almighty or merely swearing. I look for any movement, but if Debra wasn't quite dead before she must be now, surely – on impact her body has broken open.

And then – and then, as we watch, there *is* movement. Her body seems to fidget. And then shake all over, as if she's trying to wriggle herself up – but it's the water, the waters beneath her seem to rise, then *bulge*, and Debra is riding the crest of that bulge, and the water is solid and fleshy. It isn't water at all. It's a mountain of bodies, big animals and small, all these varied species, predator and prey and everything in between, but brothers now, all of them packed together tight. And they're writhing. Smashed as Debra's body is, it writhes along with them, for a moment it looks as if it's dancing – the dead jostle beneath, find space for her, and then pull her down.

"Oh God," says Brett again, and this time he *is* praying, and I don't want to interrupt. I have never seen him speak to God before. I always imagined it'd be a peaceful and holy thing. His body goes rigid, his face contorts with the effort of it all. God doesn't make conversation easy, the cruel bastard.

And then it's over, and Brett sags, and gasps for breath, and turns to look at me.

"God says he's not sure about this one," he says. "He needs a little time to think."

WE GO TO my cabin. His cabin is closer, but we're not going back there.

It's difficult to find things to talk about. The game has ended, and so abruptly. I ask Brett if he'd like anything to eat, or maybe a cup of tea? I could make us both a cup of tea. Brett says some tea would be nice.

Brett lies spread-eagled on my bed, but I don't mind, I like Brett. I lie next to him. The kettle boils, but I don't bother to get up.

Brett's still shivering, and so I hold him, and he holds me back, and his arms fit around my body neat and snug.

I think he's the one who kisses first. I think that's the way it is. It's very gentle, there's no tongues or anything, it's perfectly normal and nothing to be ashamed of. His silly blond streaked beard tickles me, I've always loved his beard.

We take things very slowly, we're nuzzling each other with our mouths the way we've seen the wild beasts do, it's not even sexual really. When I take my clothes off Brett doesn't object.

For a man with so long a beard I had expected his body to be hairier. There are a few growths of fur on his chest, just little ones – I twirl them with my finger.

And it's all okay, I think it's all going to be okay – and then suddenly Brett stiffens, and his mouth opens in a silent cry of pain, and I don't know what I've done, how I've broken him – I move away, and free of me his whole body stiffens, and he talks to God for a while.

Then he relaxes, properly relaxes this time. He turns his naked body to me. He smiles.

"It's all right," he says. "God says it's all right. Life will find a way."

And we fall on each other then, and we kiss, and he's so much stronger than any woman I've ever known, and yet softer somehow too. We make love, and it is love, love is what it's for – and for a moment I wonder which of us will be the one who falls pregnant at the end of this, and then I put it out of my head, and in the precious immediacy of the now all thoughts of the future seem so very far away.

THE STRANGER CARDS
NIK VINCENT

Nik's story is a superb little thriller, and I very much recommend that you pay attention to the cards and where they fall. Here a man is played, though it takes him a fair while before he realizes just what sort of game he's in.

"GOOD AFTERNOON, SIR. I'm Benedict Abernathy."

"Junior?" Gough asked, picking up a playing card and turning it face up into the stack in his hand.

"The fourth," said Abernathy.

"East coast name," Gough said, picking up another card from the broken circle on the table in front of him. He made it look effortless, even with his hands manacled.

"Originally," said Abernathy.

"School?" Gough asked, taking another card.

"Stanford Law."

"Need a new deck," Gough said.

Abernathy hadn't yet sat. His attaché case was still in his hand. His Armani suit was pristine apart from the wrinkles behind the knees from the drive from his office in San Francisco to San Quentin. Abernathy looked at the circle of cards with one card at its centre. They were old, greasy and dog-eared with crease marks.

Gough never stopped playing.

"We should go over the details of your appeal," said Abernathy.

Gough picked up the centre card.

"We're done here," he said.

"There's a very limited window of opportunity," said Abernathy.

"Just bring the deck," Gough said.

He turned another card into his hand. It was a king. He gathered the remaining cards and pushed them into their ragged box.

"Guard?" he called.

JAMES GOUGH WAS convicted of killing twenty-seven men in seventeen states. The only connection between the killings was the weapon and the way it was used. The locations appeared to be random. The victims were not known to their killer. They did not have jobs or family circumstances in common, or race, age, religion or sexual orientation. They did not share hobbies, education or political affiliations.

James Gough was convicted after being apprehended in the act of slaughtering his final victim by police officer brothers living in the neighbouring apartment.

"WHAT DO I do?" Abernathy asked his senior partner at Hatch, Willow and Lombard.

"It's a twenty year old case," said Marilyn Cusack. "Gough's getting the injection. This is pro forma, pro bono stuff."

"I have to do something," said Abernathy. "It's his final appeal."

"You're an idealist, Ben. So what did the client ask you to do?" asked Marilyn.

"He asked me to bring him a deck of cards," said Abernathy.

"Then show a little humanity," said Marilyn. "Jeez, Ben. How hard is that? He didn't ask you to save his life. He asked you for a deck of cards."

Abernathy dropped his head.

"You should be ashamed," said Marilyn. "Get the man a deck of cards, Ben, and while you're at it, grow a set."

"Are you dismissing me, Ms Cusack?"

"Not quite," said Marilyn, taking her jacket from its hanger. "First, I'm buying you a drink. It'll be the first of many before this is over. He plays solitaire?"

"Not the conventional version. He picks cards from a circle. A four then a ten, a five, eight, king, seven, eight, ten, two, nine, jack, king. Then he stopped. He boxed the remaining cards."

Marilyn smiled.

"You don't have to impress me with your eidetic memory," she said.

"You know there's no such thing," said Abernathy. "At least, you lose it if you don't use it. It's just an old habit."

"An old habit that got you a 4.0 grade point average, top of your class at Stanford Law, and this case."

"So I get to be responsible for sending Gough to his death," said Abernathy.

"He killed twenty-seven people," said Marilyn.

"And I can't stop his execution," said Abernathy. "But I can give him a deck of cards."

"It's what he wants," said Marilyn. "By the way, it sounds like he was playing Clock Solitaire, a kid's game."

"BENEDICT ABERNATHY THE fourth," said Gough.

"Sir," said Abernathy.

The old playing cards were arranged on the table. Abernathy put his attaché case on the aluminium chair and opened it. He took out a deck of cards. They had been unsealed and checked by a correctional officer, but were otherwise brand new. They were premium casino quality.

He handed the deck to Gough.

Gough took the box and put it on the table. He continued to play his game.

"You can call me Jimmy," he said.

There were only three piles in the circle when Gough turned over the king. He stopped, gathered the remaining cards and boxed them. He placed the battered box on Abernathy's side of the table.

"Fair exchange," he said. "You should play a round or two. Settles the mind."

"I don't know Clock Solitaire," said Abernathy. "We need to talk about the appeal."

"Time Patience, he called it, the man who taught me. He was close to death, too," said Gough. "I'll show you how."

"You're on death row, sir," said Abernathy. "Time is pressing."

"Call me Jimmy," said Gough. "I've had my time. Humour me. Let an old man teach you something. Learn some patience. Time Patience." He chuckled, a soft, warm sound.

Abernathy remembered the shame he'd felt sitting in Marilyn Cusack's office.

"Show me," he said.

Gough took the new deck of cards from its box and shuffled them.

"This game's all about the passing of time," he began, "and whether it will ever end. Sometimes it do and sometimes it don't. That's how he taught me with that very deck." He gestured at the old cards. "There's four suits in a deck and thirteen cards in a suit. That's twelve spots on the clock and time left over for eternity."

"The centre stack?" asked Abernathy.

"You catch on quick," said Gough.

He dealt the top four cards.

"First the queen spot," he said. "That's north, women, heaven, twelve o'clock." He dealt the next four cards and put them on the table. "Next comes south at six o'clock."

"Hell," said Abernathy.

"Don't interrupt," said Gough.

He dealt four more cards and placed them at three o'clock.

"Then east and west for balance."

He placed the next four cards at nine o'clock.

"Then comes the ace spot, at one o'clock, the queen's right hand. That's for parents, for wisdom, for time gone by," said Gough.

Abernathy wanted to correct him. If the queen was at twelve o'clock then one o'clock was to her left. It was to the player's right. He said nothing.

Gough continued filling the spaces around the clock.

"Then comes the jack at eleven o'clock, the queen's left hand. That's for the kids, for innocence, for time to come," said Gough.

Four cards remained in Gough's hands.

"See these four cards?" he asked. "They're for all eternity. They're the king cards."

He placed the stack of four cards in the empty space at the centre of the clock.

"That's you, the player?" asked Abernathy.

"Lord, no," said Gough. "They're the stranger cards. They're the beginning and the end. It's what happens in-between what counts. If you pick up the last stranger card and there's still cards face down, there's no forever. Play the last stranger card right at the end, that takes you into eternity."

"So how do we start?" asked Abernathy.

"We start by dipping into all eternity," said Gough. He picked the top card off the centre stack and turned it into his hand. It was a four. He took a card off the four position on the clock: a queen. He took a card from the twelve position: a nine.

Abernathy watched as the cards piled up in Gough's hand.

"It's simple," he said.

"The best things are," said Gough. "Birth, love, death. Take the old cards. Play until you reach eternity."

Gough took the final eternity card from the centre of the clock. It was a two. He continued to play.

"Let me make the best appeal I can for you," said Abernathy. "Give me something new to work with."

Gough held up the final king. There were five piles of cards still on the table.

"I'm a dead man," said Gough. "I don't remember what I did, nor why. I only know what they told me. Play the game, Benedict Abernathy the fourth. Reach for eternity. See how it feels."

Abernathy put the ancient deck of cards in his attaché case. He talked as he watched Gough play several more rounds of Time Patience. But none of them played out, and Gough didn't answer any of his questions.

"You got it?" Gough finally asked.

"I've got it, sir," said Abernathy. He'd got it almost as soon as Gough had begun playing.

"Call me Jimmy," said Gough. "You sure you got it, now?"

"I've got it," said Abernathy.

"Guard?" said Gough, boxing his new deck of cards.

ABERNATHY SAT AT his desk waiting for the call. He'd filed the paperwork. And he was sure of the outcome. He waited, a rock in his gut, sweat collecting in the armpits of his Zegna shirt, despite the air conditioning.

He remembered his meetings with Gough. He heard the old man's words: *You should play a round or two. Settles the mind.*

Benedict Abernathy opened his desk drawer and took out Gough's beaten up deck of cards. He took them out of their box and shuffled them. He cleared a space on his desk and began to lay out the cards. As he made the clock, he remembered Gough's words. Then he began to play.

The first round did not play out, nor the second or third. The games only took a matter of minutes. Abernathy became engrossed. He set the cards out in the same way, every time, replaying Gough's words. After an hour, the rock in his stomach started to melt.

He began to play slowly, stacking the cards meticulously. He placed the compass cards a little wider than the number cards so that the circle turned into a star. It made it easier to recognise which stack was which when the piles began to disappear. As he slowed down, Abernathy's eidetic memory kicked in, and he remembered the card sequences of the games.

Still, no round played out.

Abernathy began to wonder what the probability was that a round might play out.

He was working out the odds on a legal pad when Marilyn Cusack walked into his office. She did not knock.

It was several seconds before Abernathy realised that someone was standing in the room. He looked up. There was silence between them for a moment.

"The call came in?" he asked.

"Yes," she said.

"When will they execute him?" he asked.

"May twenty-second at midnight," said Marilyn.

"I'll attend," said Abernathy.

"Of course, Ben," said Marilyn.

"Thank you," said Ben.

"Put that away," said Marilyn. "Come for a drink."

"Thank you," said Ben, again.

On May twenty-second 2012, Benedict Abernathy sat in his room at the Best Western in Novato, waiting to drive out to San Quentin for James Gough's execution.

Marilyn Cusack had insisted that he take time off afterwards to recover. He had made no plans, but he knew he didn't want to be at the office or at home. He wanted to be somewhere anonymous.

He sat on the bed and took out Gough's old cards. He hadn't played since the afternoon the call had come in. It had helped. Abernathy shuffled the cards and began to lay them out, remembering Gough's words. They came easily to his mind, like a mantra.

This game's all about the passing of time, and whether it will ever end.

Abernathy played slowly for an hour, as if it was a ritual. He remembered the sequences of the cards that he played. When he played an ace, he thought about his parents, his mentors. He thought about Marilyn Cusack. When he turned up a queen he thought about the girls he'd loved, from Priya Kupertharmal in fifth grade to Beth Geter, who had left for Baltimore three months ago and didn't want a long distance relationship. When he played a jack he thought of Gerard and Stephanie, his younger siblings, and of Elizabeth, his older sister's baby.

The kings made him cringe.

9-queen-2-10-ace-4-king... 9-10-ace-7-queen-jack-7-6-king... ace-8-10-6-7-9-jack-9-3-5-5-queen-ace-6... A long run. 8-queen-king... 7-8-2-2-4-4-3-jack-2-10-3-5-8-3-jack... So close.

Benedict Abernathy wondered if he'd make it to the end of the game at last.

4-6-5-king.

The king was his ticket to eternity.

He smiled. He put the cards in their box and dropped it in his attaché case. He checked his watch. There was time to shower and change before the fifteen minute drive to the prison.

"I NEED A drink," he said. "It's all over the internet, TV, everywhere."

"It's okay, Ben. It's the culture we live in." Marilyn put on her jacket as she spoke, and minutes later they were sitting in the bar.

"It's a copycat killing, right?" asked Abernathy. "Why not do it the night of the execution? He killed using Gough's method, in his honour, so why wait?"

"Who knows?" said Marilyn. "Who knows if it was a copycat? The press gets hold of these things and twists them. It could be a coincidence."

"Maybe the killer couldn't do it that same night, because he was at the execution," said Abernathy. "But why San Diego?"

"You can't torture yourself," said Marilyn. "You're not responsible. And, not for nothing, you're not law enforcement. He'll be caught and prosecuted to the full extent of the law."

"Like James Gough was," said Abernathy.

Marilyn gestured to the bartender.

"Just remember, you're a defense attorney," said Marilyn. "You're one of the good guys."

"I was there that night," said Abernathy as the bartender poured more drinks.

"I know, Ben," said Marilyn. "I can see the effect it's having on you."

"No... I mean I was in San Diego the night of the copycat murder," said Ben. "I left the prison at about one in the morning. I got in my car and I drove all night. I don't know how, but I ended up in San Diego... At least I woke up there the following day with a sore head and no memory."

"Huh," said Marilyn.

"Is that all you can say?" asked Abernathy.

"What do you want me to say, Ben?" asked Marilyn.

"Nothing," said Ben. "I just want you to get drunk with me."

"That I can do," said Marilyn.

"It's good to have you back," said Marilyn. It was seven-thirty on Abernathy's first day in the office after his vacation. "I'm finishing for the day, and I want to catch you up on some things. Buy me a drink."

"You're the boss," said Abernathy.

"Bet your life," said Marilyn.

"You heard that your copy-cat turned into a serial?" asked Marilyn during their second drink.

Abernathy looked at her.

"It seems to be local, though."

"San Diego?" asked Abernathy.

"California," said Marilyn. "It hasn't hit the press, yet. There was a fatal stabbing in Arcadia. It looked domestic, but some bright spark made a connection to the San Diego murder."

"How did you find out?" asked Abernathy.

"You don't get to be senior partner at a law firm with offices in five cities without making a few contacts," said Marilyn.

There was a long pause.

Marilyn caught Abernathy's eye.

"No," he finally said.

"You okay, Ben?" asked Marilyn.

"Just tired," said Ben. "When was the murder?"

"June twenty-eighth. I'm surprised you didn't hear about it. You were in Los Angeles, right?"

"Visiting my sister," said Ben. "Maybe thirty minutes from Arcadia. I didn't hear."

"I guess not," said Marilyn.

HE'S FOLLOWING ME around. It's not a coincidence. Someone knows I let Gough die, and he's following me around. I was the attorney of record, Gough's last hope. I got him executed. It's retribution, and now people are dying because of me.

The killer was at the execution. He followed me to San Diego. He knew I was in Los Angeles, so he picked a target close by.

Benedict Abernathy rehearsed what he would say. He thought about saying it to Marilyn Cusack. She might understand. He could get the list of witnesses at the execution. But what if it wasn't a witness? What if it was one of the picketers standing outside San Quentin with a placard? Was there a list of those people too?

It was too out there. It sounded ridiculous in his mind. If he said the words out loud... He was an attorney. He was very junior. He had a career path mapped out. He'd get fired.

He'd wait. There'd be another murder, maybe in San Francisco.

There was nothing.

He scoured the press for news of murders, of stabbings. He looked at all the local news feeds for California. He made contacts in the homicide division. Nothing matched Gough's M.O.

BENEDICT ABERNATHY'S HEAD buzzed. He felt nervous and twitchy. It was the same feeling he'd had when he'd woken up in San Diego. The same feeling when he'd got home from staying with his sister in Los Angeles.

He showered and dressed. He thought the blackouts had stopped. He thought they were stress related, because of Gough, the execution. That was three, four months ago. He tried to remember what he'd done over the weekend. It was a blank. He checked his phone. It was switched off. When he turned it on there were texts and messages. He'd missed the Giants/Dodgers game on Saturday. Hell! How did that happen? He loved baseball, and rarely missed a home game. He didn't even know the score. He'd also missed taking the Fillimore Art Walk with Penny on Sunday, yesterday, and she was pissed.

Two days. I lost two whole days.

"YOUR COPYCAT JUST went national," said Marilyn Cusack.

"What?" asked Abernathy.

They were back in the bar. He hadn't wanted to come, but when she'd seen the look on his face Marilyn had insisted. It had been a long day, making calls, excusing his absence from the game to his buddies, sucking up to Penny. Mostly he felt relief.

He was only half-listening to Marilyn. He was watching the news scroll along the bottom of the screen on the tv above the bar.

MAN SLAIN IN COPYCAT HOME INVASION MURDER IN ROCKY FORD COLORADO SUNDAY...

Then the screen changed to show a young woman reporter standing in front of police tape at a city apartment building.

"Can you turn up the volume?" Abernathy asked the bartender.

"Twice married father of one, Spencer Hackford was slain in his home right behind me, here in Rocky Ford. His father Stanley Hackford and son Elliot were visiting Colorado Springs during yesterday afternoon when the home invasion took place. They discovered the body of Spencer Hackford and raised the alarm. This is the third murder bearing the hallmark of serial killer James Gough, executed at San Quentin on May 22nd."

Queen, queen, jack, ace, king. Abernathy shook the thought out of his mind. He'd never seen those cards come up in that order in any of James Gough's rounds of Time Patience, or any of his own. It was just the mention of his client's name, and the buzzy feeling in his head.

"Turn it off, please," said Marilyn.

"This wouldn't be happening if I'd got the sentence commuted," said Abernathy.

"Sure it would," said Marilyn. "This shit always happens. The man's a psychopath. You think he wouldn't be killing anyway?"

MAY 23, SAN Diego CA.
June 28, Arcadia CA.
September 9, Rocky Ford CO.

Abernathy started a list. He began to add details. At least he wasn't being followed. It was a relief. But if he could fit together enough of the details, maybe he could find a pattern. All the victims were men, all married, but the third had been married twice. All had parents still living. Two were fathers of only children.

He went online to find out whatever he could about the victims. He checked their memorial pages, Linked-In, Facebook, YouTube. He Googled them and their families, their colleagues, even the schools they'd attended. He made charts of their birthdays and their parents' and wives' and children's birthdays. He listed the towns they'd lived in, where they were born, their cellphone providers and their death dates. He compared the charts. Nothing fit together.

The details swam in his head constantly.

Time passed. He counted the days. There had been thirty-six days between the first and second murders. Thirty-six days passed. Seventy-three days passed, marking off the time between the second and third murders. One-hundred and nine days passed, marking off the time between the first and third murders. It was the week before Christmas and there hadn't been a fourth murder.

On December twenty-first at the end of her regular staff meeting, Marilyn Cusack asked Abernathy to stay behind for a few minutes.

"Tell me something about James Gough, something weird or funny from one of your meetings," she said.

"I'm sorry?" said Abernathy.

"Listen, Ben," said Marilyn. "I've drawn one of the named partners for secret Santa. It's my worst nightmare. What do you buy Leonard Lombard for Christmas when he can, literally, afford whatever he wants? But he likes stories. Stories and deodands. Do you even know what a deodand is? Except for a high scoring SAT word?"

"It's an object that causes a person's death," said Abernathy.

"Good for you, Mr Eidetic Memory. But I was hoping you could give me a great lawyer story," said Marilyn. "What about that game Gough played? Did you find out if it was Clock Solitaire?"

"I'll be right back," said Abernathy.

He returned two minutes later, and handed Marilyn James Gough's old deck of cards.

"Give him this," he said. "It's the deck of cards Gough played with. It was Clock Solitaire, but he called it Time Patience. He learned it from the man who gave him this deck, and he swapped it for the new deck of casino cards he asked me for."

"You're a life saver, Ben. Thank you," said Marilyn.

"It's nothing," said Ben. "I just want to forget about it now."

"You're sure you don't want them as a... keepsake?" asked Marilyn.

"Absolutely sure," said Abernathy.

BENEDICT ABERNATHY WOKE up with the weird buzzy feeling in his head. A feeling that he hadn't had in seven months. He tried to sit up, but his neck and back ached, and he seemed to be wearing shoes. He opened his eyes. He was not lying in his bed at home.

Abernathy scrambled into a sitting position and looked around. He did not know where he was. He was surrounded by people, too many people.

"You okay, dude?" someone asked. He looked like a student... older, maybe a grad student or a drop out.

"No," said Abernathy.

"Where you headed?" asked the man.

"Why?" asked Abernathy. "Where am I?"

"Wow, dude, you musta been trippin'," said the man. "You're in Texas. San Antonio airport. There was a big storm yesterday. No flights in or out."

The colour drained from Abernathy's face. He didn't have any luggage. He searched through his pockets and found a plane ticket for San Francisco, dated April third.

"Today's the fourth?" he asked.

"All day long," said the man. He looked over Abernathy's shoulder. "Hey, San Francisco. Me too. We're on the same flight. Should be any time now."

The flight took a little over three and a half hours. The fifteen mile cab ride downtown from the airport took another hour in traffic. Abernathy was disorientated, and exhausted. He needed to go home to shower and change before he could show up at the office. He found his phone. It was turned off. When he turned it on the battery was fully charged, but there were calls and messages dating back three days. Marilyn Cusack's secretary had called him repeatedly.

The apartment was too quiet, and the effects of his blackout were freaking Abernathy out. He turned on the TV, and went to the bathroom. He stood under the shower for twenty minutes, trying to remember. Nothing.

He pulled a robe on and walked back through the apartment towards the welcome sound of the TV.

"... in San Antonio, yesterday. This is thought to be the fourth of the James Gough copycat murders. Now over to Carey Coulson for the sports news. Carey?"

Abernathy sat heavily on the couch. He reached for the remote and switched to an all-news channel. There it was, scrolling across the bottom of the screen.

FOURTH COPYCAT MURDER IN TEXAS. FIFTY-TWO YEAR OLD WIDOWED FATHER OF TWO KILLED IN HIS SAN ANTONIO HOME, WEDNESDAY.

Jack, jack, king, four, three.

Benedict Abernathy shook his head. Cards. Why couldn't he stop thinking about cards.

7-8-2-2-4-4-3...

Four, three: April third. The date of the murder in San Antonio was four three. The sixth and seventh numbers were the date.

Abernathy slumped on the couch and let his head drop back. He closed his eyes. The sequence of cards from the game of

Time Patience he'd played on the day of Gough's execution began to run through his mind.

9-queen-2-10-ace-4-king.

There was no sixth number. Four numbers. Five digits.

9-10-ace-7-queen-jack-7-6-king.

There was no sixth number, but there was a sixth digit. Six for the month of June.

Ace-8-10-6-7-9-jack-9-3...

The sixth number was nine and the seventh was three. The third murder was committed on September ninth. The sixth and seventh digits were both nines for September ninth.

What do the first five digits mean? What has five digits? Abernathy sat for a moment. Then he got up to find his laptop. His legs felt like jelly, and he couldn't swallow.

He found his laptop and sat down again. It took three attempts to type, 'what code has five digits' into Google. Six of the results on the first page referred to zip codes.

Abernathy tried to breathe. He tried to swallow. He tried to type the first set of five numbers into the search field followed by 'zip code'. He had to backspace several times before he got it right.

92104 was the zip code for San Diego. 91077 matched Arcadia. 81067 was for Rocky Ford and 78224 was for San Antonio.

Abernathy threw the laptop to one side. It dropped to the floor as he staggered to the bathroom and threw up in the toilet. There was no vomit, only bile and mucus. He hadn't eaten. He had slept afterwards. He didn't remember what he'd done or how he'd done it. But he knew.

Benedict Abernathy crawled from the bathroom to his bed, and slept fitfully for a few hours. The buzz in his head was less when he woke. The memory of what he had learned came back fast. Then the card sequence started to play in his mind again.

He got out of bed, and, still dressed in the robe, he found his way back to the couch, grabbing a legal pad and pencil on the way. First he wrote out the card sequence of the single game of Time Patience that he had played out to its conclusion. Then he bracketed and circled the cards he could account for. The first two murders were solved.

He wanted to know everything about the killings in Rocky Ford and San Antonio.

His cellphone began ringing at eight-fifteen. He switched it off, and worked.

Spencer Hackford lived at 35, 56th street, apartment 8. He had been married and divorced twice. He had a son and both of his parents were still living. His father resided at his address. His mother suffered from Alzheimer's and lived in a residential care home.

He drew too many blanks on the latest murder. It was too soon. He scoured the news channels and the internet, but there was too little information.

Abernathy closed his laptop.

HE REMEMBERED JAMES Gough's words, *I don't remember what I did, nor why. I only know what they told me. Play the game, Benedict Abernathy the fourth. Reach for eternity. See how it feels.*

Twenty-seven murders. Gough had played the game to its conclusion seven times. Who would the twenty-eighth victim have been? Who had lived when he should have died? Who didn't get his shot at eternity?

Abernathy opened his laptop and typed 'James Gough' into the search field. He would have to wait for more information on his own fourth victim to work out what all the cards meant. And while he waited, he could study Gough's case. He could work out the card sequences that drove Gough's killings, and maybe, just maybe he could find the missing stranger.

The cards... Who gave Gough the cards?

Oh my God! Gough's cards!

Abernathy switched on his cellphone and dialled Marilyn's direct line at the office.

"Marilyn Cusack," said Marilyn.

"It's Ben Abernathy."

"Where the hell have you been?" asked Marilyn.

"Don't ask questions," said Abernathy. "Just tell me, did you give Leonard Lombard Gough's deck of cards at Christmas?"

"Of course I did. I printed off the instructions for Clock Solitaire from the internet and slipped them in the deck. I wrote on the gift tag, 'Play James Gough's game with this killer deck of cards'. He loved it... Are you still there, Abernathy?"

BENEDICT ABERNATHY HAD killed four times. But it wasn't him, it was the cards. He knew that if he could learn to live with himself, he would never get caught. He knew that he would never learn to live with himself until he had destroyed Gough's deck of cards.

Christmas was more than three months ago. Time was wasting.

Abernathy switched off his phone and opened his laptop. He typed 'Leonard Lombard' into the Google search field.

ALL THINGS FALL APART AND ARE BUILT AGAIN

HELEN MARSHALL

When there is next to nothing left, some will still play out of a sense of desperation, or for the very few resources that remain. Here Lydia is a pawn, passed between players, but she has an inner strength and a sense of survival. Helen's bleak story holds poetry too, and shows why many consider her to be one of the most exciting new writers in genre.

THEY WERE OLD devils then, all of them, old the way all old men were, with steel hair and skin like damp paper dried too quickly, with knuckles that bulged like crab apples and cracked and pained them when the weather was cold. Old devils. They sat in the back room, drank whiskey, tossed knucklebones and smoked cigarettes they rolled themselves. The oldest of them had red fingers stained purple with nicotine. His starved body – it was a time of famine, after all – would shudder as he dragged the smoke out, held it in the cauldron of his lungs, and released with a choking sigh.

Old men they might be, but they were devils nonetheless. Lydia – known once for her beauty and now for her heavy pour – recognized them at once.

Lydia had inherited from Mother a paper theatre, which she kept in her hovelly little house in the middle of the city. The theatre was beautiful, ornamented in blue and lavender and green. It presented another world: a world of feasting where a foil moon glittered in a sky filled with silver, angled stars. Lydia had lost Mother's actors many years ago but replacements of one sort or another had come to occupy the stage. Her favourite was a pewter devil, cold to touch and shiny where she held it, no bigger than a thimble. It had come out of a Christmas cracker – a strange place for it, perhaps, but Lydia supposed that devils got up to all sorts of no good and perhaps showing up in a Christmas cracker, the last of its kind, a fine one too, all wrapped in crepe paper, was just one more instance of it.

The devils were called Jack, Old Jack, Smiling Jack and Jack the Handsome. They were pure brimstone thugs: not good men but red men, red from head to toe, letting whiskey pour over their red lips, never tipping, never smiling, never kindness for the ones serving, used up by the world and done with the use of it. Lydia understood this about them. It was the same for her. Once she had been beautiful. She had been married then, to a man with clear blue eyes and horn-rimmed glasses that gave him the scholarly air of a teacher. She had been taken in by his shy smiles, his sweet innocence. But time had worn the varnish off both of them, and the years of want had turned him cruel.

The devils were cruel too. They were cruel and they were hungry, but Lydia loved them anyway.

THE GAME THE devils played was knucklebones. This was what Jack the Handsome – her favourite, aptly named, with his red patent leather shoes and moustache silver as frost – told her on the first day of serving.

"Knucklebones, hey? Mother played. Before she died," Lydia said.

"Not like this," drawled another – Old Jack – humourlessly. That one wore a red Panama hat pulled down at the front. Of all of them, he frightened Lydia most. She got the feeling when his eyes landed on her that a horde of flies had alighted on her skin. "None play as we do," he said. "None but one and that weren't your mother, to be sure."

"Aren't you hungry?" she asked. "How can you play like that, all day?"

"Today we play, so tomorrow we may eat. Now pour us a drink and mind your tongue. There's good meat there to make our supper, if you aren't careful."

So Lydia poured out the whiskey for them, and none said a word further as she watched. The four knucklebones flew up in the air.

"Venus and the Vulture," said Jack (just Jack) and Old Jack patted him consolingly on the shoulder.

"It goes that way for all of us at one point or another," said the other.

Lydia watched them throw, and as she stood there, dead on her feet, watching the devils with their knotted fingers scrabbling after the bones, there was a thing that Lydia remembered.

It had been early in her marriage when this thing happened. One night she had come home several hours after her shift. She had told that husband of hers the city bus had broken down. He had been sleepy and charming then, blinking at her through the horn-rimmed glasses, and smiling like a little prince. He told her to sit, and she sat. He poured her a drink, and she drank it. Then he took her little finger carefully between his thumb and forefinger.

"Lady, lady, lady," he said coaxingly, lovingly even, "this little piggy went to market."

She was almost lulled by the sweet dreaminess of his voice. But only almost. Almost because he got it wrong, and her husband was not a man to get things wrong. She knew he was supposed to be playing that old game with the toes, as Mother had when Lydia was young. But Lydia didn't want to correct him. After all she'd walked three miles in her heels already, so her feet were aching. There were, she imagined, ugly blisters growing like mushrooms on the underside of her big toe. It would be better if he played with the fingers, better, yes, than seeing her poor feet.

He did the next finger – the little piggy who stayed home, chuckling mildly about how *she* should've stayed home too, just like the piggy – and the next finger too, the one circled by Mother's amethyst ring. She laughed, then, because she didn't want him to see the blisters. And his voice was *so* sweet, sweet enough that she was smiling up at him when he reached the little piggy who had none, and he snapped the finger back so viciously that it made a sound like dry wood cracking under the weight of heavy snow.

This was the first time she saw the snake, you see. Had she known about the snake she never would have smiled like that for him. She never would have let him sit her down.

The day after it happened, that finger swelled up like a sausage until she could get barely get the bus change from her purse. But it wasn't the pain she remembered, not the sharp flare or the dull throb. It was the sound her finger made. The sound and the look of it. The way he had jammed it up at that awkward, horrible angle – upright like a flagpole.

And this memory came to her when Lydia saw the devil playing knucklebones. Old Jack tossed the bones up in the air – they gleamed like old teeth, floated in the air like the Cheshire cat's smile – and as he went to catch them on the back of his hand (like Mother had, Lydia remembered, when she used to play), his fingers turned up, one by one by one just as Lydia's had when her husband was cruel. Except with the devil, there was no awful crunch, just the red fingers curling into a terrible, backward fist, curling back so his hand looked like an overturned beetle, the fingers all twisting the way no fingers, no human fingers can twist, around the knucklebones when they fell.

Old Jack counted the pips carefully as the bones lay on the back of his big, red hand. When he announced the number, the other Jacks nodded. They sipped their whiskey. The knucklebones passed between them.

Jack the Handsome smiled at her.

WHEN THEY HAD finished and the cups were overturned, the whiskey bottle empty, Old Jack touched the brim of his red Panama hat, and declared Jack the Handsome the winner.

Lydia took Jack the Handsome home that night. There was no reason for it, really, except that he had smiled at her as he threw the bones. When Lydia took off his jacket and unbuttoned his shirt, his bare chest was red – as red as a hot plate. His fingers left red marks where they touched her skin: her neck, her shoulders, her breasts, her buttocks. She wondered if he would turn her red inside as well, first with his fingers, and then with his prick, like a roman candle burning on a starless night.

When it was over, she felt shy. She turned away from him, and hid her body – old as well, her skin pale and loose as a badly pressed shirt – beneath the covers. He said very little. His silence was red too.

After he had left, Lydia stood on the sagging porch and smoked a half-used cigarette she had saved. The cigarette tasted the way Jack the Handsome tasted. Everything tasted of ash. She looked at the midnight sky which was black and empty. There had been stars once. She remembered there had been stars when she was a child and not just in the paper theatre – but that was a long time ago, and she had lost so many things since then that the stars seemed to be the least of what had gone missing.

The cigarette burnt to the filter after a few puffs, and Lydia produced a second, which she lit upon the glowing stub of the first. She did not go inside.

Inside Mother would be waiting.

*   *   *

"Atropos and the Hound," called Jack as his bones came down and his fingers curled around them. "A bad sign."

Mother had died many years ago.

Lydia remembered the smell most of all, heavy and earthen: rotting chestnuts in the autumn. Mother had not had an easy sick bed. The disease ate her away piece by piece. Her face grew wan and tallow and her fingers curved into hooks. Lydia had sat by her when she could, and had poured cool water into a spoon which she would place between Mother's cracked lips.

Mother whispered things to her sometimes, "I remember when you wanted to be a dancer, dearest, when will you dance again, oh, when will you dance again?"

Lydia had never wanted to be a dancer, or if she had once, it had been as a child in the days Mother had fashioned the theatre for her. That dream had been abandoned so long ago that it meant nothing to her now. She supposed it was the pain that made Mother say those things, or the disease, or perhaps it was merely that the dream had lived within Mother for a very long time, and both those things had scraped away the silence that prevented her from speaking about it. In any case, Lydia's feet had all the grace of birds with broken wings, and wherever the fancy may have come from, there was no chance of it amounting to much in this late stage of the game.

When Mother died, Lydia had buried her in the local cemetery in the heart of the city in a small plot. There were only a few who wore black that day and left flowers by her side, most of them old women from the neighbourhood who would join Mother soon enough. They huddled together, mumbled their prayers. And then there had been a sound, a wild howling, and at first Lydia had taken the sound for grief. In that awful moment, she had wished it had been *her* making that sound, that *she* had summoned up that long, soulless shriek for the mother who had washed her and fed her and brushed her hair. Lydia's lips had been clenched furiously shut. It had not been her.

But it had not been *them* either. The women had glanced fearfully at one another.

Then Lydia saw – feral dogs, a hungry pack of four. The leader was a mean old mutt, his hair a matted mess of dirt and filth over a raw, skeletal form. His lips turned up in a hideous grin, tongue lolling, that same look of stupid cruelty she would see on her husband's face in the years to come. The dog had looked at her with a red spark of hatred in his eyes.

That look had said, *This place is ours now. You may have claimed it once, but you are no longer strong enough to hold it.*

That look had said, *Bury your dead here, and we shall dig them out again to gnaw upon their bones.*

That look had said, *This is what famine brings.*

The women had scattered before the dogs, and their black dresses had fluttered in the wind like the wings of crows.

Years later, Lydia told that story to her husband. He had laughed at this, gently, and he had taken her hand in his. "They're taking back all the old spaces," he had said to her. "Wild boars in Berlin, I've heard, and wolves in the alleyways – all manner of things that we thought we had banished, they're coming back, I've heard, they're all coming back. Oh, lady, even in the heart of the places we tamed, there's a hunger growing."

It was not so long after that Lydia had stabbed her husband seven times and left him in the same cemetery. She hoped the dogs had found him. She hoped they had kept their promise.

SOFTLY, SOFTLY, LYDIA entered the house, ash thick on her fingers from the cigarette. The light from the porch was weak and watery, touching the old wooden table, the chipped rims of the tea cups and bowls. Beneath the window sat the old paper theatre, the stiff curtains curling with age, the drawn balcony fading with the first bloom of rot. The evening's half-light seemed to set the silhouette of the silver devil dancing.

Mother sat nearby with her blind eyes fixed upon the scene, watching the temptation of a cut-out princess – all the stories with devils were stories of temptation – an ancient quilt piled over her knees, just as Lydia left her. Mother's mouth was a ruined mess, black as a crack in the earth, and her eyes rolled white as smoothed pebbles.

What have you been up to this night, dearest? Who have you been seeing?

"Please don't ask me, Mother."

You were a beautiful child once.

"We were all beautiful children once," Lydia told her. She plucked the devil from the stage and set him upon her palm. The little fellow seemed to wink at her, and the expression sent an odd fluttering through Lydia's belly.

Do you still love me, child?

"Of course, Mother."

You needn't love me anymore if you don't want to. I'm old and ruined and of no use to anyone. Then, almost querulously, *You buried me once.*

"That was a long time ago."

Lydia kissed the devil once, her lips touching upon his lightly shining shoulders, and then she went to bed. Mother did not sleep. Hunger gnawed at her. Lydia could hear her moan through the shut door.

"Has it always been like this?" Lydia asked her husband once. They had eaten very little that day, but they still remembered what it had been like to feast. There were bad days, yes, but there were still good days. Some. And, because the hunger was not so bad, he spoke to her as the scholar.

"Once there were stars in the sky," he told her.

"I remember."

"Once there was enough to eat," he told her.

"How did things change?"

"I cannot say." He held her lightly in his arms then, and he stroked her hair. His skin was soft, warm and the touch gentled her. "There is a story I read once, in an ancient book."

"When?"

"A long time ago."

"What happened?"

"There was an ancient kingdom."

"How ancient?"

"Shush now, and listen," he whispered into her ear. "A famine came to the ancient kingdom, but the king was very wise. He divided the people and he said to them that on one day they would play so that their hearts would be light and on the other day they would eat so that their stomachs would be heavy. In that way, the people survived and the king helped them through their suffering."

"Did the hunger abate?" she could not help but ask.

"It did not," he told her, "they played and they starved for seven years."

"And at the end of it?"

"The king feared for his people. They had grown old and tired and you could count the bones of their ribs like tally sticks. He saw how hungry they were, how close they were to becoming wild things – the gleam in their eyes when they looked on one another. So he took half of them, the best half, those whom fortune had favoured in their throws, and he sent them to find a new land where there would be enough food to feed them."

"Did they find it?" she asked, shivering. His fingers were now gently kneading her breasts, rolling her nipples into hard little pearls.

"I don't know," her husband said, and he said very little afterward, for his mouth was against her neck, and then her lips, and it frightened her to feel his kiss even though he was still a good man. It frightened her how close she would let his teeth come.

LYDIA DID NOT speak to Jack the Handsome in the days following. There was no reason to speak to him. She let the red silence grow between them in the long hours as she served the whiskey and watched them play. Watched them toss the knucklebones between them one after another.

"Aphrodite," Old Jack would call.

"The King in Waiting," said Jack the Handsome.

"And Carrion for me, least lucky of all," said Smiling Jack.

Lydia stood by Jack the Handsome while they played. She served his drink first. She cleared his glass last. She let him touch her sometimes, and then counted the marks on her skin afterward. It wasn't happiness, but it wasn't loneliness either. She felt she was a pinhole. Someone was pressing a lidless eye to her, never blinking, staring upon the world as she did. Inside her, she could feel something coming to life as she watched him play, something stirring. Perhaps it was desire, possibly terror even, but it was more than she had had before, more than the numbness and so she nurtured it.

When the evening was through, they never left any coins for her even though they had become, over time, her only customers. She did not mind. They were red men, after all, hungry men, old men, and while such things might have mattered to her a long time ago they didn't matter much anymore.

Jack the Handsome went with her sometimes – not every night, but on the nights when he was the victor. He never offered and she never asked, but he went with her anyway, and Lydia would let him strip the dress from her body and cover her nakedness with his own bright red flesh. As she did this, she would sometimes hear Mother pounding her ancient fists against the table in the other room, shrieking, *Daughter, where are you? I cannot find you!* or else, *I'm so hungry I think I might die!* They were words from a nightmare.

"Was it always like this?" Lydia would ask Jack the Handsome.

"There have always been times of feasting," he would say slowly, his voice raw as smoke, "and times of famine. It is the way of things."

And even as Jack the Handsome touched her neck, her shoulders, her breasts, her buttocks, Lydia would imagine the flesh falling away from Mother's hands until only the bone glinted there – oh, the mess she would have to clean up when all this was finished, the mess of loose skin piled like creased receipts on the table. On these days she wished the dogs had found Mother, had dug her out and gnawed at her bones as they had promised, had broken her up and licked the marrow from the wreckage so that her legs could not have carried her home again.

THE SUN ROSE sluggish and late after another starless night and spread a thin, gray light upon the city. Lydia rose and washed her face, and took the city bus to work. The devils sat where they always sat, the four tumbled bones lying on the scarred table top. But this time, as Lydia fetched the bottle of whiskey and, leaning in close, began to pour, Old Jack stopped her, his backward fingers curling fast around her wrist.

"Someone is sick with a brood of puppies," he drawled, and the brim of the red Panama hat shaded his eyes so Lydia could not tell if he meant it kindly or not.

"What?" she asked.

"Someone is growing heavy and ripe," said Jack.

"Someone is blossoming," said Smiling Jack.

Jack the Handsome said nothing.

Lydia did not know what to make of this. Her body was barren as Zoar, like a field that had been salted by the enemy. Nothing could grow there.

That night, even though Jack the Handsome emerged the victor once more, he did not return to Lydia's bed. Instead, as she opened the door to her house, lonely, longing for his red breath, his red touch, there was Mother, waiting.

Someone is coming to dinner, Mother said, and she sniffed the air through nostrils that had been eaten ragged by time.

"No, Mother," she said, "I'm too old for that. No one is coming to dinner."

Someone's coming, Mother replied, *and sooner than we'd like. There won't be enough to feed all of us. This is a time of famine, dearest, and the smallest will have to go hungry.*

"THE ROBBER BRIDEGROOM," said Old Jack with a snarl as he cradled the bones in the upturned bowl of his hand. He had played badly that night, and he knew it. There would be no way to recover.

LYDIA HAD ONLY felt like this once before. Back then, her stomach had grown fat and jellied as an egg sac. Her breasts had been heavy with milk. It was a bad time. She had been able to bring little enough home, and her scholar of a husband had only sat and read his books. But when he saw the milk leaking from her breasts, oh, how her husband had loved her then, unknowing, ignorant, but appreciative of the gifts that early motherhood had bestowed upon her. He had sucked her dry, and licked the juices from her. "Oh, lady, how pretty you are this morning," he had said to her. "How I wouldn't mind it at all if you stayed by my side today. Off to work so early? Off to catch that damned bus of yours?"

"Yes," she had replied meekly.

"Stay with me."

"There will be no supper on the table," she tried to tell him.

"Come here, and we'll dance away the hunger, won't we, lady? Come here and I'll show you the steps."

"You might hurt me," she said.

"I might hurt you if you don't," he told her, grinning a boyish grin. "You've been growing so fat, you must have something on you, mustn't you? Now come share with me, won't you? Come let us have a taste."

And so she had stayed that day, she had stayed, and they had danced a while just like he promised. He had touched her, and his teeth had stayed close, and at one point he had stuck his tongue between her legs. As she had writhed on the bed, his tongue down there, his mouth so close to what was growing inside her, she had called out again and again. "Don't touch her," she had cried. "Leave her be!"

But it was a time of famine, as Jack the Handsome had said, and so he had only cried in return, "Oh, lady, so hungry, I'm so godawful hungry!"

When the dancing was all done and the blood had run between her legs in a steady flow, she had wept for hours while her husband snoozed in the sticky bed, that boyish smile still touching his lips. She had wiped the salt from her eyes, she had wiped the blood away as well, the balled-up tissue stained pinkish as a rose when she let it drop into the basin. She had taken the knife to him afterward. Oh, he had screamed and he had pleaded, but she had carved him up all the same. When it was done, she had taken what was left of him to the cemetery, and all around her the red trees had shed their leaves, but she did not mind. She had laid out the bones where the wild dogs could find them. She had thrown no dirt on him lest she spoil the taste.

It was a time of famine, after all, and she knew they would be hungry.

They would be hungry, and she didn't want him stumbling home on his own.

*   *   *

"THE GAME IS yours," said the three Jacks to the fourth. "Let your victory bring you comfort. May you find good meat in the hunt."

THERE WAS A knock in the night, and Lydia woke in her bed, afraid, suddenly, that her husband had returned after all, a nightmare that would seize hold of her sometimes, most often in the autumn when the smell of wood smoke reminded her so vividly of the red on the trees, the red on her hands, the necklace of blood she had carved for him. But the knock was soft, polite, and Lydia knew it was not him. Jack the Handsome. He smiled when he saw her, that big, red smile of his, and she kissed him though it hurt her to do so.

"It's true," she told him, "what the others were saying."

"I know," he said.

"I suppose it was the only way I could think of to get fat," she tried to joke. Her body was wicker-thin anyway, the baby hardly an acorn inside of her.

Inside, she could hear Mother beginning to call within the house. *Who's that, dearest? Who's at the door?* She pulled Jack the Handsome away, and her hand burned as it touched him, but she didn't care much.

"What are we going to do?" she asked him, and she hated her voice for trembling.

"We shall find a land of feasting," he said to her. "Do you trust me?"

She thought about this for a while.

"No," she said.

"Do you love me?"

"No," she said.

"Will you come with me?"

"I –" she began, but inside Mother was beginning to pound the table. Her hands had whittled down to bones these days, all of her had rotted away, and Lydia could not stand to look at her anymore. "Where would we go?"

He shrugged his red shoulders bitterly. "This has always been the way of it. Once we lived in a better place, but our hunger was too great and so we played, and we played, and then half of us were sent away. And it has been the same ever since. We went to the red place. We built our kingdom among the dead, but when the famine came again, they feared our teeth and we sent them scurrying before us like rats. Then we followed them too, those of us whom fortune favoured with our throws, we followed the dead out of Hell, and we built our kingdom in the place they came to. This is how it is, and how it was, and how it ever shall be. We are hungry, we are terribly hungry, and we have eaten the moon and the stars and all else we could find here, but fortune has favoured my throw, and –" and here he staggered to a halt, and the red silence pushed in until she feared he would not finish, but he mustered himself carefully and spoke again. "I would take you with me."

"Where are the others?"

"They have fed me as best they can. I shall carry them."

And she saw that his belly was full beneath his shirt, that it bulged and squirmed like a sack of kittens.

"Where shall we go?"

"It does not matter. You must come. The little one will starve here."

Without a reason for it, Lydia began to cry. She did not love him. She did not love him. The one she loved was inside the house. Mother had played little piggies with her and dreamed of her dancing. Mother had made a paper theatre to house that dream and keep it safe – and even if a devil lay at the heart of that dream, still it was beautiful, that world of silver, angled stars untouched by hunger.

But she knew as well that Mother was dead. Lydia had taken to setting the latch on the door as she slept, cautious of Mother's blind snuffling like a pig searching out truffles. She tiptoed through the kitchen, careful not to wake her, fleeing if she stirred. If she went inside now she would see Mother sucking at her fingertips, her teeth pitting the joints, but too old to break through to the marrow inside. They would be crumbling to jagged pieces even as Lydia watched. *Dearest?* Mother would say. *Is that you? Have you brought something for me?* She was a broken, brutal thing but Mother could be quick too – and dangerous. More than once her claws had carved bright lines across Lydia's stomach, lines that welled up red and bloody. And Mother had licked at her fingers afterward.

So Lydia answered Jack the Handsome, "I will go away with you."

And she did, one hand in his, the other clenched tight around the amethyst ring in her pocket. It was a hard lump that tasted of salt, as she herself tasted of salt – salt and age and everything wasted in the world. But the sight of Jack the Handsome burnished her to the dull, red glow of a penny. She did not love him. She did not love his bright red teeth, and she feared for the thing inside her, and as well, for the place they were going: a place as beautiful and fragile as crepe paper. But still she went.

"I will live again," Lydia thought. "We will carry what we have in our bellies, the both of us, and where we go we shall bring our children forth into a time of feasting."

But as they passed the graveyard, she saw in the dark place the red spark of hatred.

That look said, *Your scent is heavy, and I shall not lose it. I shall follow where you go.*

That look said, *My children are starving, and your flesh is sweet.*

That look said, *You cannot be rid of us.*

And as Jack the Handsome took her from that place, the wails of dogs followed them, bright and anguished, the sound of things driven wild, of things left behind, the sound of the terrible emptiness that cannot be shed.

LEFTY PLAYS BRIDGE
PAT CADIGAN

Like the rules of bridge, this story is complex. The reader is advised to pay attention to what is happening between the moves, what the cards are saying about that which is taking place outside the game. At first glance, Pat's story may not appear to be a horror story, but it is. Very much so. Within the moves and countermoves there is a darkness that leads to a powerful and shocking conclusion.

"I ALWAYS SWORE I'd never play this game," Diana said, forcing a smile as she sat down at the card-table across from Camille. Her sister's answering smile had a hard edge. A smile with teeth in it, as their foster-mother Mrs. Blore would say, even if none were showing. Just about all of Camille's expressions were like that.

"Yeah, I tried to teach her," Camille said, "but she could never get the hang of it. She'd always rather sit in a corner playing solitaire."

"Maybe tonight will be different," said Kerry on Diana's right. "I think it's really nice of you to sit in while Linda's away."

"It certainly is," said Mrs. Blore as she took the seat opposite him – no, *her*, Kerry was *she* and *her*, she corrected herself. She didn't think of Kerry any other way, with her cloud of black, curly hair, her perfect olive skin, unblemished even by minor acne, and her natural grace. But they'd grown up in the same apartment building and gone to the same school; she'd known Kerry before she had begun her transition and it was hard to break the habits of a lifetime, even a lifetime of only fifteen years. Kerry didn't hold it against her if she slipped but Diana knew how much she appreciated the extra effort not to.

Abruptly, she realised Mrs. Blore had said something to her. "Sorry," she said, looking down as her face grew warm with embarrassment. "I, uh, just stepped out for a second."

"Our dreamy girl, out gathering wool again." Mrs. Blore's dark brown hand over hers was as warm as her voice.

"Our *woolly-headed* girl," said Camille, mimicking her tone. "No wonder you two get along so well."

Diana stiffened, her face burning now. Her foster mother gave her hand a quick squeeze before she picked up the rubber-banded deck of cards at her elbow. "I said, swearing you'll never do something isn't just tempting fate, it's teasing it till it bites you."

"Me and Diana don't believe in fate," Camille said.

"Is that right?" Mrs. Blore removed the rubber band and put the cards down in front of Diana. "If you haven't changed your mind, give these a good shuffle. Half a dozen times. We want to make sure they're all mixed up."

The cards felt slick under Diana's fingertips and she prayed she wouldn't spill them all over the place. Camille was a lot better at this but Diana didn't envy her skill. She'd learned it from their father and he'd played more than cards with her. *Only* her, though; it didn't matter that they were identical twins, their father had made it clear Camille was his favourite, referring to her as *my daughter* and *my little princess,* while Diana had always been *the other one,* or, on occasion, *Lefty.* Even his pervert friends had thought he was crazy. But the judge had said he was sane enough for thirty years in the state pen.

To Diana's relief, she managed to shuffle six times in a row without incident and slid the cards back to Mrs. Blore, who passed them to Kerry with the same instructions. Kerry hesitated, raising her perfect eyebrows.

"Like I said, we want them all mixed up." Mrs. Blore turned to Camille. "Your turn next."

Camille made a show of flexing like a comedy piano player and then popping her knuckles one at a time while Kerry winced. Diana waited for Mrs. Blore to tell Camille she could stop showing off; instead, the woman pointedly ignored her.

"Thank you, dear," Mrs. Blore said when Kerry finished and gave the deck to Camille. "The new manicure is lovely, by the way."

Kerry beamed with pleasure, spreading her hands out on the table. "Thanks, Mom. I never thought my hands would ever look so nice."

"*Oh,*" Camille said, pretending to be hurt. "I thought you were talking to *me.*"

"Best way I know of to quit biting your nails," Mrs. Blore said cheerfully, still ignoring her. "You'll see – this time next year, you won't need extensions."

Camille refused to be discouraged. "*I* want to get extensions."

"Your claws are long enough," Mrs. Blore chuckled.

"I meant *hair* extensions," Camille said. "Dreadlocks would look great on me, don't you think?" She pushed the deck back at Mrs. Blore, twisted one long strand of shiny, auburn hair into a tight tube, and held it up next to her face. Diana felt a small pang of regret for having cut her own hair off short. "See? I think they'd look as good as yours. And I wouldn't tie mine back, I'd leave them loose. All the way down to my butt."

This was all because Kerry had called Mrs. Blore *Mom,* Diana knew. Camille had promised to slam Diana's fingers in the heavy front door if she ever used the M-word. The threat was completely unnecessary – she had no desire to call anyone *Mom* – but there was no point saying so. Camille would only think she was giving her an argument. Easier to just go along with her. She was used to Camille's possessiveness, she understood it.

But Camille didn't like *anyone* calling Mrs. Blore *Mom* and she couldn't understand that at all. If someone like Kerry, whose family had thrown her out when she was twelve, wanted to feel like this was a real family and not a foster home, so what?

"Little girl," Mrs. Blore said to Camille, never looking away from the cards she was shuffling, "how on *earth* are you gonna keep seventy-seven commandments when you can't even remember *ten?*"

"*Huh?*" Camille's incredulous expression was deliberately ugly. Her ultimate diss, *You're so unimportant to me, I don't care how I look to you.* She didn't seem to realise that nobody knew it was an insult and wouldn't have cared if they had. "What are you *talking* about?"

"I rest my case," Mrs. Blore said and began to deal, pausing only to slap Camille's hand lightly when she started to pick up her cards. "Card etiquette – wait till the deal is finished."

The tap wouldn't have killed a fly but Camille made a show of rubbing her hand and inspecting the skin for damage.

"The brown won't rub off," Mrs. Blore said, still unruffled.

Diana pressed her lips together to keep from laughing. Sometimes Camille was like a Disney villain, like Cruella de Ville. Or the evil fairy from *Sleeping Beauty*. What was she called? Maleficent. Meet my sister, Maleficent. It worked even as a middle name. Camille Maleficent.

"Dreamy girl," Mrs. Blore said, pretending to call from a distance. "Come back, play is about to commence."

Diana smiled a bit sheepishly, looking from Mrs. Blore to Kerry and back again, skipping Camille, who picked up on it immediately.

"Over here, sis! In the chair across from you? That's not a mirror, it's your *identical* twin sister." She banged hard on the table.

"Amp it back already." Mrs. Blore's friendly tone had acquired an edge. "She knows you're there, you're partners. You're North, she's South."

"Why does *she* get to be South?" Camille said immediately. "I'd make a *much* better South than her. Hunny-chile! What you-all doin' up heah in the big house? You knows you ain't no house –" Camille saw Mrs. Blore's face and cut off suddenly, folding her hands over her cards. "I'm sorry, that was over the line even for me." She looked up again, her face solemn. Diana would have bought it if she hadn't known her. "I promise I'll behave."

"That's good," Mrs. Blore said serenely, "because you done used up *all* yo' slack, *hunny-chile*. Don' rile me less'n you wants house-arrest fo' a *week*." Pause. "Is that clear, *yo*, or should I threaten to bust a cap in your ho ass?"

The shock on Camille's face was 100% genuine. Diana sneaked a glance at Kerry; she was studying her cards as if she had never seen anything more fascinating.

"What?" said Mrs. Blore. She looked around the table, giving Diana a secret wink. "You think no one ever talked trash to me before? Please. Or like you kids say when you don't think I can hear you: *bitch,* please."

"Seventy-five cents for the swear jar." Kerry spoke quietly, never taking her eyes off her cards. "Fifty cents for the b-word, twenty-five for her ho ass. Unquote," she added as Camille gave her a dirty look.

"Worth it." Mrs. Blore chuckled as she got up and went to the glass bowl on the kitchen counter, digging in her jeans pocket. "Oops, no change, I'll have to put in a dollar." The swear jar was exact-change only, a policy that even Mrs. Blore herself adhered to. "*Still* worth it," she said, returning to the table. "Anybody else got something to say? Fat jokes, maybe?"

"*I'd* like to play cards," Kerry said. "I move we skip any further preliminaries and go directly to bridge."

"I second it," Diana said. Camille looked at her and she shrugged.

"Moved and seconded. All those in favour, don't say a damned word." Mrs. Blore picked up her cards. "Just using up that dollar," she added, as Kerry looked pointedly at the swear jar.

THEY PLAYED A few hands of what Mrs. Blore called pre-bridge while she talked about major and minor suits and the difference between balanced, semi-balanced, and unbalanced. Diana remembered most of it from the times Camille had tried to teach her by force. The problem hadn't been an inability to keep everything straight. It was simply that Camille was a card-player and thought Diana was, too, just because she'd seen Diana laying out cards by herself. She'd assumed it was solitaire and Diana had let her. It was easier than trying to explain.

Camille had always been an enthusiastic game-player, all kinds of games – board games, computer games, even roleplaying games (though that had been a very brief infatuation). Cards, however, had always been her absolute favourite, even before their father had started dealing her into his high stakes games. The social worker had said he'd used cards to reel her in, something Diana would always feel guilty about. She couldn't help thinking that if she had made the effort to share her sister's enthusiasm, she might have learned to like cards the way she did and things might have been different.

Everyone had told her it was normal to feel that way but she was wrong – there was nothing she could have done. She wanted very much to believe that. But the dark secret she still couldn't bring herself to confess to anyone was that she'd been glad their father had kept Camille too busy to play with her. She hadn't known what was really happening, couldn't have imagined it in a million years. She'd just been relieved not to have to play with Camille, who was a bad loser and an even worse winner. (The even darker secret – that as bad as she felt about what had happened to Camille, she was still glad their father hadn't chosen her over her sister – was something she couldn't even admit to herself yet.)

And what was the big deal anyway? At the end of every game, all you got was points, which Diana didn't think was much of a payoff for what was little more than arithmetic. Cribbage and gin bored Diana silly and she absolutely loathed poker – their father's game. She could tolerate spades and hearts because there had to be more players, and she actually enjoyed whist in spite of always being partnered with Camille. Her sister had thought she could simply move her on to bridge. But as soon as Camille started talking about contracts and suit rankings and HCPs, Diana felt her brain glaze over along with her eyes. She couldn't help it. But it was okay – their father was in prison and nothing like that could happen to Camille under Mrs. Blore's roof. It was perfectly all right for her not to play cards.

She had not expected Camille to give up and accept she just wasn't a bridge player; her sister didn't work that way. Camille didn't accept things, things accepted Camille. But apparently her desire to play bridge far outweighed her desire to force Diana to play with her. She settled for insisting Diana hang out in the same room, supposedly so she could socialise and not feel left out.

As if. Most of the conversation was card patter and even if it hadn't been, it wasn't easy getting a word in edgewise around Camille. If she sat as close to the table as Camille wanted, the other players got nervous. They probably thought she was there to help Camille cheat. If her sister really expected her to do something like that, she was in for the second biggest bridge-related disappointment of her life but Diana didn't think that was it. More likely, Camille was hoping she'd learn the game by osmosis so she could be drafted as a fourth when needed. Diana countered by making sure she always had something to read. Mrs. Blore let her use her iPad, which gave her access to more books than could have fit in the room she shared with Camille. Even better, Mrs. Blore didn't put any of them off-limits; bookworm heaven.

She might have been less resistant to whist, where luck mattered as much as skill and the bids were little more than veiled hints as to what kind of cards you held. In bridge, luck began and ended with the deal and bidding was a complicated code – the Stayman convention, the Blackwood whatever-it-was – to tell your partner how good your cards were, or weren't. Except everyone knew the code, which meant all the players knew what you were saying, so what was the point?

But despite all this, here she was, sitting in voluntarily because the one other bridge player in the house was spending a week with her aunt and uncle, deciding whether to move in with them. If she did, Diana would be stuck in this chair unless the next placement wanted in; she could only hope. At least Mrs. Blore was a much better teacher than Camille; Diana wouldn't have to worry about getting her ass kicked every time she made a mistake. Even if it was an especially stupid mistake.

They were on their third practice hand before Mrs. Blore introduced the dummy; by then, Camille was so impatient she could hardly sit still. The dummy was something else that baffled Diana. You had to have four people but only three of them could actually play. And the dummy's cards were all face up, which meant everybody got to see half the deck, albeit not the same half. That seemed exceptionally weird to Diana and she said so.

"It *is* quirky, isn't it?" Mrs. Blore said. "Legend has it that four English nobles were playing bridge in their favourite pub and they ordered some drinks. Service was so slow that finally one of them decided to go see what the hold-up was. He was one of those cocky, over-confident types –" she glanced briefly at Camille. "And threw his cards down face up on the table, saying he had such a good hand, his partner could play it for him."

"That didn't *really* happen." Camille's skeptical expression turned doubtful. "Did it?"

"I hope so," Diana blurted before she could think better of it. It was the first thing she'd ever found even remotely interesting about the game.

"Me, too," Kerry said with a bright smile. "I think it's neat when you hear why you do something instead of just doing it because it's a rule."

"So go read a book," Camille said, shifting in her chair. "I thought we were gonna play bridge, not get a recap of *Downton Abbey.*"

"A little more patience, if you please," Mrs. Blore said.

"Then tell her to bid." She jerked her chin at Diana, who looked helplessly at Mrs. Blore. She couldn't see anything bridge-like in the cards on the table in front of her.

Camille opened her mouth to say something else and then shut it again when Mrs. Blore raised her index finger. "The bids are, one club, one diamond, and pass, in that order," she told Diana, pointing at herself, Camille, and Kerry respectively. "What do you think would be a good bid?"

"Two clubs. No, I mean two diamonds. Two diamonds," she said quickly, refusing to look up at her sister.

Mrs. Blore patted her arm. "Two hearts." Camille responded with two spades, Kerry passed, and she was back on the hook again with even less idea of what to do.

"Just pass," Camille said to Diana. "You don't know what you're doing anyway."

"Give her a break and stuff a sock in it," Mrs. Blore said.

Camille put on her smug princess face. "I'm not wearing any."

"I'll loan you one of mine," Mrs. Blore replied cheerfully, "with my foot still in it."

They all laughed, even Camille, who tried not to. "She's right, though," Diana said, careful not to laugh too much. "I *don't* know what I'm doing."

"Nobody's born knowing squat. You be patient with yourself. No matter who else is impatient with you," Mrs. Blore added, looking sideways at Camille.

"I'm *trying*," said Camille defensively. "But this is taking so long that by the time we're ready to play for real, it'll be time to go to bed."

"Not if we stay up a little later than usual."

Camille brightened immediately. "Really?"

"Sure," Mrs. Blore said, smiling. "We got the whole house to ourselves. We can be a little bit naughty and stay up late. Even sleep in some tomorrow morning."

"Careful," Kerry said, impressed. "You don't want to go too far over to the dark side. You might not find your way back."

"I'll leave a trail of bread crumbs," Mrs. Blore chuckled.

"That didn't work out so good for Hansel and Gretel," Diana said.

"Good point," said Mrs. Blore, laughing again. "You got a better idea?"

Diana shrugged one shoulder. "Cards?"

She didn't feel any more confident when they moved from pre-bridge to actual play, stumbling through bidding without any help for the first time, sure that she was messing up. Kerry and Mrs. Blore won the auction; Diana was relieved for all of a second, until she realised that meant she had to lead the first trick before Mrs. Blore could lay out her cards as the dummy. She found a two and tossed it into the centre of the table.

"Now, would you say I had a balanced, semi-balanced, or unbalanced hand?" Mrs. Blore asked her as she sat back in her chair.

"Um..." Out of the corner of her eye, she saw Camille look upward and mouth, *Gimme strength*. "Semi?"

Their foster mother smiled gently and touched the nine of hearts, the only card she had in the suit. "Try again."

Diana winced. "Right. Even just one singleton makes it unbalanced."

"How do you not remember that?" Camille demanded. "Try this – you and I are a doubleton. They're both singletons –" she pointed at Mrs. Blore and Kerry. "They're always unbalanced, not us. Well, unless all you've got besides a doubleton is singletons."

"Really," Mrs. Blore said. "And how many suits would you be playing with?"

"Around this table? Just three," Camille replied. "You and Kerry are singletons, we're a doubleton. Three suits."

"Uh-huh. And what suits are those?"

"Well, we're hearts. Kerry could be a diamond, she's all shiny now. And you..." Camille made them wait. "You'd be a club." Another much briefer pause. "Because we joined you."

"Very clever, little girl." Mrs. Blore looked at her through half-closed eyes.

Camille looked smug again. "You thought I was gonna say something else, didn't you?"

Abruptly, Kerry sat up and tapped the two cards in the middle of the table. "We're all waiting on you. What'll it be, follow suit or trump already?"

To Diana's surprise, Camille was actually rattled. She scanned her cards as if she were seeing them for the first time.

"Spades are trump, in case you forgot," Kerry added. "And the game is bridge."

Frowning, Mrs. Blore pursed her lips and gave her head a barely perceptible shake. Kerry looked innocent and said nothing else. Diana couldn't help smiling; she pressed her knuckles quickly against her mouth as if she were thinking very hard. Not quickly enough, however, judging by the coldly poisonous look on Camille's face. *Let it go,* she pleaded silently. *You won when you got me playing this rotten game – can't that be enough?*

* * *

AFTER THE DEAL had gone once around the table, Mrs. Blore called intermission and asked Kerry to make popcorn. "A couple of great big bowls," she said. "It'll go nice with the cherry-peach iced tea."

Camille said she had to go to the bathroom and hurried upstairs. Before anyone could ask her to do anything, Diana thought as she got four glasses out of a cabinet. She started to take out a pitcher as well but Mrs. Blore told her the tea was already made and waiting in the fridge.

"This is a great big chore for you, isn't it?" she said as Diana filled the glasses with ice cubes.

"No, of course not," Diana said, surprised.

Mrs. Blore laughed. "I meant bridge."

"Oh. Well..." She floundered, trying to find the right words. "It's not so bad – you're a better teacher than Camille. But I don't think it'll ever be my favourite thing."

"It doesn't have to be. It's just very useful to know." Mrs. Blore smiled at her obvious bewilderment. "Millions of people play bridge all over the country, all around the world. All kinds of people. The Supreme Court justices play bridge."

"They do?" Kerry was wide-eyed as she placed one bowl of popcorn on Mrs. Blore's left and another on Diana's right.

"Probably. Considering their pedigree and what schools they went to, I'd bet money on it. They all probably get together every Friday and Saturday night without telling the Chief Justice. That gives them an even eight players, two full tables they can swap around. Nobody wants to play with the boss."

Diana finished pouring the tea and sat down again. "You also sell this game a lot better than Camille."

"Honey, I'm not teaching you this game to please your sister. Bridge is useful for meeting people and getting to know them. And the best way to find other players is to join a bridge club."

"I play online sometimes," Kerry said.

Mrs. Blore made a disdainful noise. "Forget it. You don't know who you're playing with online. You know that picture of the dogs playing poker? Could be them." She frowned. "And when do you have time to waste online?"

"It's just once in a great while," Kerry said, looking nervous now. "A really, *really* great while."

"Uh-huh." Mrs. Blore glanced up at the ceiling. "That girl wants to make sure all the ice-cube trays are refilled and back in the freezer before she comes down again. Listen – the both of you. If you're gonna make it in this world, you gotta be able to play the game, whatever that may be."

"And the game is bridge?" Diana made a face. "I'm sorry, I don't think I could –" she was about to say *stay awake,* and then caught herself. "I don't think I could ever be that good a player."

"Practice. That's all it is. You just gotta get used to seeing the cards in a certain way and learn the language. Learn how other people speak it, find out what they're saying. You'd be surprised at who shows up at my club's regular Wednesday night games, and what I find out from them."

"I'm already surprised," Diana said. "You're the first person who ever told me to play cards. Everybody else is always saying I should stay in school, study and get good grades so I can go to college."

Mrs. Blore chuckled. "If that's what everyone else says, then I don't have to say it, too."

"Say what?" Camille was sitting down again and helping herself to a handful of popcorn.

SHE SHOULD HAVE known, Diana told herself. The cards had been warning her and she had failed to take them seriously because she hadn't imagined Mrs. Blore's dollar-store bridge cards could actually be saying anything. Not this soon, anyway.

She should have known better about that, too. Handling a deck of cards was like a radio tuner looking for stations. At first the cards were just all over the place and it was just random noise. But eventually they adjusted to the environment, became acclimated to the hands touching them, the style of shuffle, the rhythm of the deal.

How long that took depended on the cards and the number of people who touched them. Some decks made sense in less than an hour; others might babble for days or weeks, even months. Generally the more different people who handled a deck, the longer it took for the noise to die down. Even just one other person could impede the most prodigious deck and cards that had previously been coherent often shut down in unfamiliar hands, so she hadn't given much thought to all the spades and diamonds that kept turning up. Not even the two of diamonds, which was rarely out of her sight, appearing either in her own hand or face up on the table in the dummy's. Ignoring that one made her the real dummy.

Only she hadn't really ignored it as much as she'd taken it for granted. The two of diamonds was her frequent flier, the card most likely to show up for her even amid random noise. Or if didn't show up, it would somehow be conspicuous by its absence. But it was always connected to her, a constant reminder that no matter how whole and unto herself she might feel on her best day, she had come into this world in terms of Camille and she would continue to exist that way. Her own body proved it.

As far as Diana was concerned, the two of diamonds simply took up space. It told her nothing she didn't already know, certainly not about her past or present and very little about the future. Even in its original form in the tarot, it offered no new information: *Profound but ill-advised partnership; no marriage is possible.* When she'd been much younger, she'd thought this had meant Camille would make it impossible for her to get married. Later she had read it as referring to the differences between them, the greatest and most insurmountable being that Camille had been their father's favourite and she had been the other one. It even trumped their peculiar physiology.

Trumped. It was her deal, she realised and picked up the cards.

"More tea?" Camille asked. "It's really good tonight." She picked up the pitcher and started to refill everyone's glass.

That definitely counted as unusual but Diana had been more focussed on having to make the first bid. Maybe she should pass regardless of what she held, then tell Camille she was just taking her advice because she still didn't know what she was doing. The idea made her smile inwardly as she dealt the last four cards, and then suddenly the table was awash in ice cubes and peach tea.

Everyone jumped back and Kerry immediately went to get the mop while Diana and Mrs. Blore grabbed the glassware before it could fall and break, taking it to the sink, while Camille stood wailing, "*I'm sorry, I'm so sorry, it was an accident!*" over and over.

She was still wailing when Kerry returned with the mop and bucket, and continued while Diana grabbed a roll of paper towels for the table. Mrs. Blore took it from her and handed her some cloth dishtowels instead, waving away Diana's protests about stains. "Honey, they're *already* stained. Iced tea might be an improvement. And will you quiet down?" she added, turning to Camille who did so, flinching slightly. "It was an accident, we get it. Now wash the pitcher and glasses and make some more tea."

Camille hesitated, still looking fearful, then did as she was told. She wasn't faking that, Diana knew. When they'd still lived at home, an accident like that would have meant a backhand blow to the face for whomever was within reach, guilty or not; kids needed discipline no matter who they were, the favourite or the other one. Diana couldn't help flinching herself when she knocked something over or broke something. Their first week with Mrs. Blore, she'd broken two glasses in as many days; the first time, she had automatically shrunk into a half-crouch with her arms covering her head and waited for the open hand or the fist. When nothing happened, she lowered her arms to see Mrs. Blore with a dustpan and broom. "Did you cut yourself, honey?" she'd asked in that warm, gentle voice as she swept up the fragments. "Don't worry, they sell these four for a buck at Louie's Dollar Shop and frankly, I didn't like that particular shape much anyway."

Mrs. Blore went on talking to her for twenty minutes, until she finally unclenched and un-tensed enough to stand up straight. Her reaction was one that Mrs. Blore was all too familiar with, and when Diana had understood she was saying that her father's idea of discipline was a genuine you're-under-arrest crime, she had burst into tears. And then the next day, when she had dropped another glass, she'd done the same thing. Mrs. Blore hadn't minded; it took a while, she said.

Diana took the saturated towels to the sink, where Camille had finished washing everything out and was now filling the pitcher with fresh water. Her expression had gone from fearful to put-upon. "Do you want me to make the tea?" Diana asked her in a near-whisper.

"What, you think I don't know how to make tea?" Camille asked loudly.

"No, I was just offering," Diana said annoyed, still keeping her voice low.

"I *know* how to make *tea*, it's not rocket surgery," Camille said, even more loudly.

"Fine, fine," Diana said, speaking at normal volume now. "I was just offering to help you."

"Our dreamy girl," Camille said, mimicking Mrs. Blore again. "Always dreaming she can help someone." She gave Diana a wide, fake smile, lips closed but with plenty of teeth as she dropped several bags of Twinings Peach and Cherry Blossom into the pitcher. "I've got this. There's nothing you can do. As usual."

Stung, Diana turned away to see Mrs. Blore looking mournfully at the pile of wet cards on the table in front of her.

"I'm afraid these have had it," she said. "I thought they were plastic-coated. Either I was mistaken –" she held up several cards wadded together; the one completely visible to Diana was the two of diamonds. "Or we actually wore their coats off. And I'm sorry to say that's the only deck we have. I guess bridge night just turned into movie night –"

"Not so fast!" Camille said cheerfully. "Super Twin to the rescue *again!*" She was holding up a package of Bicycle cards with blue backs.

Diana's jaw dropped. "Those are mine!" She grabbed for them and Camille danced away, hiding them behind her back.

"Uh-uh-uh, sis, they're mine."

Diana was livid. "You *liar!* I *know* you saw me with them –"

"Oh, come on, you think you're the only person who owns a deck like this?"

Abruptly, Mrs. Blore was between them. "Separate corners! *Now!*"

Diana started to protest, saw the expression on their foster mother's face, and obediently retreated to the far corner of the kitchen.

"Okay, now what's the story? You." She pointed at Camille. "Where did you get those cards?"

"At Louie's Dollar," Camille said, putting on a prim innocence. "They sell them for fifty cents."

Mrs. Blore turned to Diana, her face neutral. "And you say otherwise?"

"I say she's a liar. She knows I keep them under my pillow, inside the pillowcase. That's where she got them."

"Like you're the *only* person who plays solitaire?" Camille laughed.

"*You've* never played solitaire in your life!"

"Oh, just because *you* never saw it doesn't mean it didn't happen," Camille said, her expression turning cold. "*Lots* of shit happens that you never know about!"

"That'll be a dollar," Mrs. Blore said, gesturing at the swear jar.

"Worth it," Camille said, just the way Mrs. Blore had said it earlier. She found four quarters in her pocket and made a move toward the counter.

"Not so fast." Mrs. Blore held out her hand. "I'll take care of that for you."

Camille reluctantly gave her the coins. "So, what? You gonna keep us in separate corners all night? Hard to play bridge that way."

"Won't be any bridge if you took those cards from your sister."

"I didn't," Camille said, lifting her chin defiantly. "And I can prove it. Go upstairs and look. Her precious cards are still in her precious pillow case. Go ahead, you'll see."

"Oh, I'm staying right here, little girl, I don't want to come back and find your bodies on the floor." Mrs. Blore turned to Diana. "Would you mind if Kerry checks?" Diana shook her head.

Kerry left the kitchen and was back in a few seconds. "Diana, your deck is right where you said," she told her, looking apologetic. "I opened the box – they're blue backs, like those." She nodded at Camille.

"Did you see a tiny star inside the flap?" Diana asked. "I drew a five-pointed star in blue ink inside the flap."

"I'm sorry, I didn't notice," Kerry said, even more apologetic.

"Well, that's easy." Mrs. Blore took the box from Camille, opened it, then looked at Diana, shaking her head.

"There – that proves I'm innocent," Camille said. "Even though the burden of proof is on the accuser. We both know that, don't we, sis?"

"Why did you buy a deck just like mine?" Diana asked her darkly.

"There are thousands of decks just like yours all over town, so what? I've been falsely accused," she said to Mrs. Blore, looking hurt. "What are you going to do about it? You'd never let *me* get away with sh – stuff like that. You'd put me under house arrest for a week –"

"Enough already," said Mrs. Blore. "Let's call it a misunderstanding and a mix-up. *A mix-up,*" she repeated, looking a warning at Diana.

"Okay, it's a mix-up," Diana said after a moment. "But I'd still like to know why she bought a deck just like mine."

"How do you know *you* didn't buy a deck just like *mine?*" Camille said evenly. "You don't know, maybe I had this one first."

Diana opened her mouth to ask how she just happened to have them on her but Mrs. Blore looked another warning at her and she backed down.

"I'm ruling this is all just an innocent mix-up," Mrs. Blore said. "And the swear jar is buying this deck from you." She took the deck from Camille and gave her two quarters. "You can buy another one at Louie's. Save yourself some trouble and choose a different colour. Diana, you're sentenced to go on playing bridge. Anybody got a problem with that? Because I don't care," she added as Camille started to answer. "Decision of the foster mother is final."

"Like it ever isn't," Camille muttered.

"And don't you forget it," Mrs. Blore chuckled. "Now let's get rid of that mess on the table."

As SOON AS Diana touched the cards, she knew for certain they were hers.

To save time, Mrs. Blore dispensed with passing the deck around, shuffling it herself, then dealing. Diana kept her attention fixed on the cards accumulating in front of her. She could feel Camille looking at her, the pressure was practically physical, but Diana refused to meet her gaze. She knew she couldn't trust anything she saw there, whether it was a brazen admission or a wounded denial. The truth would only be in the cards.

And she was right. These *were* her cards. Camille had simply swapped out the decks. That was why she'd bought identical cards. Identical cards, identical twins. Except Diana knew the difference. Nobody else would – no one else in the house could tell one deck from another, including Camille. But she didn't have to because she knew Diana could. And there wasn't a damned thing Diana could do about it, which was something they both knew.

Because how would it sound if she told Mrs. Blore what was really going on? *These really* are *my cards, Camille bought a deck that looks exactly like mine just so she could switch them. Make her give them back.* Yeah, right. Even Mrs. Blore would think she was crazy and she'd probably end up in restraints or doing the Thorazine shuffle, like the seventeen-year-old psycho in the first foster-home they'd gone to. While Camille went around claiming *she* was the normal one.

Diana could practically hear her. *It wasn't really* me *that Daddy liked to play with, she just* wishes *it were. I let her say whatever she wanted because she'd start screaming and yelling if I tried to contradict her. But she's so messed up I just can't play along with her fantasy any more.*

Oh, yeah. That was Camille, all right. Making her out to be the screwed-up twin and covering her own batshit crazy with a smiling mask. She'd made a bad mistake cutting her hair, Diana realised. She had only wanted to look completely different, to make sure everyone knew which was which, and she'd ended up locking each of them into an identity there was no escape from.

When she and Camille had looked exactly alike, everyone identified them together, as the twins, not as the A one and the B one. Except for their father, of course. He'd always been able to tell his little princess from the other one because he knew the special circumstances of their birth, that they were mirror twins. Camille had been on the right and Diana was her reflection, with everything backwards. Even her internal organs were the wrong way round. "Her heart will *never* be in the right place," he would say, "not like my little princess. For all we know, even her eyeballs see things backwards."

That had only been him, though, and he was locked away where he could never do it again. No one else could tell just by looking which was which. But now she'd made it easy, and it wasn't going to be the little princess and the other one, it was going to be the nice, normal one and the batshit crazy one, not just to their father but to everyone. And there was no doubt as to who Camille had decided to be.

"Diana, honey?" Mrs. Blore said.

She blinked. "Oh, sorry."

"Oops, she did it again," Camille sang. "Because she's not that innocent."

Diana frowned at her hand; apparently she had arranged it into suits on automatic pilot. And there it was, as usual, the two of diamonds, proclaiming that ill-advised partnership. Along with the two of spades, warning her about gossip, deceit, and betrayal, the five of spades, telling her to beware of troublemakers in a happy home, and as if she hadn't already gotten the message, the Queen of Spades, the bossy, domineering, malicious woman. It was the only picture card.

"Well, *shit*," she said, then clapped a hand over her mouth.

"Swear jar," everyone said in unison.

She sighed as she got up and went to the counter, where she stood for a long time fishing in all of her pockets, until she was sure no one was looking at her.

The crash made them all jump. "Oh, jeez, I'm sorry!" Diana cried, flinching a little.

"Well, *that's* a mess," Camille said over her shoulder, without moving.

Kerry and Mrs. Blore both started to get up but Diana waved them down. "I can manage," she said, getting the dustpan and broom from the cabinet under the sink. "I'll have it cleaned up in two shakes. Really."

"Just be careful of all that glass," Mrs. Blore said.

"Don't worry," she said happily, sweeping the largest fragment into the pan and heading toward the trash bin just to the left of Camille's chair. "I can do this without cutting *myself*."

She took the cards with her afterwards. She didn't think anyone else would want to play with them again even though the plastic coating made them easy to wipe clean.

AUTHOR BIOS

Pat Cadigan has won the Locus Award three times, the Arthur C. Clarke Award twice for her novels *Synners* and *Fools*, and the Hugo Award for her novelette, 'The Girl-Thing Who Went Out For Sushi.' While her novels are all science fiction, she has also written two nonfiction movie books and several media tie-ins, and her short fiction runs the gamut from lighthearted fantasy to hard-edged horror. A former Kansas City resident, she lives in gritty, urban North London with her husband, the Original Chris Fowler.

Mexican by birth, Canadian by inclination, **Silvia Moreno-Garcia** lives in beautiful British Columbia with her family and two cats. Her speculative fiction has been collected in *This Strange Way of Dying*. Her debut novel, *Signal to Noise*, about magic, music and Mexico City, will be released in the spring of 2015. She tweets @silviamg and blogs at silviamoreno-garcia.com

Paul Kearney was born in Northern Ireland in 1967. He studied Anglo-Saxon, Middle English and Old Norse at Oxford University, and has been an English teacher, a bartender, and an Army Officer. His first novel was published in 1992, and he has been writing professionally ever since. He lived for several years in the United States, and in Denmark, but at present he and his wife make their home in a croft beside the beach in County Down.

Yoon Ha Lee's collection *Conservation of Shadows* came out from Prime Books in 2013. Her short fiction has appeared in Tor.com, *The Magazine of Fantasy and Science Fiction*, *Clarkesworld*, and *Lightspeed*. She lives in Louisiana with her family and has not yet been eaten by gators.

Rebecca Levene has been a writer and editor for twenty years, working in the games, publishing, TV and magazine industries. Her new four-part epic fantasy series, The Hollow Gods, launched in July 2014 with *Smiler's Fair*.

Helen Marshall is an award-winning Canadian author, editor, and doctor of medieval studies. Her debut collection of short stories, *Hair Side, Flesh Side* (ChiZine Publications, 2012), was named one of the top ten books of 2012 by *January Magazine*. It won the 2013 British Fantasy Award for Best Newcomer and was shortlisted for a 2013 Aurora Award by the Canadian Society of Science Fiction and Fantasy. Her second collection, *Gifts for the One Who Comes After*, will be released in the autumn of 2014. She lives in Oxford, England where she spends most of her time staring at old books.

Libby McGugan's first novel, *The Eidolon*, has been nominated for the 2014 British Fantasy Best Newcomer Award. She recently emerged from a writing cave in Glasgow with the second book in the *Quantum Ghosts* series, *The Fifth Force*, for some fiddle playing and emergency medicine work. *The Sugar Pill*, another medical-based short story, was published in the serial fiction magazine *Aethernet*.

Gary McMahon is the acclaimed author of nine novels and several short story collections. His latest releases are the novels *The Bones of You* and *The End*, and a short story collection titled *Where you Live*. His short fiction has been reprinted in various 'Year's Best' volumes. Gary lives with his family in

Yorkshire, where he trains in Shotokan karate and likes running in the rain. You can find Gary at www.garymcmahon.com

At night, when the lights are dim and the creepy crawlies scuttle through the shadows, **Hillary Monahan** throws words at a computer. Sometimes they're even good words. A denizen of Massachusetts, she's most often found locked in a dark room killing internet zombies or corralling basset hounds. *Mary: The Summoning*, her YA horror novel about four girls who summon Bloody Mary, was published by Disney-Hyperion in fall of 2014.

Gary Northfield has written and drawn mad, jolly comics for kids for over 10 years now, including Derek The Sheep for the *Beano*, Max The Mouse for *National Geographic Kids*, Little Cutie for *The DFC* and Gary's Garden for *The Phoenix*. He has a book out called *Terrible Tales of the Teenytinysaurs* from Walker Books (2013), and his comic strips Derek the Sheep (2008) and Gary's Garden (2014) have been collected into books with Bloomsbury and David Fickling Books respectively. His new fiction book series, *Julius Zebra*, will be out 2015 from Walker and Candlewick Press.

Benjanun Sriduangkaew writes fantasy mythic and contemporary, science fiction space operatic and military, and has a strong appreciation for beautiful bugs. Her short fiction can be found in Tor.com, *Clarkesworld*, *Beneath Ceaseless Skies*, *Solaris Rising 3*, various Mammoth Books and best of the year collections. She is a finalist for the Campbell Award for Best New Writer.

Ivo Stourton is a writer and lawyer. He has published two previous novels with Random House, *The Night Climbers* and *The Book Lover's Tale* and one science fiction novel with Solaris, *The Happier Dead*. He lives with his wife in London.

Robert Shearman has written five short story collections (*Tiny Deaths, Love Songs for the Shy and Cynical, Everyone's Just So So Special, Remember Why You Fear Me,* and *They Do the Same Things Different There*), and between them they have won the World Fantasy Award, the Shirley Jackson Award, the Edge Hill Reader's Prize and three British Fantasy Awards. His background is in the theatre as resident dramatist at the Northcott Theatre in Exeter, and regular writer for Alan Ayckbourn at the Stephen Joseph Theatre in Scarborough; his plays have won the *Sunday Times* Playwriting Award, the Sophie Winter Memorial Trust Award, the World Drama Trust Award, and the Guiness Award in association with the Royal National Theatre. He regularly writes plays and short stories for BBC Radio, and he has won two Sony Awards for his interactive radio series, 'The Chain Gang.' But he's probably best known for reintroducing the Daleks to the BAFTA winning first season of the revived *Doctor Who*, in an episode that was a finalist for the Hugo Award.

Melanie Tem's work has received the Bram Stoker, International Horror Guild, British Fantasy, and World Fantasy Awards and a nomination for the Shirley Jackson Award. She has published numerous short stories, eleven solo novels, two collaborative novels with Nancy Holder, and two collaborative novels and a short story collection with her husband Steve Rasnic Tem. She is also a published poet, an oral storyteller, and a playwright. Solo stories have recently appeared in *Asimov's Science Fiction Magazine, Crimewave,* and *Interzone,* and anthologies such as *Black Wings* and *Darke Fantastique.* The Tems live in Denver, CO, where Melanie is executive director of a non-profit independent-living organization. They have four children and five grandchildren.

Tade Thompson's roots are in Western Nigeria and South London. His professional background is psychiatry with interests in anthropology. His short stories have been published in small press, webzines and anthologies. Most recently, his story 'The Madwoman of Igbobi College' appeared in Interfictions Online. He lives and works in South England and has been known to haunt coffee shops, jazz bars, bookshops, and libraries. He is an occasional visual artist and tortures his family with his attempts to play the guitar. His novel *Making Wolf* will be published by Rosarium in 2015. He releases random tweets at @tadethompson and blogs at tadethompson.wordpress.com

Lavie Tidhar is the author of *A Man Lies Dreaming*, *The Violent Century* and the World Fantasy Award winning *Osama*. His other works include the *Bookman Histories* trilogy, several novellas, two collections and a forthcoming comics mini-series, *Adler*. He currently lives in London.

Nik Vincent began working as a freelance editor, but has published work in a number of mediums including advertising, training manuals, comics and short stories. She has worked as a ghost writer, and regularly collaborates with her partner, Dan Abnett. Nik was educated at Stirling University, and lives and works in Kent. Her blog and website can be found at www.nicolavincent-abnett.com and she tweets @N_VincentAbnett.

Chuck Wendig is a novelist, screenwriter and game designer. He's the author of many published novels, including but not limited to: *Blackbirds*, *The Blue Blazes,* and the YA *Heartland* series. He is co-writer of the short film *Pandemic*, the feature film *HiM*, and the Emmy-nominated digital narrative *Collapsus*. Wendig has contributed over two million words to the game industry. He is also well known for his profane-yet-practical advice to writers, which he dispenses at his blog, terribleminds.com, and through several popular e-books, including *The Kick-Ass Writer*, published by Writers Digest. He currently lives in the forests of Pennsyltucky with wife, tiny human, and two dogs.

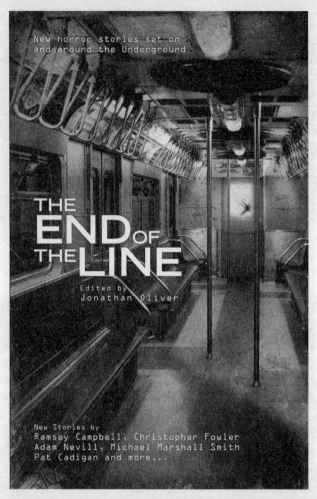

New horror stories set on and around the Underground

THE END OF THE LINE

Edited by
Jonathan Oliver

New Stories by
Ramsey Campbell, Christopher Fowler
Adam Nevill, Michael Marshall Smith
Pat Cadigan and more...

In the night-black tunnels something stirs, borne on a warm breath of wind, reeking of diesel and blood. The spaces between stations hold secrets too terrible for the surface world to comprehend, and the steel lines sing with the songs of the dead. The End of The Line collects some of the very best in new horror writing in a themed anthology of stories set on, and around, the Underground, the Metro and other places deep below. This collection of 19 new stories includes thoughtful, disturbing and terrifying tales by Ramsey Campbell, Christopher Fowler, Mark Morris, Pat Cadigan, Adam Nevill and Michael Marshall Smith amongst many others.

 WWW.SOLARISBOOKS.COM

Follow us on Twitter! www.twitter.com/solarisbooks

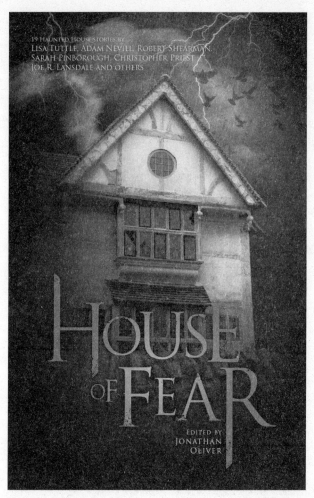

19 Haunted House stories by
LISA TUTTLE, ADAM NEVILL, ROBERT SHEARMAN,
SARAH PINBOROUGH, CHRISTOPHER PRIEST,
JOE R. LANSDALE AND OTHERS

HOUSE OF FEAR

EDITED BY
JONATHAN
OLIVER

The tread on the landing outside the door when you know you are the only one in the house. The wind whistling through the eaves, carrying the voices of the dead. The figure glimpsed briefly through the cracked window of a derelict house. Critically-acclaimed editor Jonathan Oliver brings horror home with a collection of haunted house stories by Lisa Tuttle, Stephen Volk, Terry Lamsley, Adam L. G. Nevill, Weston Ochse, Rebecca Levene, Garry Kilworth, Chaz Brenchley, Robert Shearman, Nina Allan, Christopher Fowler, Sarah Pinborough, Paul Meloy, Christopher Priest, Jonathan Green, Nicholas Royle, Eric Bown, Tim Lebbon and Joe R. Lansdale.

 WWW.SOLARISBOOKS.COM

Follow us on Twitter! www.twitter.com/solarisbooks

Audrey
Niffenegger
Dan
Abnett

Alison
Littlewood

Storm
Constantine

Will Hill
and others

An
anthology
of the esoteric
and arcane

Magic

They gather in darkness, sharing ancient and arcane knowledge as they manipulate the very matter of reality itself. Spells and conjuration; legerdemain and prestidigitation – these are the mistresses and masters of the esoteric arts.

From the otherworldly visions of Conan Doyle's father in Audrey Niffenegger's 'The Wrong Fairy' to the diabolical political machinations of Dan Abnett's 'Party Tricks', here you will find a spell for every occasion.

Jonathan Oliver, critically acclaimed editor of The End of The Line and House of Fear, has brought together sixteen extraordinary writers for this collection of magical tales. Within you will find works by Audrey Niffenegger, Sarah Lotz, Will Hill, Steve Rasnic and Melanie Tem, Liz Williams, Dan Abnett, Thana Niveau, Alison Littlewood, Christopher Fowler, Storm Constantine, Lou Morgan, Sophia McDougall, Gail Z. Martin, Gemma Files and Robert Shearman.

 WWW.SOLARISBOOKS.COM

Follow us on Twitter! www.twitter.com/solarisbooks

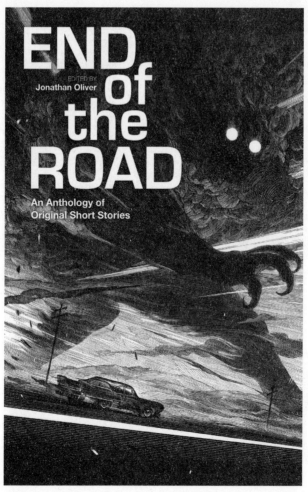

An incredible anthology of orginal short stories an exciting list of writers including the best-selling author Philip Reeve and the World Fantasy Award-winning Lavie Tidhar.

Each step will lead you closer to your destination, but who, or what, can you expect to meet at journey's end? Here are stories of misfits, spectral hitch-hikers, nightmare travel tales and the rogues, freaks and monsters to be found on the road. The critically acclaimed editor of Magic, The End of The Line and House of Fear has brought together the contemporary masters and mistresses of the weird from around the globe in an anthology of travel tales like no other. Strap on your seatbelt, shoulder your backpack, or wait for that next ride... into darkness.

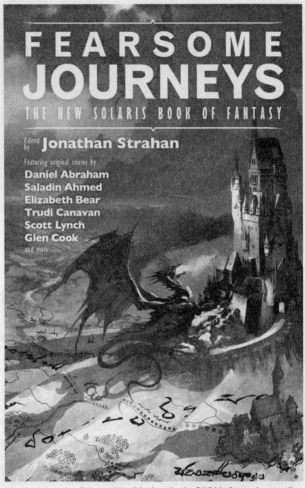

FEARSOME JOURNEYS
THE NEW SOLARIS BOOK OF FANTASY

Edited by **Jonathan Strahan**

Featuring original stories by

Daniel Abraham
Saladin Ahmed
Elizabeth Bear
Trudi Canavan
Scott Lynch
Glen Cook
and more

How do you encompass all the worlds of the imagination? Within fantasy's scope lies every possible impossibility, from dragons to spirits, from magic to gods, and from the unliving to the undying.

In Fearsome Journeys, master anthologist Jonathan Strahan sets out on a quest to find the very limits of the unlimited, collecting twelve brand new stories by some of the most popular and exciting names in epic fantasy from around the world.

With original fiction from Scott Lynch, Saladin Ahmed, Trudi Canavan, K J Parker, Kate Elliott, Jeffrey Ford, Robert V S Redick, Ellen Klages, Glen Cook, Elizabeth Bear, Ellen Kushner, Ysabeau S. Wilce and Daniel Abraham Fearsome Journeys explores the whole range of the fantastic.

 WWW.SOLARISBOOKS.COM

Follow us on Twitter! www.twitter.com/solarisbooks

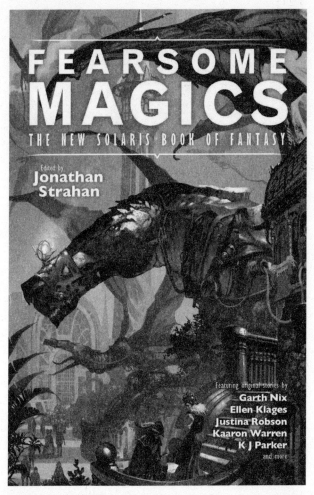

EDITED BY JONATHAN STRAHAN

THE BEST SCIENCE FICTION & FANTASY OF THE YEAR

VOLUME EIGHT

INCLUDING STORIES BY **K J PARKER** // **NEIL GAIMAN**
GEOFF RYMAN // **GREG EGAN** // **M JOHN HARRISON**
CAITLÍN R KIERNAN // **E LILY YU** // **MADELINE ASHBY**
TED CHIANG // **JOE ABERCROMBIE** // **IAN MCDONALD**

From the inner realms of humanity to the far reaches of space, these are the science fiction and fantasy tales that are shaping the genre and the way we think about the future. Multi-award winning editor Jonathan Strahan continues to shine a light on the very best writing, featuring both established authors and exciting new talents. Within you will find twenty-eight incredible tales, showing the ever growing depth and diversity that science fiction and fantasy continues to enjoy. These are the brightest stars in our firmament, lighting the way to a future filled with astonishing stories about the way we are, and the way we could be.